"GODDAMN, I'M A GOOD COOK!" I HOLLER.

"You're super hot," Eddie says like James Brown.

"A bad-ass mo-fo," I tell him.

"A kicking, killing, slamming, jamming, crazy cooking Italian." We toast my restaurant's anniversary again and howl our laughter at the night sky.

"But you know," Eddie says and leans in close. "You'd taste better than anything down in that silly restaurant of yours." He breathes warm breath onto my cheek. "I want to ravage you until you're as creamy as this here goose liver." He nips at my neck. "I'll whip you into a frenzy of mashed potatoes."

I laugh into his ear. He smells like olive oil. His hands find their way under my chef's jacket.

"You are as rich and creamy as eggs benedict," he says. "Crème brûlée has nothing on you."

"What else?" I beg. This is our joke. The only way into me is through food. He reads me like a menu.

"You are as tender as a lamp chop. As spicy as the best tagine." He nuzzles, kneads, and tickles my tingling skin. "You are as voluptuous as uh, uh . . . Oh hell." He stops and looks at me. "What do the French call those purple things?"

"Eggplants?"

"Aubergines!" he says triumphantly and slides my checked pants over my hips.

ALSO BY HEATHER SWAIN

Eliot's Banana

LUSCIOUS
LEMON

HEATHER SWAIN

New York London Toronto Sydney

An *Original* Publication of POCKET BOOKS

DOWNTOWN PRESS, published by Pocket Books
1230 Avenue of the Americas
New York, NY 10020

ISBN: 0-7434-6488-5

First Downtown Press trade paperback edition October 2004

10 9 8 7 6 5 4 3 2 1

DOWNTOWN PRESS and colophon are
trademarks of Simon & Schuster, Inc.

Manufactured in the United States of America

Designed by Jaime Putorti

For information regarding special discounts for bulk purchases,
please contact Simon & Schuster Special Sales at 1-800-456-6798
or business@simonandschuster.com

ACKNOWLEGMENTS

For everything they do for me, my love and gratitude go to Dan, Barbara, Richard, Tanya, Chris, Lucinda, Jason, Katie, Laura, Heidi, Marybeth, Anne, and Emily. Thank you also to Amy Pierpont and Megan Buckley for your constant support and endless encouragement.

FOR MY MOTHER

And if the earthly has forgotten you,
Whisper to the silent earth: I flow.
To the rushing water say: I am.

—Rainer Maria Rilke,
Sonnets to Orpheus

CHAPTER
ONE

Up on the roof, Eddie stands in front of me with a champagne bottle sticking out from between his thighs like a green glass penis. "Very funny," I say, but of course I laugh, because I always laugh at Eddie's antics.

Thick, blond hair falls across his green eyes as he struggles with the wire casing, then the cork. He looks up, shakes the hair out of his face, and flaunts a cunning smile. "We have to celebrate, darling!" He wrenches the cork from side to side and gyrates his hips, mumbling, "Come on, baby. Come to daddy."

"Jesus, Eddie," I say. "Are you fucking it or opening it?"

"It's the only way I can get it, sugar."

"Sugar?" I say with a snort, but I like it and he knows it.

I turn and look over the edge of the roof as he works on the cork. In the distance, the Brooklyn Bridge shines golden in the failing late spring sun. Five stories below, yellow cabs, black town cars, and graffiti-covered delivery trucks roll through the congested grid of East Village streets. They compete with rollerbladers, bicyclists, and pedestrians. The sidewalks are crowded with hipsters, tourists, dog walkers, baby pushers, old women pulling shopping carts, and bums asking for change. I love this neighborhood. These are my people—the ones who choose to be in this tiny corner of the world because they find beauty in its roughness, just as I do.

"Oh, yeah. Oh, yeah," Eddie moans as he works on the cork. "I can feel it now. Here it comes."

"Do you need some help?" I ask him, then tease, "from a professional?"

"O ye of little faith," he says in his sweet southern drawl. Ever since I've known him, Eddie's liked to pretend he's some hayseed straight off a cotton farm, baffled by big-city ways. But the truth is, he's been kicking around New York for the past ten years and is more citified than I am, and I grew up here. Plus, his soft gentile hands with their perfectly manicured nails and the '85 Krug Brut champagne he's opening expose him as a fourth-generation Princeton grad and grandson of a textile magnate from the great state of Georgia.

"Here it comes," says Eddie. "Just a little more. Oh, oh, oh!" He stands up straight and juts his hips forward as the cork arcs into the evening sky. Champagne shoots out from between his legs, and he howls with delight. There's nothing Eddie likes more than a party, even if it is just the two of us on a roof.

Never to be outdone by him, I grab the bottle and bring it to my lips. Let the bubbles tickle my nose before I take the first greedy gulp. The champagne scratches my throat and lingers sweetly on the back of my tongue. Before I can take another swig, he scoops me up, one arm under my knees, the other across my back, and gallops around the roof, singing, "Happy Anniversary!" to the tune of the *Lone Ranger* theme song. We twirl in circles. The sunset blurs. Water towers, chimneys, and satellite dishes spin. Horn honks, tire squeals, laughter, and shouting burble up from the streets and meld into an urban symphony.

In Eddie's arms, I am perfectly suspended between the earth and sky. Nothing's holding me down. I could fly away and soar past the just-rising moon with my hair on fire and my arms spread wide like a human shooting star over Manhattan. Then we collapse, champagne splashing, tiny plates of hors d'oeuvres crashing, onto a white tablecloth spread over the warm tar of the roof. In the center is a huge bouquet of yellow roses. Eddie's gift to me on my restaurant's first anniversary.

He props himself up on one elbow beside me and pants, "You did it, Lem. Congratulations!" He raises the frothing bottle to his lips.

He's right. I have done it. After ten years of regrets, mistakes, stupid moves, and pure dumb luck, I've gotten what I want. No one expected this from me, least of all myself. I came into the world as a colicky, jaundiced baby with fuzzy blond hair like a troll. My parents named me Ellie Manelli but called me Lemon, which isn't much better. They left me behind with my grandmother and four aunts in Brooklyn to pursue their beatnik lifestyle, then ended up on the bottom of a river. When I hit eighteen, I took off from the cloistered streets of my small Brooklyn neighborhood to traipse around Europe with every other lost soul looking for some semblance of self. I returned defeated and spent years wandering from job to job, never happy, never satisfied, until I decided to stop grousing and waiting for something to happen. A year ago, a shoe store went out of business on the bottom floor of this building, and I opened my restaurant, Lemon, named after me.

Now suddenly, I've became the new It Girl of the New York cooking world. Various trend-spotters have dubbed Lemon "hot" and part of the "downtown scene." I've been declared a "hip young chef" to watch. A picture of me, complete with my blond hair streaked blue to match my Le Creuset saucepans, graces the pages of *Gourmet* magazine this month to celebrate our anniversary.

I don't know how it happened. Who turned out to be my fairy godmother. Or if the karmic scales finally tipped in my favor. If I weren't such a cynic, I might claim that every experience in my life has led me to this shining moment, but I think that's bullshit. All I know is, my luck in life has changed, and it's about damned time.

"How about some of these here whores de vors?" Eddie asks. He pops a piece of foie-gras-covered toast into my mouth. The goose liver melts slowly, and I moan happily. He lays a roasted hen-of-the-woods mushroom and goat cheese phyllo purse on my outstretched tongue. When I'm done with that, he tosses me a bright green cerignola olive. I swallow the fruity salty brine, then wash it all down with more champagne.

"Goddamn, I'm a good cook!" I holler.

"You're super hot," Eddie says like James Brown.

"A bad-ass mo-fo," I tell him.

"A kicking, killing, slamming, jamming, crazy cooking Italian." We toast again and howl our laughter at the night sky.

"But you know," Eddie says and leans in close. "You'd taste better than anything down in that silly restaurant of yours." He breathes warm breath onto my cheek. "I want to ravage you until you're as creamy as this here goose liver." He nips at my neck. "I'll whip you into a frenzy of mashed potatoes."

I laugh into his ear. He smells like olive oil. Always like olive oil. My love for the past five years. Who ever thought it would last this long? I met Eddie when I was a sous-chef at a fake Italian restaurant on the Upper West Side. He came to sell olive oil from his import business to the executive chef, a lazy cook and a lout with horrible hygiene. Eddie saw through the pretense of the oversalted ossobuco and rubbery tagliatelle. I only saw his eyes, green and laughing, sharing a joke with me. I handed him a slice of my roasted red pepper ciabatta dipped in his best extra virgin oil, and he licked his lips.

His hands find their way under my chef's jacket. "You are as rich and creamy as eggs benedict," he says. "Crème brûlée has nothing on you."

When I first started going out with Eddie, I figured we'd have a few laughs, drink a few bottles of wine, and eventually part with no hard feelings. Looking at us, you'd never think that we would last. Eddie is every inch the prep school brat, certain of entitlements from the world. I embody my Brooklyn upbringing, complete with the huge chip on my shoulder carried proudly like an epaulet. But beneath our facades, each of us is as ornery as the other one. Maybe that's what keeps us together.

"I could turn you into soup," he says and flicks the snaps of my bra.

"What kind?" I grab his soft earlobe with my sharp teeth.

"Vichyssoise." He draws the word out as if it's luxury.

I look up. The sun has set, but the stars are hidden by the glare of city lights. The moon is lonely, with only red-tailed jets to share the sky.

"What else?" I beg. This is our joke. The only way into me is through food. He reads me like a menu.

"You are as tender as a lamb chop. As spicy as the best tagine." He nuzzles, kneads, and tickles my tingling skin. "You are as voluptuous as uh, uh . . . Oh, hell." He stops and looks at me. "What do the French call those purple things?"

"Eggplants?"

"Aubergines!" he says triumphantly and slides my checked pants over my hips.

My hands find him.

"I am merguez!" He rolls the word across his tongue as if he is some conquistador, and we wail at the moon.

"Now," I say, and I mean it. "Now!"

Eddie doesn't need to be told twice. He's there already. Away we go. Again, the sky blurs and sounds merge. Everything falls together like all matter sucked deep into a big black hole. My mother at the bottom of the ocean waves her bony hand, her hair is seaweed strands, she rides an electric eel. My father, buried beneath the Greenwood soil, rolls over in his grave and tells the beetles to shut their tiny eyes. This is it!

Tonight is my night, and I could devour the world. Catch it by the heels. String it up in a tree from a looping snare. Skin it, fillet it, sauté it. Serve it on a platter with bitter wild leeks and potentially poisonous mushrooms shaped like flying saucers. Surround it with delicacies of the rivers and the sea. (Gifts from my long-dead mother.) Exotics from my larder. (One thing from every place I've ever been.) An eclectic stew of me.

I let go a whoop, a holler, a self-satisfied scream for all the world to hear. I am a T-Rex skulking. A warhead launching. A woman to be reckoned with. Watch out, I warn, as I roar with delight. Nothing can stop me now!

EGG & SPERM

Ping! Waxing and waning ovaries release a half-life on the twenty-eighth day of May. *Swoosh!* A squirming sperm army advances at the right hour on a rooftop in Manhattan. Both hurl through space and time until one of those brave swimmers unites its chromosomes with that spaceship egg. Cosmic matter flies. Reenacts the universe from black hole to big bang to self-sustaining planet circling the sun. And suddenly, there you are.

Or are you? Exactly when will you be you? At what moment do you exist? At the instant of collision? Or when this ever-dividing organism of replicating DNA finds a uterine wall in which to implant? Does it take your mother's knowledge to make you you? What about her love? Has God breathed life into you, even though on your own, outside of her body in which you grow, you would be doomed? Or does God have anything to do with it?

Have you been here before? Brought back through some karmic cycle of never-ending life? Do you have something to prove in this go-round? Past transgressions to rectify? Or are you brand-spanking-new to this tiny planet, held secure by gravity in the midst of forever?

Never mind, never mind. Who cares? You have no say. At this point, everything about you is completely predetermined. So you float, free-form, waiting patiently for discovery while your parents pant beyond you, no different than the two humping mice nestled in the chimney shaft three feet away. Your parents are oblivious to your existence. Unknowing of the changes awaiting them in the form of you. This is the way you are brought into the world. This is the way you are loved. Welcome.

CHAPTER
TWO

Franny, plate the shad roe!" I yell over a whoosh of fire off the grill high enough to singe my eyebrows. Then I get the hell out of the way as Ernesto tosses sweetbreads searing in one skillet, flips the sea bass grilling in another, and plops a medium-rare filet onto a waiting plate with his bare hands.

Around us, the kitchen is chaos. Smells of meat, fish, chicken, vegetables, coffee, chocolate, and sweat assault the muggy air. Kirsten and Lyla rush in the double swinging doors.

"The place is a madhouse," Kirsten says. She is sleek and fast, a lithe petite dancer who could balance a meal for eight on top of her pirouetting head. She checks her ticket against the food waiting in the window and quickly grabs what she needs.

"Mel double-seated me, and I'm dying," Lyla answers in her booming alto voice, better suited for belting out Broadway tunes than reciting tonight's specials.

"Did you see the line?" Kirsten asks.

"They're all the way around the corner," says Lyla. She lopes, long and lanky, out the door, plates of steaming food loaded onto her arms.

Beside me, Franny flails spatulas, tongs, knives, and towels as if she is Lakshmi, the four-armed Hindu goddess of wealth. She slows down just long enough to carefully spoon quivering fish eggs onto a bright blue dish of lemon caper sauce with tiny orange blossoms scattered over the top. Her crazy red curls spiral out from beneath her ever-present Chicago Cubs baseball cap. She's been wearing it when she cooks since I met her in Nice during our junior year abroad.

Franny and I were roommates in a decrepit flat that we shared with six other exchange students. We immediately hated each other. I thought she was a loudmouthed American hell-bent on getting as much mileage out of her Eurail pass as possible. She thought I was the worst kind of New York snob who only wanted to befriend the French. We were each right about the other, but we found a startling affinity in the kitchen.

One day while I was trying to re-create a daube niçoise that I'd had at a tiny café in the old city, Franny poked her finger in my sauce and declared it needed orange peel. I begrudgingly added it, and the stew was excellent. After that, we gravitated to the kitchen together, silently dancing around one another as we cooked. I'd chop onions and garlic; she'd add celery and herbs. I'd salt her sauces; she'd deglaze my pans. Together we churned out dinners that quickly became famous with our other roommates, and Franny and I became friends. I've never met another person whose cooking style and sensibilities complements mine so well. Franny is invaluable to me in this kitchen, even if she is a huge pain in the ass some of the time.

Behind me, Ernesto, my old flame, mans the grill. He's still as beautiful as the first day I saw him, with shoulders like a T-bone in the center of a steak, long legs, and a perfectly round butt. Skin the color of a hickory nut and a strong, square jaw. I met him in a hotel steakhouse in Midtown that catered to expense-account assholes. He was already an old pro then, with hands as tough as catcher's mitts from years of burns, cuts, and scars. He's barely older than I am, but he's worked steadily since he slipped into New York from Ecuador when he was just six- teen. However, unlike most men who work in kitchens, Ernesto is a good guy who saves his testosterone for the woman in his bed. He's also one of the best grill men in New York, with the grace and timing of an expert flamenco dancer.

Then there's Makiko, quietly huddled over a ginger pear crème brûlée, working as carefully as a watchmaker with her tiny blowtorch, mint leaves, and sugared violets. With her deli- cate Japanese features and whispery voice, she's often mistaken for a mousy pushover, some submissive mincing geisha girl. But I've seen her mad, her black eyes fierce beneath a heavy shag of half-blond/half-black bangs. Makiko knows how to hold her own in an American kitchen.

When I started this place, I put together the best crew I'd ever met. Franny and I hadn't cooked together since we'd dragged ourselves across Europe, a trip that left our friendship in shambles. Despite our falling-out, I never lost track of her. When it came time to open Lemon, I enticed her away from a busy bar in SoHo. She wasn't hard to convince. Ernesto walked out of a giant Italian joint in the Bronx and brought his cousin Manuel, fresh off the plane from some tiny Ecuadorian hill town, to do our prep and clean up. Makiko came with me from a pan-Asian monstrosity dedicated to fusing the worst of all cuisines. I stole Melanie, the hostess, from a bar down the street where I used to drink after my shifts at the last bistro where I worked. And I pinched Kirsten and Lyla from my favorite pseudo-diner on the Lower East Side.

I cajoled, bribed, and promised all of them anything they wanted to come work with me. Swore to them that we would be chummy. Comrades in our quest for dazzling the chow hounds and foodies, the Emeril LaGasse watchers and Nigella Lawson wannabes who come in every night and comment on the temperature of the wine and whether the chicken is organic or not. I claimed that I would be a different kind of chef, never making empty vile threats with a shining cleaver poised above my head nor running a revolving door of support staff through the kitchen.

Of course, over the past year, I've broken every one of those promises. Repeatedly. I've hired, fired, and lost twenty-three waitstaff, bartenders, and line cooks, often due to my own stupidity and shortsightedness. I've consistently overruled Franny and Ernesto, even though they usually have better judgment than I do. Scared Makiko witless with my temper tantrums and threatened Melanie more times than I care to admit. But in the end, they've stuck by me through all of my transgressions, trespasses, fits and starts, firings, yellings, and bad-mouthing. I'm grateful to them for their loyalty. I admire them for their brazenness to stay. Of course, I'll never tell them that. They'd think I'd been slurping absinthe from a sippy cup.

An order comes across the printer for three radish and butter sandwich appetizers. I quickly slice a warm baguette and slather the soft insides with butter, then shove my hand into an empty radish container on the prep line.

"Manuel!" I holler toward the back. "Where the fuck are the radishes?"

By the time I've said it, he's abandoned his sink full of giant pots and scrambled over boxes of passion fruit and mangoes and bags of basmati rice and disappeared into the walk-in.

The printer grinds away more tickets. I rip them off and call the orders. "Baby greens, beet and endive, two roasted pepper goats. Mushroom tart, sausage sampler, lamb shank, trout, and rare filet. Another radish. Is there a freaking radish lovers' convention in town tonight or what? Manuel!"

"*Sì*. Got it!" he calls from the back.

While I wait for him to slice the radishes, I lean against the counter and close my eyes. My feet ache, my back hurts, my head is pounding. I have an oil slick on my forehead. I'm getting a zit on my chin the size of a cantaloupe. And I'm running on about two-and-a-half hours of sleep. This has been my state for over twelve months, and there's no end in sight. How could this all be worth it? I ask myself every night.

Then the peppery fragrance of the freshly chopped radishes hits my nose, and I am back at my grandmother's kitchen table in Carroll Gardens. On warm spring Saturdays we munched tissue-thin slices of red radishes stacked on crusty buttered baguettes with a pinch of kosher salt and squeeze of fresh lemon. My grandmother grew the radishes behind her house in a small garden next to my mother's pear tree. They were always the first vegetables of spring, when the dirt was warm and moist from all the rain. The baguettes came from Monteleone's Bakery on Court Street, the place where my grandfather worked for thirty-five years delivering bread all around Brooklyn. Those sandwiches are the reason I started this restaurant.

After ten years of whoring myself to other chefs in five different countries; of slinging hash, burning my arms, crying into soups; of swatting the greasy hands of horny fry cooks away from my ass while holding cookie sheets against my chest like armor; of enduring insults, propositions, come-ons, and blackmail in fifteen different languages across two continents, I swore if I ever had my chance . . . Chance, schmance. What was I waiting on? Some long-lost uncle to keel over and leave me a million bucks? When the shoe store went out of business on the bottom floor of this building, I was there, Johnny at the rat hole, as Eddie's father would say. I signed the lease. Put down the money from my parents' insurance policy, left festering in a low-yield savings account. Agreed to let Eddie invest some of his inherited loot. And took a loan—the number so big that it made me dizzy. That's how I opened Lemon, the place where I can cook what I want with the people I love.

"The sweetbreads!" Franny yells.

Ernesto's across the kitchen, getting more trout from the reach-in. But I'm right there, so I rip the pan off the heat and scoot the delicacies onto a waiting plate, perfectly garnished by Franny with lardons and curly endive. I hand the plate off to Kirsten, who scurries in and out of the kitchen like a nervous cat. Franny, Ernesto, and I grin slyly at one another.

It's a miracle that we pull it off every night. We've purposefully bucked the traditional structure of the restaurant kitchen. No garde-manger, no saucier, no rigid system of who does what. At this restaurant there are no coke-addled ex-cons who've made a life going from kitchen to kitchen like pirates jumping ships. No egomaniacal misfits who only find solace in the hot exclusivity of a cooking staff. We flattened out the hierarchy and got rid of the regimen. The result is a kind of controlled chaos, but none of us would have it any other way. Lemon is a success, no doubt, because of the weird symbiosis among Franny, Ernesto, and me.

I look around the kitchen again. Manuel has already built the radish sandwiches. The orders are all on the grill, and the salads are up. There's nothing moldering under the heat lamps in the window. Everything seems momentarily in control, so I pull the bandanna off my head and run my fingers through my matted sweaty hair. "I'm going out front!" I yell as I swing open the kitchen doors.

I can't stand not knowing what's going on in the dining room. I realized early on that a restaurant is only partly about making food. I'm in the business of satisfying all the senses: sight, sound, smell, and touch as much as taste. Everything has to be perfect, or nothing will be. So every night, I have to make sure the tables are set correctly, the flowers are right, the music is at the ideal volume. I have to see how people look as they bite into their entrees. Are they smiling? Drinking? Laughing? Are the waitresses keeping everyone happy? I know my checking-up makes the staff crazy, but I don't care. Maybe after another year I'll trust things are running smoothly without my constant vigilant oversight, but not yet.

The clatter of pans and sizzle of oil from the kitchen recede as I step into the dining room. I let out a long breath. I love this space. I spent months and months scouring flea markets all over the eastern seaboard for every last detail until I nearly drove Eddie batty, but I knew exactly what I wanted.

Diners laugh, talk, and stuff their gobs at beat-up wooden tables surrounded by funny old mismatched chairs from other people's kitchens. Giant gold gilt mirrors and stained-glass windows discarded from churches, estate sales, old inns, and defunct restaurants line the lime green walls. Overhead, chandeliers from Atlantic Avenue antique shops are turned down low. Some are simple, with small crystals dangling like diamond earrings. Others are ostentatious, with gaudy cut-glass-crusted appendages that remind me of little girls' unicorn collections. Tin flowerpots, lace doilies, candelabras, and old picture frames decorate every flat surface. It's a mishmash, a gallimaufry, a jumbled-bumbled mess. It's the personification of me, and that's just the way I like it.

On the edge of the bar, I reorient a green glass vase that once belonged to Little Great-Aunt Poppy. The flowers release the heady fragrance of lilies into the air. Peonies the size of baby heads droop prettily from the vase. Giant spires of hollyhocks stand up tall and proud above a mist of Queen Anne's lace. My florist, Xiao, gets it right every night.

Then I notice Lyla and Kirsten idling by the drinks station while Mona, the bartender, holds up a bottle of Grey Goose vodka in one hand and a Mr. Boston gin in the other.

"Wait," says Mona as she ponders the liquor. She looks like a white-trash trailer-park Gidget in her tube top and Union '76 truck-stop hat. "Which one does a sidecar use?"

This is what I get for hiring a twenty-something diva wannabe for a bartender. I groan and start for the bar, ready to toss Mona out by the nostrils. The girl cannot get it together. Can barely remember what goes in a gin and tonic, let alone a sidecar.

I've regretted hiring her from the first day that she sweet-talked her way into the job, telling me how much she needed the work if she was going to stay in New York and keep her band to-gether. I've always been a sucker for the strugglers with a dream. Plus, I was in deep shit, having just fired my last bartender, who turned into a lush and a thief after three months on the job.

Every time I swear I'm canning Mona's ass, Eddie points out that she's gorgeous and that cute girl bartenders win points with the weekend steak eaters. But enough is enough. She's backing up the whole damn dining room. I stomp across the room, tak-ing in a deep breath, ready to let Mona have it, but I'm stopped in my tracks when Eddie saunters in the front door.

Time bends and slows when Eddie comes into a room. Something in his Deep South manners, his leisurely assured walk, his drowsy lingering grin, drags the fabric of the cosmos back to an era of long hellos and longer good-byes. It's not as if he thinks he owns the place. More like he's certain that you're glad to have him around. I'm sure that's why his import busi-ness does as well as it does, given what a lazy ass he is at heart.

Melanie, the hostess, normally wound up and ready to pop, visibly relaxes when Eddie comes in. Her shoulders ease. Her motions become as languid as Blanche DuBois's. She greets him with a kiss to each cheek as if everyone has been transported to the Left Bank. She chats with him, tosses her head back to laugh at his silly wisecracks. The people waiting for her attention don't resent Eddie's intrusion. He offers them a little shrug and an apologetic smile. They stand back to listen in to his conversation as if they are each his new best friend. Melanie pats an empty barstool behind her, but he shakes his head and points toward the back of the house. He wants to see me.

Eddie ambles along with his hands in his pockets and a lopsided grin on his face. He wears his usual southern-schoolboy-gone-bad uniform, wrinkled khaki pants with a white T-shirt under the same untucked, unbuttoned blue oxford cloth shirt that was balled up on the roof a few hours ago. He has the sleeves rolled up to his elbows, showing off the curly blond hair across his forearms as if he's been out chopping wood instead of yukking it up with the best chefs in the city over samples of first-press oils.

I forget about Mona and the botched sidecar. Forget about whether the sweetbreads are too rubbery and whether the walk-in will go on the blink tonight. I watch Eddie shake his hair out of his eyes, then survey the place. He nods at every table packed with happy eaters, reveling in their ravioli, bingeing on beef cheeks au jus, loving life that offers them fresh lima beans in a sweet-pea cream. Watching Eddie evaporates all my fury.

He spots me and breaks into a huge smile. Walks toward me with open arms, drawling the words, "Darling! I hear your roof is on fire!"

"Jesus, Eddie," I say. "You're so freakin' cheesy."

"Drunken goat," he says.

Then, just as I'm ready to step into his hug and bask in his sweet olive smell, I hear Mona say, "Does vermouth make a martini dry?"

17

Now I've got no time for Eddie's sweet-talking, good-old-boy slap-and-tickle. I close in on him and grab him by the collar, dragging him with me to the back, pleading with him. "You've got to tend the bar before I kill Mona. She doesn't know the difference between a mojito and her skinny white ass!"

"No worries, Lemon, darling," he says, but promptly plops himself down on a barstool and asks for a glass of his special stash of '97 Altesino Brunello red.

"Eddie!" I whine.

"It's all under control," he assures me. "Mona and I will not let you down." He winks at her, and she winks back as she uncorks the wine. Eddie tells her how to mix the drinks, and I go back to scanning the dining room, making sure everything else is perfect.

Once Lyla and Kirsten have hurried off with their cocktails, Eddie turns to me and says, "Oh, by the way, my mother says to tell you congratulations. She's been showing off the *Gourmet* article to her gardening club today."

"That's nice," I say absently as I try to decode the facial expressions of every eater. Chefs are fundamentally insecure people, always trying to bowl everyone over with the food they create. I'm no different. If I could, I would run up to each table and ask, Do you like it? Is it the best thing you've ever eaten? Which, of course, is really a way of asking, Do you like me?

"Speaking of my mother," Eddie adds inelegantly. I try to ignore him, but he says, "She and my father want to come up for a visit."

It's not that I don't like Eddie's parents. They're perfectly fine people, but the few times I've been around them, I've gotten the distinct feeling that I'm not the girl they'd imagined for Eddie. Before I can protest, make excuses, forcefully refuse, Melanie grabs me by the elbow.

"Critic at table four," she whispers fiercely.

18

I glance over at the unassuming couple Mel is nodding toward. "I don't recognize either one," I tell her.

"I'm pretty sure she's the new critic from the *Post*. I called Bryan at Bistro Jeanine and described her. He says that's the one. See, she's writing notes under the table."

"Christ," I mutter. "Like they fool us. What'd they order?"

"To start, the fennel apple salad for her. Seared sea scallops for him. Then the lamb and the trout."

"It'll be fine," I tell Melanie with some new kind of crazy megalomaniacal self-confidence. Usually I'd flip out if there were a critic in the house. I'd dash into the kitchen to personally inspect, taste, and plate every item going out to a critic's table. But right now I'm so beguiled by my own success that nothing can touch me. "Anything else?"

Mel frowns at me uncertainly, but I'm feeling so good tonight that I stick with my pronouncement that everything will be fine. "Well," she says. "We're booked until ten-thirty tonight and Sunday brunch is full for the next four weeks. Must've been that *Gourmet* article."

I shrug. "Who knows?" But I think, Who cares? I deserve every ounce of this attention. If the critic from the *Post* doesn't agree, then too bad for her.

The front door opens, and a laughing group of six walks in. Melanie immediately strides across the room, her arms outstretched as if she's greeting her dearest old friends. They smile. Look eager. Ready for our food. Eddie has turned around to chat with Mona, who leans across the bar to flirt shamelessly with him. I let it go, for now. I don't have time to play the jealous girlfriend. I've got to get back to the kitchen to wow these new diners with some culinary delight.

As I throw open the kitchen doors, I find Franny and Ernesto locked in a kiss over the grill. Makiko looks at me and shakes her head with feigned disgust. "Like a Tokyo love hotel in here," she says.

"You filthy sluts!" I yell. "Get back to work before I can your lazy, good-for-nothing asses!"

Franny gives me the finger, and Ernesto says, "Jealous?"

"Hardly," I say as I tie my bandanna on my head and scoot back behind the prep line. "You two deserve one another." Although I say it like an insult, I mean it in the nicest possible way, and they know it. The printer cranks out a never-ending ribbon of new orders. I take a deep breath, but before I start the call I grin, deeply satisfied with my good life.

ZYGOTE

In the past two weeks, you have divided and divided again until you resemble a mulberry. This cluster of cells holds everything that will be you. You have traveled through the channels of your mother's swampy womb, laid your roots, and burrowed in for the duration of your stay. You mother has tucked you beneath a protective lining, to keep you safe and snug inside her.

Despite her first protective act, she remains an unwitting accomplice to your existence. She goes about her daily life (on her feet twelve hours a day, slugging back margaritas at two A.M., sleeping only a few hours, then waking to terrifying fears of failure) as if silently daring you with her debaucherous behavior to live. And you do, you live, you tenacious blastocyst. Sending out your signals that she ignores. Your subtle signs of life. Her swollen breasts like water balloons left on the tap too long. A vague queasiness she associates with stress. That off-kilter sway when standing still, as if in a tipping boat. You bide your time, patient and enduring, going about your business of becoming an embryo.

CHAPTER
THREE

W hat'd you bring?" Grandma asks without looking up from
the cabbage rolls she's making on the wooden table. The
same table with scratches on the legs and a yellow-checked oil-
cloth cover that's been in the center of this kitchen since I was a
kid. The smell of onions and garlic, simmering tomatoes, and
pork fill the room. My stomach rolls over, and my underarms
prickle in the heat.

"You bake a pie?" Aunt Adele asks as she takes the pan from
my hands.

My four aunts bustle in the tiny kitchen, stirring pots, cut-
ting vegetables, and getting in each other's way. The older they
get, the more alike they look. Each one has the same olive skin
and thick jet-black hair with a few strands of gray chopped into
different variations of a bob. It was Grandfather Calabria's hair.

My grandmother, mother, and I were the only three towheaded northern Italians in the midst of the all those dark
brooding Calabrisians on my mother's side and the back-
slapping, joke-telling Manellis from Modena on my father's
side. I'm the only one among my dozens of cousins who burns
in the sun, gets freckles across my nose, and can't eat more than

one hot pepper without sticking my head under the faucet. I've always been the quiet one. The left-out one. The different one. The orphan.

Eddie plants a quick kiss on Grandma's cheek. "You look gorgeous today, Miss Annie." He pulls a bottle of Piaggia Carmignano out of a paper sack. "I brought you a little blood of Christ."

"Sacrilege!" Grandma throws her hands to the heavens, but she smiles slyly. "You Baptists have no manners."

"I was raised Episcopalian," Eddie tells her.

"How're your parents, Eddie?" Aunt Gladys asks as she comes out of the pantry, carrying three jars of homemade pickles. My aunts are fascinated by tales of Eddie's sprawling Georgian family, which I'm sure they picture sitting on old rocking chairs on some spacious veranda, sipping mint juleps beneath a Confederate flag.

"They're fine, thank you. They'd like to plan a visit," he says with his eyes on me.

I turn away quickly just as my cousin Deirdre takes my pie from Aunt Adele. "So pretty, with the crust all braided around the edges like that. You're so talented, Lemon." She sets it on the speckled Formica counter next to three other pies and a chocolate sheet cake.

"How much you charge for a piece of that pie at your restaurant?" Aunt Mary asks from the kitchen table, where she snaps green beans with cousin Sophie.

"Hi ya, Eddie," Sophie says and waves a bean.

"We don't serve it at the restaurant," I tell Mary.

"Why not?" she asks.

"Too pedestrian," I say with a shrug.

My grandmother looks up and notices me for the first time. "Good Lord, Ellie Manelli. What's with the hair?"

I hate it when she uses my name instead of calling me Lemon like every one else. "You like it?" I ask sarcastically and run my fingers through the blue streaks.

"No," she says and turns back to Eddie. "You bring me some oil?"

The first time I invited Eddie to a family dinner, he expected to find a gaggle of hot-tempered Sophia Loren look-alikes, slugging back bottles of Chianti while feasting on platters of thin-sliced prosciutto and huge bowls of fusilli simmering all day in a secret-recipe ragu. For about an hour he tossed around words like *fagiola* (which we call beans) and *buccatino* (which we call mozzarella balls) in his thick Georgian drawl until my aunts laughed at him and my grandmother asked repeatedly what the hell he was talking about. He figured out pretty quickly that despite our name and ancestry, we're much more Brooklyn than Italian. Still, my grandmother appreciates the good stuff when it comes to Eddie's oils.

He takes out a slender blue glass bottle with a cork. "First press," he says. "From a little orchard in Puglia. It's nice and sweet. Good on ripe tomatoes. And look at this." He pulls a small flask of aged balsamic out of the bag. "I got this near Modena from a man on a mule. He said his grandfather made it in a huge vat in a barn. Of course, I assumed he was pulling my leg, but he took me there and sure enough, there was his old granddad, stirring a giant tub of vinegar. They served me some twelve-year over fresh strawberries with a little bit of powdered sugar on top."

"Strawberries and vinegar?" my grandmother scoffs. "Sounds terrible."

"Your mother probably ate it in the old country," Eddie says. He loves his version of my family's past. Stone farmhouses, orchards, goatherds walking through the hills.

"Listen to him," says my grandmother. "The old country! They were lucky if they got tripe. They had nothing."

"When you going back to Italy?" Aunt Joy asks Eddie.

"Mid-August is the next trip," he says. "I wish Lemon would come with me."

I roll my eyes and turn away. I'd love to go with him, and he knows it, but I can't leave the restaurant now. Things have gotten nuts. We're booked all the time, and I'm still perfecting the brunch menu. It would be wonderful, though, to abandon it all for a few weeks. Trek through small villages with Eddie, discovering little gems like this aged balsamic. Every bottle he brings back has a story.

I used to figure I was just another part of his southern-boy fascination with things Italian. A way to aggravate his mother, who keeps waiting for him to come back into the fold and increase the family fortune rather than piss it away on oil and vinegar. But Eddie is committed to his business, regardless of how little money he earns. So the least I can do is try to make his investment in Lemon pay off.

"You want a glass of wine?" Eddie asks Grandma. He takes two jelly jars from the shelves.

"Yeah, why not," she says. "Jesus died for me too, you know."

"Mother!" says Gladys. My grandmother shrugs indifferently and laughs at her own blasphemy.

"You're getting lots of good press lately," Deirdre says to me. "I read that *New York Times* article with your recipe for pound cake."

"They named her one of five new chefs to watch," Eddie says as he uncorks the wine. "Called her 'Luscious Lemon.' The guy couldn't stop gushing about the pound cake."

"What's so special about your pound cake?" Grandma asks.

"Nothing really," I say, because next to my grandmother, everything I do in the kitchen is all poofy nonsense.

"She uses bergamot preserves in the batter," says Eddie. "Then she tops it with an Earl Grey–infused crème anglaise and blueberry coulis. It's definitely luscious. Just like her." He reaches over and wraps his arm around my waist. I elbow him in the ribs.

"It's mostly Makiko's recipe," I say.

"I read the review you got in the *Post* a few weeks ago," Aunt Joy says to me. "How do you cook a beef cheek anyway? I didn't even know cows had cheeks."

Aunt Adele's grandson Jessie snickers from the stool by the stove. "Butt cheeks," he says.

"Hey, Jessie, you watch your mouth." Adele shakes a finger in her grandson's face. "Get outta here. Go play with your cousins." Jessie slips off the stool and scurries out of the room. "I swear Billy teaches that child no manners."

"Billy was always such a nice boy," Gladys says.

"He was not," says Sophie. "Lemon, you remember what a jackass Billy could be?"

"He just put up a good front for the adults." I open the refrigerator to see what's planned for brunch.

"Billy was all right," says Grandma. "That kind of orneriness skips a generation. Jessie is just like Adele."

"I wasn't that bad," Adele says. The rest of the room bursts into laughter. "Oh, get out of here." Adele snaps a dishtowel at her sisters. "You all were just as bad as I was."

"You were all juvenile delinquents, from what I hear," I say.

"Your mother was the worst," says Joy. The rest of my aunts gaze at me wistfully as they nod in agreement. I hate that look.

"So what kind of pie is it anyway?" Grandma asks me as she puts the last cabbage roll into a casserole dish and wipes her hands on her stained apron.

"Strawberry rhubarb."

"I haven't had a good rhubarb pie in a long time," says Grandma. "Mine stopped growing out back years ago."

"It used to grow right up the side of the building," I tell Eddie. "When we were kids, we'd dare each other to pull if off and take a bite."

"Whoever could eat the biggest piece without spitting it out was the winner," Sophie adds.

"Y'all must've been real bored," says Eddie.

"Like you and your brother were discovering brain surgery down in the swamp," I say.

"Your aunt Natalia used to have rhubarb in her backyard, but of course she wouldn't let anyone at it," says Joy.

"How do you know what grew in Natalia's yard?" I ask.

"My girlfriend Ferdie's place looked out into Natalia's yard. I saw the rhubarb," Joy explains.

"You asked her for some?" I ask.

"Yeah. Thought I'd make a nice pie for Ma. Natalia wasn't using it, but she said no."

"Maybe she was going to use it," I point out.

Joy, Adele, Gladys, and Mary all snort and scoff.

"A Manelli girl?" Adele says.

"Cooking?" Joy adds.

After my parents died, my mother's sisters and my father's sisters began a petty war of insults and digs across the neighborhood streets. The Manellis never forgave Grandmother Calabria for taking custody of me, and so they took issue with every decision she made. If she sent me to Catholic school, they thought public was better. If she didn't force me to take piano lessons, she was spoiling me. If I showed up at church in pants instead of a skirt, she was negligent. Of course, all my cousins would get in on it, too. The Calabrias fighting the Manellis.

Leaving me in the middle, feeling like all the discord was my fault.

"Where'd you get your rhubarb, Lemon?" Grandma slips the cabbage rolls into the oven.

"Farmer's market in the city."

"How much'd you pay?" Adele asks.

I ignore her and pull a covered dish out of the overstuffed fridge. "What's this?"

"What's it look like?" says Grandma. "It's cucumber salad."

"Who else is coming?" I pick a slippery cucumber out of the bowl and pop it into my mouth. Vinegar and sugar sting my tongue. Bile creeps up the back of my throat, and I swallow hard.

"I don't know." Grandma plunges her hands into soapy dishwater and starts washing pots. "The usual, I guess. Your cousins Tom, Anthony, Sam, Cindy, Angela, Amy, Joe."

"Amy has to work," says Aunt Mary.

"You invite Rick and the baby then?" Grandma asks.

"Yeah, sure," says Mary. "He'll probably stop by."

"Is Aunt Livinia coming up?" I ask. My grandmother's one remaining sister has lived in the basement apartment here since I was thirteen. In the past few years, she's retreated farther and farther into her little dark hovel downstairs. I rarely see her now.

"She hasn't been up here for almost a month," says Grandma.

"What's wrong?" I ask.

"She's old."

"Let me do that." Eddie rolls up his sleeves and bumps my grandmother out of the way.

"Such a gentleman," Grandma says as she dries her hands. "When're you going to marry my granddaughter?"

I glance up at the old owl clock tick-tocking above the sink. "That only took three and a half minutes," I mutter.

"Just as soon as she'll have me," Eddie says with a wink.

My aunts all look at me eagerly. I stick my head inside the refrigerator again. I learned early on that the best defense against my aunts' constant prying is to ignore them.

"You know your cousin Cindy just got engaged," Aunt Gladys says.

"Is she pregnant?" asks Mary.

"Just because both your girls were bursting the seams of their wedding dresses . . . ," Gladys says to Mary.

Sophie laughs. "Who wasn't pregnant when they got married in this family?"

"Anyone ever heard of birth control?" I ask from inside the fridge.

"Not pope-sanctioned," Joy jokes.

"And we're such good Catholics," Mary adds.

"Well, she's not pregnant," says Gladys. Then she giggles and adds, "At least not yet."

"Give her till the honeymoon," Mary says, and they all crack up.

Except for me. I've always found their constant joking about the fertility of the Calabria clan annoying. As if the only thing a woman in our family is capable of doing is having babies, and like that's such an accomplishment.

"You're the only one left, Lemon," says Joy.

I pull out a platter of red peppers, tomatoes, prosciutto, and mozzarella. The smell of the cheese turns my stomach, and I shove it back in. I never thought I'd see the day when I was sick of food, sick of cooking, sick of tasting. All this hoopla over the restaurant is beginning to wear me down. Eddie's pointed out repeatedly that I probably need a break and more help, but I can't afford those things yet. I have to keep going until we're running smoothly and turning a profit; then I'll think about hiring more staff and taking some time off.

"I heard from Trina," Aunt Adele suddenly announces, which stops the room dead. Even I come out from the fridge. Trina's the youngest of the grandchildren after me. She was a surprise, a miracle baby by all their estimations, but she's been a constant source of heartache for Aunt Adele, and yet she remains doted on and adored.

"When?" Aunt Mary asks.

"Yesterday," says Adele.

"You didn't tell us," Joy gripes.

"I'm telling you now," says Adele.

Everyone waits, no one moving.

"She's coming home," Adele says, and her eyes fill with tears. My aunts smile at her, misty-eyed and soft, then they're laughing like hyenas, throwing their arms around Adele, and patting her on the back.

I'm not so sure this is good news. Trina has been out in Seattle, finding herself, for the past two years. An endeavor that landed her in detox twice before her twenty-first birthday.

"Maybe Lemon could give her a job," Gladys says.

I let that comment pass. "What time do you think we'll eat?" I ask my grandmother. My eyes are heavy, and I'm exhausted. Every day in the late morning I feel this way. A few days I've even slipped off into the storage room and had a quick nap on top of the flour sacks.

Grandma adds salt to the noodle pot. "Why? You got somewhere you need to be?"

"Thought I might lie down for a while," I say.

This stops my aunts yammering about Trina.

"You sick?" Adele asks.

"She's working too hard," says Gladys.

"It's all those late nights," Joy adds.

"You have to take time off," Mary warns. "Or you'll burn out."

Eddie looks at me carefully.

"I'm fine," I say. "Just tired."

"Go in my room," says Grandma. "Turn on the air conditioner if you want. I'll get you up when everything's ready."

Eddie walks me to the hall. "You okay?" he asks with his hand on the small of my back.

"God, I'm fine," I snap at him. "I want a little nap, and everyone acts like I'm on my deathbed." As soon as this comes out, I realize how bitchy it sounds, and I wonder what my problem is. "I'm just tired," I say more kindly. "Will you be okay down here by yourself?"

Eddie laughs. "Of course," he says and kisses my cheek. I know it's true. My family adores Eddie. "Enjoy your nap," he tells me as I lug my tired body up the stairs.

Nearly everything in Carroll Gardens has changed since I was a kid, except for my family. When my cousins and I were growing up, everyone and everything on the streets was the same— Italian. The bakery, the shoe store, Leopoldi's Hardware, Dr. Cornelio the dentist, the Catholic church. Virgin Mary statues graced the front of nearly every building. Old men sat on metal folding chairs in their undershirts outside the social clubs where they played cards in the afternoon. Women yelled at kids from apartment-building windows.

Now most of the Italian families, including all of my Manelli relations, have sold their brownstones for a small fortune and moved to the Jersey suburbs or Florida. Carroll Gardens has become a hip Brooklyn neighborhood full of young couples, trendy bars, and overpriced knickknack shops. But the Calabrias never change. My four aunts still live within five blocks of one another. I think they see it as a personal triumph that they're still here, especially when the Manellis jumped ship. I mark it up to the hideous stubbornness that runs in my family.

I draw the shades in Grandma's room but leave a window open and the air conditioner off so I can smell the mock orange scent floating up from the garden, which settles my stomach a little. As I lie down, fuzzy chenille pom-poms on the ancient light blue bedspread push into my skin, but I'm too tired to care. Sleep these days overwhelms me. Pulls me under like anesthesia. One second I'm awake, the next I'm dreaming. Each time I wake up, I'm groggy and queasy, as though the sleep wasn't enough and my body wants more. Begs me to close my eyes again. On my grandmother's bed, I fall into a heavy, almost drunken sleep, and immediately I'm dreaming my old dream of the train.

The train is fancy, not like the dingy Amtrak cars of my childhood, with their worn orange seats and graffiti everywhere. The conductors wear white gloves and little hats. They walk through the aisles of red velvet seats, smiling at the passengers. There is a dining car with tablecloths and candles where my parents sit and drink wine from pretty glasses and laugh with their heads tossed back as prairies pass by outside the windows. They are glamorous. More Myrna Loy and William Powell than Norma and Giovanni from Brooklyn. And it's clear, they are deliriously happy on that train.

The scene switches to outside. The train is big and black and powerful. It speeds through the dark night, whistle blowing lonely and forlorn. Charging ahead like a blind bull. Smoke pours out of its stack, and the whistle screams. Up ahead is a bridge spanning a deep ravine over a tiny river that looks like a small blue thread winding through minuscule trees below. I'm there. Standing on the bridge, waving my arms frantically, trying to get that train to stop.

The conductor sees me. His mouth is a big black O, his eyes round and white. I'm small and in the way. He pulls the brake, but it's too late. The train is coming too fast. It hits a bump. The front wheels jump, and the engine smashes through the side of the bridge. Smoke trails behind it as it plummets. Then the coal car plunges over the edge. A small man with a shovel flies away. Passenger cars, one by one, go over. Faces appear in the windows. Hands press against the glass. These are the ghoulish faces of long-lost children, grainy, black and white, staring icily ahead. The children scream, and I wake up, heart pounding, palms sweating, the chenille spread wadded in my fingers.

When I get my bearings, I realize that the screaming children are outside in the garden behind the house. Out the window I see that some silly fight has broken out between my cousins' kids under my mother's pear tree. Little Megan and her twin Rosie tug on opposite ends of a doll while Jessie and his brother Adam throw hard green pears from high in the branches of the tree. My cousin Angela stomps out the back door, shaking her finger and scolding the kids. As quickly as it started, it's over. Megan gives up the doll, Adam and Jessie stop throwing pears, and they all go back to happily playing again.

The noise of the kids out back is the sound of my childhood in this house. Before my parents died, all my cousins, Manellis and Calabrias, congregated here every Sunday. Even though many of my cousins had bigger yards or better toys or Atari, everyone loved coming to my grandmother's house. There were always cookies or cakes, and my grandmother gave us free rein of the entire house and yard.

We'd find old clothes in closets and put on plays. Make jalopy cars from abandoned toys in the basement and race them down the quiet street. Hold huge games of hide-and-seek from the basement to the attic. Those were the times when I was the happiest and missed my parents the least. Then they died, and the rift between the families happened. From then on, I had to choose where to go on Sundays. No matter what I chose, I felt bad. As if I'd let one side down. Plus, I was always sure that the other side was having more fun without me. In a way, it was a relief when the Manellis started moving away a few years later.

Now it's another generation out back. I'm the only one beside Trina who hasn't done my part to keep the Calabria family going. Even my mother (the black sheep, the oddball, the one who claimed she would be childless forever) had me when she was twenty-three.

I glance above Grandma's dresser, where two pictures of my parents hang with all the other family portraits. One photo is the formal black-and-white glossy from the cover of the only album my parents recorded. My father cradles his upright bass with a lit cigarette between his first and second fingers as my mother looks over her shoulder from the piano. Both gaze seriously out at no one. This picture was used at their funeral, on an ornate plant stand between the two closed caskets.

The other picture is their wedding photo, snapped by a friend as they walk out of City Hall. My mother wears a short yellow dress and carries a lazy bouquet of daisies. My father's in a natty blue pin-striped suit and black Chuck Taylor sneakers. She smirks at the camera, and my father tosses his head back, laughing, as if she were the funniest thing in the world. I'm in that picture, too. Hidden beneath the empire waist of my mother's yellow wedding dress. Every time I look at that picture and the beguiling grin on her face, I wonder what made my mother do it. Marry my father and have me. Was she happy?

Everyone else in the family made lives that revolved around their kids. My aunts quit whatever jobs they had as soon as they got pregnant, then got down to the business of being wives and mothers. I've known since I was a kid that I'm too much like my parents to want that life for myself.

My parents left me behind with my grandmother from the time I was a year old. They'd tour with their jazz quartet for a few weeks, come home to play clubs around the city, then take some time off to rehearse and be with me. Even as a small child, I resented them for this arrangement and convinced myself they didn't love me enough to stick around. My grandmother would have none of my complaining, though. "Of course they love you," she'd say when I'd question why they weren't home with me. "They just have other lives." I couldn't help but imagine those other lives as much happier without me.

My aunts did nothing to dispel that notion. I overheard them, more than once, talking snidely about my mother.

"Anyone heard from Norma lately?"

"Has she made plans for Lemon's birthday?"

"She never has in the past."

"Remember when she tried to bake a cake?"

"It was more like a chocolate brick."

"I can do a party."

"I can bring the cake."

"I'll decorate."

And they would. Every year, every event in my life, my aunts orchestrated, sometimes overelaborately, in an effort to make up for what they perceived as my parents' lack of interest. What my aunts didn't understand was that I wanted whatever my parents had to offer, no matter how lame. But my parents rarely had a chance to arrange anything because my aunts were usually in the way, and then my parents died.

When I was thirteen, I decided that they weren't really dead. After all, I'd never seen them dead. My mother's casket was empty and my father's closed. The only evidence of them was the photo between the coffins. For all I knew, both of them were still alive and living some incognito life where I couldn't find them. Maybe they'd gone off to Tokyo or Paris, where American jazz musicians were lauded as gods. Or maybe they were right across the Bridge, in Manhattan, playing bars at night, while I grew gawky and awkward out of their sight.

My adolescent explanation for their absence made more sense to me than their horrible deaths. Could someone's parents really die in a train wreck? And not just any train wreck, but a train that smashed through a bridge and plunged into a swollen river in New Jersey? That sounded more like a bad movie or urban lore or something I would've made up to explain their absence in my life.

Before I can get too dark and brooding about my parents, I'm interrupted by my grandmother calling me. "Lemon," she yells from the bottom of the stairs. "Dinner's ready."

This is the fabric of my life. Since I was a kid, whenever I'd delve too deeply into what it meant not to have parents, my grandmother would pull me into the family. I know what they're doing downstairs. Moving purposefully around a table full of sustenance, laughing, joking, arguing. I've always been a part of this ritual, but separate, too. Trying to find my place in the midst of all the people while everyone else (including Eddie, who slipped into my family so easily) seems certain of where they belong. I look at my parents' pictures once more. They hardly knew me when they died. To them I remain forever a grubby six-year-old trying desperately to make them stay. To me they are infinitely vibrant, distant stars who never had a chance to show me where I fit in.

"Lemon?" Grandma calls again. The stairs creak beneath her steps.

It's no use trying to figure it all out now, and I don't want to make my grandmother wait. I rouse myself from the bed, run my fingers through my hair, and haul myself up. "Coming," I yell back.

EMBRYO

At four weeks you are tiny. Nearly microscopic. You have no eyes or fingers or toes. You are just a blob of tissue and a bundle of nerves. Your mother knows just how you feel. Still, she refuses to suspect you. She has too much to do. Too many steaks to sear, salads to dress, pears to poach in wine. She refuses to question. Blames all the signs and symptoms on other things so that she will not imagine you into existence.

Except that she does. At night. Lying in bed with thoughts and worries ricocheting around her mind. Some sneaking suspicion lurks. No, she thinks. Not now. Not yet. I have too much to do. You are unconcerned with her agenda. You have your own. It's made up of spinal cords and arm buds and eye bulges. You are making yourself into a person. One layer at a time. Preparing yourself for life. Forming your yolk sac from which to feed, you suck her dry. Your head tapers to a point, like a teardrop. The first of many times that you will break your mother's heart.

When she thinks of you at all, for those slender moments before she drops off to sleep, she confuses you with her own mother, who lives at the bottom of the ocean. It might have taken millennia for the ancient flow to move her. Mountains had to melt, streams had to join up to form rivers carving tricky switchbacks through the land, scooting her remains over the rocky riverbeds out to that great expanse of water spreading from continent to continent. Her bones picked clean by the kisses of fishes. Her hair bleached white by the salt. No matter. She always loved to travel. So is it you that your mother thinks of when she's drifting, in your watery home deep inside her belly, or her own mother, forever at rest in her aquatic grave? And are you two so different?

CHAPTER
FOUR

I am woozy, dizzy, muzzy-headed, and grouchy. I'm full, bloated, enormous, and on the verge of puking. I'm sick of food. Sick of cooking. Every smell is a rancid assault. Every taste turns bitter on my tongue. The thought of walking into my restaurant makes me want to lie down and sleep for days. I thought I would never burn out, but I can feel it in me. Slowly I'm sinking.

"God, I'm tired," I say to Makiko. "This week's been a bitch. I thought things would've calmed down by now." It's seven A.M., and we're walking the quiet streets of the East Village on our way to the Union Square Farmer's Market.

"I think all the press for the first anniversary stirred things up again," she says through a mouthful of Hostess Sno Ball. She brushes pink and black crumbs from her denim jacket.

"We were so busy last night that Lyla completely forgot a table," I say. "They sat there for fifteen minutes. We're making stupid mistakes like we just opened."

"At least people are coming," she points out. "It'd be worse if no one showed up."

Although Makiko's right, I can't figure why we're still not

turning a profit. Why I can't get the ordering right. Why Franny and I get on each other's nerves in the kitchen. I worry that the menu's wrong. That my food will fall out of favor, become passé, or be imitated to the point of oversaturation. A few weeks ago, I was on top of the world, so sure of myself; now every anxiety about how the restaurant could fail wakes me every few hours all night long. Orders not filled. Rotting meat crawling with maggots in a warm and muggy walk-in. Irate customers. Jeering critics. Creditors nipping at my heels.

When it's all too much, I get up. Stumble to the bathroom, nearly delirious, my bladder ready to burst. My stomach in knots, feeling like I'm going to retch. Maybe I have a bladder infection. Stomach cancer. A kidney problem. A liver dysfunction. Some horrible disease that will render me a babbling incontinent imbecile. These are the kinds of thoughts that dash around my mind as I lie awake for hours, worrying.

Until I finally give up, put on my clothes, and go back down to the kitchen to get a jump start on the day so that I don't fall any further behind. This morning I was up by five-thirty and in the kitchen by six. Makiko was already there, staring at the pantry shelves. We decided to go to the farmer's market together, hoping to be inspired by the fresh spring produce.

We walk side by side, dragging our rattling granny carts across the craggy sidewalks. Taxis cruise silently by. Shopkeepers yawn while lifting their iron gates. Garbage trucks crawl by like babies in heavy diapers. And a few blinking souls wander the streets sipping paper cups of coffee and holding folded newspapers tucked beneath their arms.

"This neighborhood looks completely different in the morning," I say. Already we've passed a Dominican bodega with porno magazines in the window. A Ukrainian sausage shop full of pig heads. A church with a homeless man sleeping on the stoop. A housing project, a kosher bakery, and a Chinese nail salon.

"It's changing, though," says Makiko.

"I know. Used to be, you could buy crack or mangos or chocolate *babka* and a *New York Times,* all in the same block."

"I remember," says Makiko. "My first apartment was on Avenue B and Eleventh. Every night when I came home, I thought for sure I'd be mugged. But it was kind of exciting, too."

"Now there are two Starbucks, for God's sake."

Makiko pulls the rest of her Sno-Ball out of its cellophane wrapper. "It's getting so tame," she says. "Just like any regular neighborhood in New York."

"Except that past nine o'clock everyone here is twenty years old. I feel like such an old woman next to all the kids coming in and out of bars with their tattoos and piercings. Jesus, listen to me. I *sound* like an old woman. I think that's why I put blue streaks in my hair, to prove that I'm not so old yet."

Makiko laughs. "I acted just like all those kids when I first came here. I thought the East Village was heaven." She shoves the Sno Ball in her mouth then pulls a Twinkie out of her bag.

"God, it's embarrassing to remember myself at that age," I say.

"I imagine you were very, very serious." She wags the Twinkie at me to make her point.

"Hell no. All I wanted was to get as far away from Brooklyn and my family as possible. As soon as I graduated from high school, I was out of here. I went to Yellow Springs, Ohio, to this little college called Antioch."

"I didn't know you even went to college," Makiko says as she nibbles around the end of the Twinkie, exposing the cream in the center.

"It was such a ridiculous choice," I say. "I was the only meat-eating, non-Birkenstock-wearing person with a vowel at the end of my name on campus. Needless to say, I didn't fit in. I only stuck it out for two years, then I got into a junior-year-abroad program in Nice."

"That's where you met Franny, right?" Makiko asks.

"Yeah. We both told our families we'd be home after a semester, but then we spent the next year and a half migrating around Europe in our pseudo-hippie gear. I had bracelets up my arms and toe rings on my feet. And bells. For God's sake. I was into tiny bells on the ends of my clothes. I jingled like a naughty cat wherever I went."

Makiko laughs and licks a huge dollop of cream from her finger. I catch a whiff of the sugar, and my stomach gurgles. "How can you eat that crap?" I ask, nodding to the Twinkie.

"What?" she says. "It's good."

"You're a pastry chef, for God's sake. My pastry chef."

She studies the little cake. "I've been trying for years to make a fancy Ding Dong, or maybe a Ho Ho." She sighs. "But they're just never the same."

"If you perfect it, we'll put it on the menu," I tell her sarcastically.

"You would though, if it was good," she says, and I nod. "In Japan, no one would ever let me try to make something as weird as this." She pops the rest of the Twinkie in her mouth.

"Is that why you came over here?" We pass Pak Punjab, my favorite Pakistani deli, where turbaned cabbies double-park for the seventy-five-cent samosas. My stomach rumbles when I think of the starchy potatoes and bits of red chili wrapped inside the flaky deep-fried dough.

"Sort of," she says. "I didn't get into college. It's really hard in Japan, and I was never good at school. I knew I wanted to

43

cook, but the system in Japan is horrible. You have to appren-
tice for years and years, sweeping floors, chopping vegetables,
before you ever get a chance to make something. I told my parents I wanted to come to New York to learn English and go to
cooking school."

"That's really smart," I say. "You had a decent plan. My so-
called plan in Europe was to whore myself to any restaurant
that would have me. Franny and I'd march into some little
tourist town, survey all the restaurants, decide which one had
the cutest waiters, then bug the chef until we were hired for any
slop job he'd give us. We thought it was great, though. Living in
hostels, drinking with the locals, learning to cook all kinds of
different food."

"Sounds fun," says Makiko, then she takes a bottle of Yoo-
hoo out of her bag and shakes it. "Why'd you leave?"

"Long story," I say. Truthfully, I thought that I would stay in
Europe forever, but it all ended quickly for Franny and me. I
was back in Brooklyn eighteen months later, burned out, broke,
and certain I'd never speak to her again.

"When I got back, I tried to stay in Brooklyn for a while," I
tell Makiko. "But my family drove me crazy. They hoped cooking was a phase for me. That I'd at least finish college or do
something normal, like marry a hairy goomba from our neighborhood and have twenty-seven kids."

"Sounds like my mom." Makiko wipes a Yoo-hoo mustache
from her upper lip. "She wants me to move back to Japan, find
a husband, have two kids, and live in her house until she dies."

"Do you ever go back?"

"I haven't been in two years," says Makiko. "I'm a bad
daughter."

"I'm not much better," I say. "My grandmother can't believe
I willingly live in this neighborhood instead of Brooklyn. To

her, this is the place her parents tried to get away from. But I love the tin ceilings and the bathtub in my kitchen. I imagine my great-grandmother giving her seven kids a bath, then scrubbing potatoes, in that kind of tub."

"Does your grandmother want you to live with her?" Makiko asks.

"No, it's not that. She can't figure out why I won't move in with Eddie. He's got a gorgeous two-bedroom co-op in Park Slope on a quaint little tree-lined street a block from Prospect Park. My aunts all palpitate at the thought of his parquet floors."

"So why don't you move in with him?"

"I don't know." I shrug. "Probably because it would be the smart, respectable, adult thing to do."

We both laugh.

"Anyway," I say. "I can't beat the commute right now. Five flights of stairs, and I'm at work. Do you like your place?"

"My neighbors are crazy, but my rent's cheap and it's close to work, so I'm happy," she says.

"Poor Franny has the worst commute."

"All the way from Washington Heights," says Makiko. "That's like an hour each way."

"She never lets me forget it," I say. "That's why, despite all my bitching about the East Village, I'll never leave."

At the corner of St. Marks and Second Avenue, I have to slow down because my stomach flip-flops, then tightens. All of a sudden, I think that I might barf. I reach out for a mailbox and steady myself.

"You okay?" Makiko asks. She holds me by the elbow.

The feeling passes quickly, and I'm ravenous. Now one of Makiko's Sno Balls sounds good. Or a doughnut. Maybe a croissant. Maybe a pain au chocolat. "I think I'm just hungry,"

45

I say. My stomach growls. I look around, desperate for a greasy, sugary doughnut fresh from bubbling oil. But there are no bakeries on this block.

"We could go to a diner," Makiko suggests.

Then as quickly as I was starving, my desire evaporates, and nothing sounds good. In fact, the mere thought of food makes me queasy again. Every trashcan near me suddenly reeks. I shake my head. "No, forget it," I say. "I'm okay."

"You sure you're okay?" Makiko asks me. "You look kind of pale."

"Can I have some of your Yoo-hoo?"

"Sure." She hands it over, laughing. I take a sip. It's all wrong. Too thick. Too chocolatey. I nearly gag. I wipe my hand across my mouth and hand her the bottle back.

"Let's just get to the market before everything good is gone," I say and walk down the street again, fighting the urge to throw up.

At the southern tip of Union Square Park, a few hard-core skate rat kids, who probably haven't been to bed yet, zip around the promenade, dodging the early risers who pour out of the subway-stop gazebos. Beneath the shady canopy of sycamore trees at the center of the park, a group of homeless men on benches stretch and yawn and rummage through their overstuffed shopping carts as squirrels and pigeons compete for crumbs. Surrounding the green space, farmers haul crates of vegetables from the backs of their trucks onto folding tables as the most ardent shoppers wait impatiently with their baskets ready.

I discovered the allure of a good farmer's market in Nice. Every Saturday, farmers from the cool hill towns carted their produce into the stalls on Cours Saleya. My skinny French paramour, Jean-Pierre of the impossibly high cheekbones and thick full lips, drove me there on the back of his motorbike, nearly panting with anticipation. He knew what kind of powerful aphrodisiac fresh food was for me. Figs, clementines, plums, eggs, fresh cheese, bread, and tiny bags of dried herbs. All of it ambrosia.

"I'm going to start over here," I tell Makiko and point to the west side of the market, where my favorite farmers set up.

"Okay," she says. "I'll catch up with you later. I want to check out the raspberries on the other side."

We part, and I walk slowly past every stall with the other early birds, mostly chefs from area restaurants. They all seem to know each other from cooking school, but since I never went to cooking school, I only know them by sight. I don't speak to them because I'm paranoid and think they probably begrudge me my sudden good fortune with the restaurant gods. We eye one another's carts jealously.

This morning the farmers' bins are filled with sugar snap peas, early beets, pints of the first red raspberries, and the last few stalks of rhubarb. A few farmers have yellow string beans, slender young asparagus shoots, pear tomatoes, and small Korean cucumbers. All of us chefs will stuff our baskets with these ingredients and hurry back to our restaurants to come up with something dazzling for dinner. I feel more pressure than ever to make inventive new combinations, to distinguish Lemon from all the others vying for the spot I've claimed at the top of the food chain.

At the far end of the market, I stop at my favorite stall. The farmers, Joe and Lionel, wave hello as they stack leeks into a lovely pyramid and dump pounds of beans into a wooden bin. I plunge my hands into a crate of garlic scapes. They wind and twist around my fingers like papery green snakes. I snap a scape in half and bring it to my nose for the fresh clean smell of grass and dirt and that familiar pungent oniony odor. I nibble on the succulent end. It starts out sweet, like chewing on a stem of clover, but then my tongue turns hot, and the bite of garlic crawls up into my nose. My stomach roils. I put the scape down.

Lionel sidles up to me and elbows me in the ribs. "I got something you might like," he says and jerks his head toward the truck. The first time Lionel did this, I thought he was trying to sell me pot. Instead he brought out a small bushel basket of wild ramps. I nearly swooned at the sight of the delicate little leeks with their dainty onion heads drooping prettily off green stems.

This time Lionel pulls a plastic laundry basket out from under a burlap sack. It's stuffed full of weedy greens. "You know what these are?" he asks.

I grab a stalk and feel a prick. "Ouch." I suck on my stinging fingertip. "Are they nettles?" I ask with awe.

Lionel winks. "I think I'm the only one who's got them."

I greedily take as many bunches as I can stuff into my cart, secretly hoping that I've beaten the other chefs to the bounty.

"What're you going to do with them?" he asks.

I lean in close. "You wouldn't believe what I have waiting in my walk-in," I say quietly. Lionel raises both eyebrows in anticipation. "There's a guy up in Vermont who does a bit of hunting," I tell him.

"You got some wild game?"

"Pheasants."

"How'd you find them?"

"Long story."

"Ah, well," he says with a sigh. "The nettles will go perfectly."

Makiko and I take a cab back downtown, then lug our heavy carts into the empty restaurant. She goes immediately to the kitchen, but I'm exhausted and want nothing more than to lie down on the floor and sleep through the next five years. Wake from my magic slumber in an enchanted restaurant that runs itself. One where I merely have to touch my golden spatula to the stove, and delicious entrees will appear. Tiny singing birds will flutter about, delivering dishes to happy diners who never complain about anything.

Last night was full of complainers. People unhappy about the wait, irritated by Mona's bad drinks, and someone even sent a steak back that was cooked perfectly medium, claiming it was too bloody. I was about to throw it in the deep fryer, but Ernesto rescued me from being such a jerk and dutifully put it back over the flame to darken it up.

Other nights are rowdy. Everyone who walks in the door wants booze and the most outrageous things on the menu. We have to eighty-six dishes, make substitutions, send Manuel hustling around town desperately searching for ingredients. They run the waitresses ragged with their desires. Keep Mona on her toes mixing oddball drinks with blue curacao, crème de Yvette, and green chartreuse. At the end, they throw down lavish tips and leave in a flurry of laughter.

Then sometimes, everyone is quiet, subdued. They hover over bottles of earthy red wines and slow-roasted meats. They linger at the tables, eating rich heavy desserts and sipping brandy or port while the waitstaff grows impatient for the tables to turn. I've tried to find the pattern. Does it coincide with the moon? The stock market? Why can't I ever get on top of the trends?

The door opens behind me, and I jump and gasp like a ninny as Franny saunters in. "Jesus," I say. "You scared the shit out of me."

"Nice to see you, too," she says.

"Sorry," I mutter. "I was just thinking."

She stops next to the hostess station and glances through the reservation book. She is dressed like a ten-year-old boy in cutoff shorts, a Sponge Bob T-shirt, and Puma tennis shoes. She is as petite and pixyish as I am buxom and blond. We've always made an odd pair.

"Looks like a another quiet night," she says, dripping sarcasm as she scans the full pages.

"We're going to get slammed," I say with a moan.

"Isn't that what we want?"

"I'm so tired," I tell her.

"You and me both." She pokes at my cart. "What'd you get?"

"Nettles and garlic scapes."

"I saw what you have in the walk-in." She takes the cart from me and pulls it toward the kitchen. "Where'd you get the birds?"

I follow her through the swinging door. "Game purveyor that Eddie found." The antiseptic smell of the kitchen turns my stomach over. Maybe I'm allergic to my restaurant.

"Let me guess," says Franny. "One of his third cousins twice removed down in Georgia shot them, then drove them up in his Ford pickup truck?" Franny unloads everything into the slop sink. In the back, Makiko focuses intently on adding flour to the mixer.

"Close. One of his clients in Vermont does some hunting on the side." I lower myself to a stool to rest for a moment, hoping my stomach will stop rolling over every few minutes.

"Are they legal?"

"Didn't ask."

Franny pulls a leaf off the nettles and nibbles carefully on the end. "Bitter," she says, and frowns. "What are you going to do with them?"

"Remember Mrs. Slocomb?"

"From the hunting lodge in Devon?" Franny asks in a horrible British accent that sounds like a cross between Queen Elizabeth and a speech-impeded Swede.

"I thought we'd stuff the birds with nettles and sausage, then bard and truss them like she used to do."

"You try it yet?" she asks me.

"No, but I think we can figure it out."

"I was planning to make a tagine with the lamb in back. It's been in the walk-in for two days."

"We can't have two specials," I say.

Franny sets her jaw and scowls at me. We've been arguing over the menu more and more. "You can make the lamb tomorrow," I offer.

"Fine. Whatever," she says snottily. "You're the boss."

I don't know what's eating Franny, but I don't feel like getting into it with her, so I haul myself off the stool and head into the walk-in. The cool air feels good against my clammy skin. I could stay in here all day. I press my cheek against the metal shelves and swallow the bitter taste in my mouth. I grab several braces of birds hanging in the back and carry them into the kitchen like Diana after the kill.

"What are those?" Makiko asks me. She rolls dough out on the counter into perfect ten-inch rounds.

"Pheasants," I tell her. "You ever had one?"

She shakes her head.

"Speaking of pheasant," Franny says. She's washing the greens. "Remember Ian?" She wiggles her eyebrows at me. Apparently she's over our tiff about the birds.

"The strapping young hunting guide?" I ask as I slap the pheasants on the counter.

"Did he know anything about hunting?" Franny asks.

51

"I think his true talent lay in finding secluded wooded areas," I say.

Franny chops the nettles with onions and chervil. "Ian liked to bard and truss your ass."

"Like you've got room to talk." I step back in the walk-in for the sausage.

"I was very serious about my job at the ol' hunting lodge," Franny yells. "Not like you, off screwing in the woods."

"In the woods?" Makiko says to me when I come out.

"I believe Franny was in the barn," I say as I dump the sausage into a bowl. "What was his name, Franny?" I snip the strings holding the pheasants together. Their floppy heads slump from loose, flabby necks.

"Ollie? Oliver? Alan? Albert?" she says.

"Such a slut," I say with a snort.

Makiko laughs from behind us.

"You were the slut," says Franny.

This is dangerous territory for us. Nearly every fight we had in Europe centered on some guy. Our final blowout was over a chef named Herr Fink, a little barrel-chested Austrian prick with fingers as thick as sausages, blond fuzz across his head, and piercing blue eyes. Looking back, I realize that our problems weren't so much about the men, though. We were too close. We lived together, worked together, and went out at night together. There were only so many men in the small towns where we stayed, so we invariably ended up competing for the few good ones.

"You slept with way more guys than I did," I say.

"Let's count them up," Franny challenges.

I wonder if this is a good idea. But, I think, maybe we've progressed. Maybe we can finally start to joke about how stupid and immature both of us were. So I say, "Fine. In Nice, I only slept with Jean-Pierre."

Every day he waited for me outside the horrid flat where
Franny and I lived. He and I had an agreement. He took me to
tiny restaurants that I would never find on my own and ordered
specialties that never showed up on the menu. In return, I slept
with him.

He'd find me the most delicious salade niçoise with tender
salty anchovies, boiled new potatoes, and grilled tuna. I'd pull
him into a narrow alleyway for a blow job. He'd drive me up
the winding roads into the hills above the city for the best
gnocchi. I'd lead him to the beach at sunset for a quickie
under the docks. He'd take me to a street vendor who made
socca, the crispiest chickpea-flour crepes, with flecks of fresh-
ground black pepper, and I'd get rid of Franny for an entire
afternoon.

At the end of the semester, it wasn't hard to leave Jean-
Pierre. We looked at each other and laughed. I'd gained ten
pounds but had never felt so sexy, with my newfound hips and
tits and full round belly. He gave me a long blue cigarette
holder. I handed him a perfect peach. I took one long lingering
look at him as he rode away. He seemed so silly on that tiny
motorbike. I knew I wouldn't miss him, but I did miss the *socca.*
The *socca* was outstanding.

"Only Jean-Pierre? That's such a lie," says Franny. She
scoops the nettles and onions into a skillet, adds rosemary and
salt, then says, "What about Ken?"

"Americans don't count," I say. "Especially him." I rinse the
pheasants under cold water. "What about you?"

"No one."

"Liar." I take a cleaver from the knife rack and sharpen it
against a whetting stone.

"I'm not a liar." Franny tastes the hot wilted nettles. She
adds salt and pepper, then gives me a spoonful. The tastes are

rich and subtle but a little bitter. I add some sugar. She tastes it and nods.

"What about Fredrique?" I ask.

"I never had sex with Fredrique," says Franny.

I raise the cleaver over the birds, then stop. I think that I might cry as I look into their small dead faces.

"You remember how fussy he was about everything?" Franny says. "I think he was gay."

"Sounds like half the guys I go out with," says Makiko.

My nose tingles and my chin quivers as I stare at the birds. How stupid. I've butchered game hundreds of times.

"What's wrong with you?" Franny asks, her arms plunged deep into a mix of sausage, nettles, raw egg, and bread-crumbs.

"I can't—" I motion to the birds. Their tiny swollen eyes, shut tight, and their pointy beaks, pale and useless now. This time I know that I really am going to vomit. I drop the cleaver and run for the slop sink. I barf on top of vegetable peels. Spit frothy bitter bile and groan.

"Jesus," Franny says and jumps away. "Did you drink too much last night, or what?"

Makiko stands behind me, pulling back my hair as I turn on the tap and stick my face beneath the cold water. "It's those stupid birds." I feel the deep and urgent need to sob.

Franny laughs. She picks up a bird by the wings and makes it dance on its skinny bare legs. Its head flops from side to side, and I feel my throat close. Franny holds the cleaver next to the wing and points it menacingly at me. "Who you calling stupid?" she says in a goofy bird voice.

I moan as my stomach churns again.

"Stop it!" Makiko tells her.

"Jesus, you guys," Franny says. She puts the bird down.

Makiko runs a dishtowel under the cold water and hands it to me. "Maybe you have the flu or something."

"You do look like shit this morning," says Franny.

"Thanks a lot." I lay my head on the countertop and close my eyes. The stainless steel cools my flushed cheeks. "God, I'm so tired."

"You should go back to bed," says Makiko.

"I can't prep all this by myself," Franny says.

"Maybe Ernesto would come in early and cover for me." I sit up. My stomach clenches again, and I swallow hard.

"That's an idea," Franny says with a grin. "Why don't I call him?"

"How long's that been going on?" Makiko asks.

"Wouldn't you like to know?" says Franny. "But I'll tell you one thing, if Lemon had told me what a good lay he is, it would've happened much sooner."

"You and Ernesto?" Makiko asks me.

"God," I moan. "It was so long ago, I can hardly remember."

The thing with Ernesto and me was nothing like what he and Franny have. We were both just bored and lonely and too tired to look outside of our gigs for some companionship. There was never much passion between us. Just mutual admiration and the need for someone warm after long hours in a small cramped kitchen. What little infatuation we had with one another fizzled quickly, and we found that we're better off as friends.

Franny has already dialed his number. "So get the hell out of here," she says to me. "You're making me sick just looking at you."

I stand up, and my head reels. "I'll try to come back by three."

"You paying me and Ernesto overtime if you don't come back?" Franny asks as I shamble toward the door.

"Fat chance," I say.

"Then get your ass back here tonight," is her half-joking reply.

Makiko glares at Franny, then she says to me, "Don't come back if you're still sick."

"I'll be fine," I say as I push through the doors.

CHAPTER
FIVE

Upstairs, I slough off my cooking clothes. I'm too tired to find pajamas among the piles of laundry on the floor.

"Hey, darling," Eddie mumbles when I crawl in bed with him. "What time is it?"

"Around nine." I snuggle my hips close to him and pull his arm around my shoulders. "I came up to take a nap."

"You sick?" he asks and presses his hand against my forehead.

"No. I'm just—" I stop. I don't know what I am. Exhausted, yes. Burned out? Truly sick? He wraps his arms tighter around my body and hugs me hard. My breasts are as tender as bruises. My stomach turns over again, then I feel simultaneously ravenous and ready to retch. I'm irritable. I'm nauseous. There's a tiny buzzing gnat at the back of my mind. A thought that has been nagging at me, but I continually swat it away. Now it niggles at me. Could I be? No way. I wriggle away from Eddie, swing my legs over the edge of the bed, and get up again.

"Where're you going?" he asks.

"Have to pee," I say.

This is stupid, I think as I march to the bathroom. It's just

PMS. And being overworked, overtired, overstupid. That's the logical explanation for the grouchiness, the fit I threw about the stupid pheasants, the tiredness, bloating, and aching boobs. The barfing? That could be something else. A virus. Nerves. Still. What if it isn't?

I shut the bathroom door and look at myself in the soap-speckled mirror. Franny was right, I do look like shit. My skin is ashy. My eyes, normally a warm hazel color, have gone muddy brown and lack any luster. The skin beneath them is grayish blue. I look worn. A little haggard. I've got no flare, no flash. All hints of luscious Lemon have vanished from my face.

I turn to the side and examine my body. The same little trundle of flesh that always sits below my belly button is there. I'll never be one of those perky girls who can run around all summer braless in a tank top and hip-huggers. I come from child-bearing stock. Broad shoulders, strong arms, and solid, capable hands. Full round breasts, perfect for suckling a babe. Sturdy legs and Botticellian hips, great for lugging infants around. It took me a long time to learn to love this body. To see myself as sumptuous and sexy. Eddie calls me voluptuous and loves to lay his head down between my hipbones where my low-slung belly is. But as I look at myself I wonder, am I losing it all at thirty?

"Lemon?" Eddie knocks on the door. "You okay in there?" He stands in the hall, yawning and rubbing the hair on his belly. When he's wet, he looks like an otter with slick fur. I half expect him to break oysters on his gut and hand me the oily meat.

I lean against the scummy sink. This bathroom hasn't been cleaned in weeks, and it's disgusting. "Eddie, what if I was—" I say, then stop.

He cocks his head to one side and blinks at me. "If you were what?"

If I say it, it might come true, and I'm not sure it would be such a good thing. Eddie and I have never discussed having kids. Plus, I'm not sure that I'm ready. How could I keep up with the restaurant if I had a kid when I can barely keep my head above water now? And Eddie? I look at him. He stands in the doorway, scratching his stomach. He claims he wants a family someday, but he's never seen a man actually take care of a baby. His father never changed a diaper, and his older brother hardly counts as the modern man, working fourteen-hour days down in Atlanta as a bond trader while his wife and the nanny shuttle their kids around in the minivan.

"I could be—" I say and stop again.

Eddie looks down at my hand resting on my belly. Then his eyes widen. He looks up at me. "Are you pregnant?" he asks in a hallowed whisper.

I bite my lips and shrug. "Could be," I say.

We look at each other uncertain.

"But I thought you were on the pill."

"I am, but—" I shake my head. Try to count up the days since my last period. All time falls into the before-the-anniversary category and the after-the-anniversary category. I know I haven't had a period since before. That was well over a month ago. Five or six weeks maybe. I pace around the little room between the grimy toilet and the door.

"I've been so busy and exhausted," I tell him. "Everything's so hectic. I know I've missed some pills. I tried to make up for them, but I could've gotten off track." Then I shake my head. "No. I couldn't be. It doesn't make sense. We've barely had sex in the past month."

"You don't have to tell me," he says with a little snort. Then he stares at me again. His eyes are bright. Worried and excited. "But is your period late? Do you feel sick?" He runs his fingers through his hair. "Have you done a test?"

I think of Franny downstairs grousing to Ernesto while she stuffs the pheasants without me. The Sunday brunch menu that isn't set. All the receipts and bills in a pile on my desk. This is not what I need right now.

"It's probably stress," I say. "Besides, I always think I'm pregnant. Every time my period's even a second late. It's the curse of growing up around a bunch of fertile Italian women who get pregnant every time the pope sneezes."

Eddie continues to watch me from the doorway. I pick up a hairbrush from the sink top and pull out wads of tangled hair from the bristles as if it's the most important task in the universe. I have to move, keep myself busy. I concentrate on the brush so I don't have to think about what might be happening.

"There's one way to find out," Eddie says. "I'll run down to the pharmacy and get us one of those kits." He hustles down the hall. "What'd you call them?" he yells. Then he's in front of the open door again, hobbling into his jeans.

I stand with a wad of hair in one hand and the clean brush in the other. "A pregnancy test," I say stupidly.

"What kind is best?" he asks me. Before I can answer he says, "I'll ask the pharmacist," then runs back into the bedroom and returns with his shoes. "Should we call the doctor? Can I get you anything else while I'm out? Vitamins?"

"But Eddie," I say. "What if I am?"

He shrugs. "A kid could be fun, Lem," he says as if we're talking about a puppy. "My mom would flip."

"Do you know how much work a baby is?" I shake the brush at him. "You think it's all fun and games, entertaining your nephew, but you get to send him home at the end of the day. Having a kid would completely disrupt our lives!"

He hops into the room and kisses me on the forehead. "We don't even know yet, so don't get all wound up." He shoves his wallet and keys into his pockets. "I'll be right back," he yells as he goes out the door.

I walk slowly to the bed and flop down. Grab a pillow and hug it to my chest. I'm not ready for this. I've just gotten to the cusp of success with my restaurant. I can't ruin ten years of hard work with a baby. Then again, Eddie's excitement is so sweet, so seemingly genuine. He looked at me with pure amazement, as if I had done something brilliant by possibly getting knocked up. As much as I deny it, there's a part of me that wants a family someday.

Sometimes I imagine having kids. When I'm cooking, baking a pie, or making meatballs like Grandma and Aunt Poppy taught me, I think about what I would say to a kid. How I would teach her the same things. Or if I had a boy, I think he would be something like my dad. At some point in my life, I think that I'll want this. A successful restaurant, an adoring husband, and a gaggle of ornery towheaded kids. Sometimes I daydream about a farm upstate. Moving Grandma in with me. Having kids who run free through fields and meadows with goats and ducks and chickens. Who paint their faces with berry juice and make mud pies on the bank of some little creek.

Other times my family daydreams are of a sprawling apartment in the West Village. My children will be city-smart, streetwise little imps who hang on subway poles and love John Waters films. And I will be forever with them. Never leave them. I'll take everything my grandmother has shown me about loving a child, and I'll revisit it tenfold on my own kids.

But not now. Not quite yet. If I had a kid now, I'd be too much like my mother. Torn between pursuing my career and trying to be a parent. I'm afraid that my restaurant would win. So I can't be pregnant. But then again, what if I am? I place my hand on my belly. "Hello in there," I say. "Anybody home?"

The front door opens, and Eddie jogs, panting, into the bedroom. "Okay." He dumps the bag of tests on the bed and flops to his stomach at my feet. There are three kinds of tests—EPT, First Response, and a generic drugstore brand, plus a bottle of folic acid tablets and a fake yellow rose in cellophane wrap.

"First of all, this is for you." He hands me the tacky little rose.

"Thanks," I say and pretend to sniff it. It smells like plastic.

"There was a line for the pharmacist, and I didn't want to wait to ask which test was best, so I got a bunch. We might want to try more than one, just to be sure." We examine the instructions on the back of each box.

"I don't think I could pee that much," I say.

"I'll get you some water." He rushes out of the room again.

"What's folic acid?" I call after him.

"Good for neural tube closure in the first three months."

"How do you know that?"

"My sister-in-law took it when she was pregnant," Eddie yells from the kitchen.

I open the EPT box and look at the instruction sheet. A cartoon woman with a perfect Y-shaped crotch holds the stick between her legs. She has no expression on her face.

Eddie comes back in the room, flushed and excited. He hands me a glass of milk. The smell makes my stomach clench. I push it away.

"Calcium," he says.

"Don't start," I warn.

Eddie takes the cap off the folic acid and slips his thumbnail under the foil top. "It's good for you."

"I might not be pregnant."

"Act like you are until you know you're not." He taps a tablet into his palm and holds it in front of me.

"We'll know in five minutes."

"So for the next five minutes—" Eddie says.

"I won't smoke any crack." I grab the test stick and head for the bathroom.

"Can I come, too?" Eddie clutches the instructions next to his chest.

"And watch me pee? Gross, Eddie."

"Like you never pee in front of me."

I stop and point the stick at him. "You act like this is some kind of game."

"You act like it's something awful," he says to me.

We stare at each other. An impasse. Which is it?

"Just let me pee alone, and then you can come in and watch the results with me," I offer.

"Fine," he says. "But do it right." He reads the instructions. "Only pee on it for five seconds."

"I know," I say as I shut the bathroom door.

"And then put the cover back over the soft tip."

"I know." I open the foil packet and pull out the purple-and-white test. It's curved to fit my fingers. An ergonomic pee stick, how convenient. I take the purple cap off the test area.

"And then lay it flat. On the sink. Don't hold it up," he says through the door.

"Okay." I drop my panties and scoot far back on the toilet so I can hold the stick between my legs and hit my target.

"Are you done yet?"

"For Christ's sake, Eddie. If you don't shut up, I won't be able to pee."

"Okay, sorry. I'm going to be quiet now."

I can hear him breathing right outside the door. "Why don't you make me some tea?"

"I will when you're done."

"I can't pee with you by the door."

"I'm not by the door," he says in a small quiet voice, as if he's far away.

"I can see your shadow through the crack."

He moves away. The floorboards creak. I relax and feel my bladder start to release, but then Eddie tiptoes back toward the door. "Eddie!" I shout. "For Christ's sake."

"Dang, Lemon, you have better ears than a hunting dog."

"Really. Go make me a cup of tea. My stomach is upset."

"Okay," he says. "Herbal only. No caffeine. And don't read the results without me."

"It takes a few minutes."

"Exactly three minutes," he yells.

I sigh. Then laugh. This is all so ridiculous. I hear the water running in the kitchen. My pee comes. I shower the stick, put the cap back on, and set it gingerly on the counter.

"Lem, where do we keep the tea bags?" Eddie calls from the kitchen.

I peek out of the bathroom door. He stands with his head inside the cup cabinet. It's amazing how he's never learned where anything but the corkscrew is kept in my place.

"Forget it, Eddie. I don't want any tea."

He pulls his head out, leaving the cabinet doors wide open and the water heating on the stove. "You done?"

I nod and wrap a towel around my body. Being half naked feels way too vulnerable right now.

"Everything go okay?" Eddie advances down the hall.

"I peed, Eddie."

He smiles at me like I'm a good dog. Then we both lean over and watch the test strip. The urine creeps through, turning the first window a pinkish mauve color.

"If both windows show a line," says Eddie.

I turn to face him.

"You're blocking my view," he says.

I wrap my arms around his middle.

"The line is coming up in the first window."

"I'm scared," I admit.

"Shhhh," says Eddie. He rubs a circle on my back. "We can handle this."

I close my eyes and imagine for just a second Eddie and me with a baby. Maybe things would be easier. Maybe I wouldn't push myself so hard then. I'd have to learn to balance. To make my life more even. "Are you ready for a kid?" I ask him.

Eddie kisses the top of my head. "Yes," he says with such confidence and clarity that I'm calmed. He picks up the test and squints at it. I squeeze my eyes shut.

"What's it say?" I ask.

"Well," says Eddie, "it's kind of hard to tell."

"It's a yes or no thing, Eddie."

"But I don't know. Maybe there's a line. It's faint. Or maybe that's not it. How long has it been?"

I grab the stick from him and hold it up to my face. He's right. There could be a line in the second window. Or maybe not. I hold it up to the light. We both squint at it.

"This is certainly anticlimactic," I say.

"Maybe we should do another one," Eddie suggests.

"I don't have to pee again."

He takes it from me. "I think that's a line. I think you are."

I grab it back from him. "No. It's too faint. It's just left over from the pee going through."

"How do you feel? I mean deep down." Eddie presses his hand against my belly and closes his eyes. "Do you think you are?"

"How would I know?"

"Because it's your body." He opens his eyes and stares at me. "Don't you know? Can't you feel it? If you close your eyes and concentrate?"

I swat his hand away. "It's not like that, Eddie."

He looks at me, skeptically. "My sister-in-law swore she knew the minute she conceived."

"Your sister-in-law's full of shit."

"Maybe she's just more in touch with her body."

"God, I hate this in-touch-with-your-body bullshit. Women drop babies into toilets because they have no idea they're pregnant."

"That's not true."

"Is so," I insist. "There was a girl in my high school who had a baby and swore she had no idea that she was pregnant. Everyone thought she was just getting fat. She was already kind of chunky. She had a period every month and the baby never kicked or moved. It can happen."

"She was in denial," Eddie says. "Didn't want to believe she was."

"Next time you're pregnant," I say angrily, "you let me know how it feels!" I drop the test in the trash and stomp out of the room.

"Lemon," Eddie calls after me. "Lem, come on." He follows me to the bedroom.

I crawl back into the bed, pull the covers up to my chin, and face the wall.

"Hey." He sits beside me. Rubs my legs. I squirm away from him and pull my knees up to my chest.

"Let's not get all pissed off at one another," Eddie pleads. "This could be one of the happiest moments in our lives." He pulls me into his body and lies down with his arms wrapped around me.

"This wasn't in the plan," I mutter.

"Sometimes the best things are unplanned."

"I don't think I can handle it."

"Of course you can," says Eddie. "You're the toughest person I know. You can handle anything. Plus you have me. We'd be great parents." We're quiet for a while and then he asks, "So what do you want to do?"

"If I don't get my period in a few days, I'll do another test," I say and realize that I'm a little disappointed. Despite all my fears about whether I want a kid or could handle a kid and the restaurant, for a moment there in the bathroom, with Eddie all excited, I was looking forward to the idea of a baby.

"Let's get married," Eddie says.

I groan. "Not this, Eddie. Not now."

He's done this four times in the last year. The first time he asked me was a joke. He'd lured me away from the restaurant for a long weekend at an old ski lodge in Stowe, Vermont. We'd seen so little of each other since I'd opened Lemon, and I was so exhausted, that we stayed holed up in our room for two days. After a strenuous and vocal round of sex, we lay tangled up on a featherbed beneath a goose-down comforter, and he panted in my ear, "That was so good I ought to ask you to marry me." I laughed, but he said, "No, seriously. I think I will." Then he slid off the bed onto his knees and said, "Lemon, will you marry me?"

"Not a chance," I said, and he looked momentarily hurt, but quickly recovered when I invited him back beneath the covers.

The next time was at the Fulton Street Fish Market at 5:00 A.M. on a Thursday. We were both loopy on too many cups of Chinese tea from an all-night dim sum joint where we waited for the fishmongers to open. We goofed our way through the market, Eddie cracking jokes, me giggling. At the height of his silliness, he picked up a red snapper and moved its sad frowning mouth to say, "Don't you want to marry Eddie?"

"Not on your life," I answered.

"You're one cold fish," he made the fish say, and we both cracked up.

He also asked me in the car on the way back from an organic farm I was checking out for the restaurant. He made an impassioned speech about how he wanted to move back to Georgia, buy a farm, marry me, and have a brood of wild children. Then once he proposed after a particularly brutal fight, when he'd left me waiting at a bar on my one night off while he finished a squash game. When I was done stomping down Avenue A, screaming at him about his pathological lateness and overinflated sense of entitlement, he took my hand, grinned at me, and asked in his sweetest drawl, "Don't you want to marry me now?"

This time Eddie looks at me straight on. "I'm dead serious."

"I know you are."

"Why not, then?"

"Because we don't even know for sure."

"So what? Even if you're not."

"This is all too much," I say. "I can't take it. I can barely keep up with life now, and you want to throw a kid and a wedding in the mix?"

"Okay," he says gently. "We'll make things easy. Why don't you just move in with me?"

"And give up all this?" I say and motion grandly to my messy hovel.

"This is no place for a baby," Eddie scolds me.

"There may be no baby," I say. The teakettle in the kitchen starts to scream. "You left the water boiling," I tell him.

He sighs. "I love you, Lemon," he says as he gets out of the bed. "Someday you'll have to say yes."

I don't know, I think as he leaves the room. Will I have to say yes? Why can't I make a different choice in my life? Why can't Eddie and I forever be lovers dedicated to good food? It'd be a hell of a lot easier that way. I suspect that I'm a much better chef than I'll ever be a mother and a wife. So what if I sometimes daydream about a family? I also daydream about having a whole string of great restaurants. And just maybe those two dreams aren't compatible. But the question comes back to me, what if I am pregnant?

I lay on my back and stare at the ceiling with my hands crossed below my belly button. I close my eyes and concentrate like Eddie said. Should I know? Do I have that power? That insight, if I just want to know badly enough? I quiet myself. Breathe softly. Listen. The teakettle whistle dies as Eddie moves it off the burner. Then I hear him in the bathroom, peeing.

I focus on myself. My breath, my rhythm. The feeling beneath my hands. Hello? I ask inside my head. I think I feel a tiny flutter in my gut. Like bubbles deep inside me. Like a fish far below the surface. Is that you? How would I know? Shouldn't I know? If I can't tell, does that mean that I'll be a horrible mother? When did my mother know about me? Was she excited, or did she dread me?

"Lemon," Eddie calls from the bathroom.

"Yeah."

He walks into the room, grinning wide, and holding the stick. "The line." He holds it out to me. Tears fill his eyes. "The line is there."

I grab the stick from him and stare at the bold purple mark, announcing my pregnancy. "Oh, dear," is all I can say.

Eddie climbs onto the bed and folds me in a giant hug. "This is so great! So amazing! So completely fucking awesome!" He pulls the covers off of me, unwraps the towel from my body, and cups my belly in both hands, then shimmies down so that he can talk into my navel. "Attention, future child, this is your father speaking."

I put my hands into his hair and stare down at him. "Pregnant?" I whisper. "A baby?"

"How're you feeling?"

I can't answer. I have no idea how I feel. No idea what to think or do. I'm overwhelmed. Stunned.

"Are you nauseous?"

I study the ceiling. Concentrate on the tiny fissures in the plaster. There's a stain up in the corner that looks vaguely like Jesus. What am I going to do? I ask the apparition.

"Hey," Eddie says. He peers closely at my eyes. "You okay? Are you freaked out?"

I nod my head. Where have all my sentences gone?

"Do you want to call someone? Your grandmother? Franny?"

"No!" I say and sit up.

"Why?"

I lie back again. "I just need some time to get used to the idea. It's so—sudden. I'm not sure what I want to do."

Eddie sits up on his knees. "Lemon," he says seriously. "You don't mean that you'd get rid of it."

Get rid of it? An abortion? When I was in Europe, I contemplated the same thing. In Vienna, my period went AWOL for two weeks. I convinced myself that my pills had failed. That the condom had leaked. That one of Herr Fink's little Teutonic fuckers had slipped through and met up with my ripe twenty-year-old egg. I was scared too death and didn't trust over-the-counter pregnancy tests, since I couldn't even read the directions.

I confessed this all to Franny while I was shut inside a coffee-shop toilet stall, retching up my morning bread and milky tea.

"What a lightweight," she said and laughed. "You didn't even drink that much last night."

"I think I might be pregnant," I whispered from the floor.

Franny was washing her hands. She turned off the tap and went so still and quiet that I could hear water slipping down the drain. I watched her shoes from under the stall door. "How?" she asked. "You aren't even sleeping with anyone."

"I have been," I said and hugged my knees close to my chest. I knew that Franny had been interested in Herr Fink. He flirted with every girl on the restaurant staff, and she confessed to me that she was smitten.

Franny didn't move for several seconds. "Who?" she asked.

"Just some guy," I lied, but Franny wasn't stupid, and I hadn't been careful. While she was stuck in the storage room, peeling potatoes with some old shell-shocked Nazi, I'd been moved up to be Herr Fink's sous-chef. I didn't even like him that much, but that didn't stop me from screwing him in the walk-in. Or the bathroom. Or on the bar after everyone else had left for the night. As if I weren't just one in a very long line of silly girl cooks and waitresses who'd had her legs wrapped around Finky's loins. It was obvious, and Franny knew it.

"Herr Fink?" she asked. I didn't answer, but I imagined her face, horrified. I was afraid she would turn and walk away.

"Please don't leave me," I begged her. Franny didn't leave me then. As much as it must have outraged her, she took me to a clinic to find out that my period was merely late. Sitting in the cold metal chair in the waiting room after I got the news, I grinned at her sheepishly. But Franny stared at me with pure disgust, then she left, and I thought I'd never see her again.

Now, as I look at Eddie, I see the sadness in his eyes at the thought of not having this child, and I realize there's no reason not to. I'm thirty years old. I love Eddie. He's right. We'd make decent parents, or at least no worse than anyone else. "No," I tell him. "I wouldn't get rid of it."

He smiles, relieved, and this makes me happy.

"I just need to get used to the idea before I'll be ready to tell other people."

Eddie grins at me and crawls down to the end of the bed. He takes my left foot in his hands and massages the tender pads beneath my toes. "It really turns me on knowing that you're pregnant, knowing that I'm the daddy." He kisses the bottom of my foot and rubs my Achilles tendon.

"Who says you're the daddy?" I ask.

Eddie grabs my knees, which makes me squirm and laugh. "Who's your daddy?" he demands as he slathers my bare skin with kisses. "Who's your sugar daddy?"

"You are!" I tell him in a fit of laughter. Then I bolt upright in bed because I know I'm going to barf again. "Oh, God," I moan as I jump up and run toward the bathroom with my hand pressed over my mouth. Eddie is close behind.

I toss the toilet lid open just in time to spew another round of frothy bile into the placid water. I come up and catch myself in the mirror. I'm puffy and pasty, red-eyed and disheveled. "Oh, Christ," I say. "What've I gotten myself into?"

Eddie stands in the doorway with his eyes squeezed shut. "You okay?" he asks, refusing to look.

I rinse my mouth out and splash cold water on my face. "Yeah," I say. "I'll be fine."

He opens his eyes and looks at me with pity. "Poor thing," he says and reaches to stroke my hair. "What can I get you? What can I do for you?"

I laugh at his sudden desire to please me.

"I should cancel my trip to Italy," he tells me.

"Don't be ridiculous," I say on my way back to the bedroom. "It's two months away." I flop down on the bed. "Not everything in our lives has to suddenly change."

He gets down on his knees beside me. "But I need to take care of you. I'll be your slave for the next nine months." Suddenly I feel better. And ravenous. "What do you want, my queen?" he asks, half joking.

"If this were all there were to pregnancy, I could get used to it," I say.

He takes my hand. "You name it, I'll do it. Anything."

"All right," I say and try to think of something that I really want. "The first thing you can do is get me a doughnut."

SIX WEEKS

For six quick weeks, you've been waiting to be discovered. Waiting to be confirmed. Living your small life, like some past criminal in the witness protection program. Going about your business. Hidden in the place where all your mother's secrets lie. You know everything about her right down to her sacred DNA, but you will tell her nothing about yourself. What color will your eyes be? Your hair? Will you be tall and lanky like your daddy or short and compact like your mama? Will you have her temper or his sense of whimsy about the world? Whose nose will be yours? Doesn't really matter anyway. Now that you are known, nothing much has changed for you. You go about your business, slowly forming.

You are a quarter of an inch long. You could sit comfortably on your mother's thumbnail. She could carry you between her toes like lint. You have buds for arms and legs, but you look like a tiny tadpole swimming deep inside her belly. An odd hunchbacked worm with a tail. Smaller than a pea.

Neural tubes close, and your brain begins to fill your head. What thoughts can you have? What dreams and desires? Do you have memories from another life?

Two tiny discs of pigment like shallow cups grace the sides of your not-yet-formed face. What will you see with those eyes? What will they give away? Will your mother know your lies, your hopes, your desperation someday?

A string of pearls down your back will become your spine. Will you stand up for yourself? Bend over backward for others? Your heart is the size of a poppy seed and already beginning to beat. When will this heart fill with love? When will it break for the first time? How much sadness will you know?

CHAPTER
SIX

"What time is it?" I sit up in bed and push my hair out of my eyes. Bright sunlight streams through the slats in the blinds. Eddie grumbles beside me as he rolls over and slings his arm around me. "Shit," I say when I catch a glimpse of the red numbers on my digital clock. "It's nearly eleven." I shake him by the shoulder. "Wake up. We're late."

"Late for what?" Eddie mumbles. He pulls me closer against him, but I wriggle away.

"Trina's welcome-home party at my grandmother's." I scramble out of bed, which makes my stomach pitch and roll.

Eddie yawns. "I forgot about that."

"I tried to get out of it, but Grandma kept rescheduling it so that we'd have to come." I kick a pile of clothes, looking for something presentable to wear. "She doesn't force anyone else to come."

"Everyone else just goes," Eddie says. "Besides, she wants to see you."

I hold up a pair of khaki pants that look like they've been living under my mattress for months. "She could come to the restaurant every once in a while." I toss the pants aside.

"It's not like she'll get time with you if she comes there. Lord knows I don't," Eddie complains.

"So I should work less?" I snarl at him.

"I didn't say that."

"I can't keep skipping shifts and expecting Franny and Ernesto to cover for me. Franny already resents the hours she works."

"Franny just likes having something to complain about." Eddie stretches his arms overhead. "Anyway, it's good we're going to your grandmother's. We haven't seen your family for a while."

I sniff a tank top hanging on the closet door handle. It smells like bacon. A BLT with lots of mayonnaise and a juicy tomato sounds better than anything ever has in my entire life. I pull the tank over head and look for a skirt inside my closet.

"I wish we could see my family more often," Eddie says with an exaggerated sigh.

I ignore him as I skim through hangers until I find an old grungy short jean skirt.

"Mom keeps asking about scheduling a trip up here."

"This is a bad time," I say as I struggle with the button of the skirt. "This can't be too tight already," I mumble.

"When's a good time?" Eddie asks.

"I don't know, Eddie. Not now. Okay?" I suck in my gut and try the button again. It closes, but the waistband cuts into my skin. "Jesus, I have nothing to wear!"

"Put a rubber band around the button," Eddie says.

I look at him dumbly. "What are you talking about?"

"Come here." He picks up one of my hair bands from the nightstand and loops it through my buttonhole, then fastens it across the button. "There," he says happily. The skirt fits perfectly.

"How the hell did you know that?"

"I saw my sister-in-law do it," he says.

"I think you've got other pregnant girls stashed around the city."

He grabs my hand and pulls me down to the bed again. "Yep, you're just one of the masses carrying Kilby progeny."

I poke him in the ribs. "Get up," I say. "We're going to be so late."

Eddie wraps his arms around my waist and hugs me. "Let's tell people today."

"No way!"

"They'll figure it out sooner or later."

"The later the better," I tell him.

He lifts my scraggly hair off my neck and kisses the warm skin below my hairline. It would be so nice to skip out on everything today and stay in bed with him.

"So, when can my parents come?" he asks.

I squirm around to face him. "Shit, Eddie. I can't deal with trying to make your mother like me with everything else going on."

"My mother does like you," he insists.

"Yeah, right. And carrying your bastard child will only endear me to her more."

He lets go of me and swings his legs over the edge of the bed. "She'll get used to the idea," he says with a laugh.

I get up and check myself in the mirror. My clothes are wrinkled and crumpled. The blue streaks in my hair are fading. I won't be able to color it again until after the baby comes. I'll have to go back to my natural blond. The picture of motherhood. Will I start wearing flowered dresses and carrying a sensible handbag, too? Will Eddie's mother deem me appropriate then?

"If you don't pick a date for my parents to come," Eddie says from the doorway, "then I'm picking one, and you'll have to live with it."

"I'll be out of town," I tell him.

"We'll follow you," he says.

"Get ready, so we can leave," I say.

"I'm serious," he warns.

"So am I," I tell him. "If we're any later, my grandmother will kill us."

As soon as we open the door to my grandmother's house, I hear laughter bubbling out from the kitchen. My aunts all have the same laugh in different tones and octaves, so that they harmonize nicely when they crack up. I wonder where my mom's laugh fit into the scales they create. Do they notice that some half tone is missing?

"It was Fat Faye's little brother," Mary is saying as we walk down the hall.

"Deanie Wayne Rauch," adds Adele.

"Fat Faye loved Elvis," Joy says.

"Thought the King himself was going to take her away from that horrible old house," says Gladys.

Mary says, "Their apartment was filthy."

"They didn't have a cent to their names," says my grandmother. "They were so poor that Mrs. Rauch made her Thanksgiving turkey out of meatloaf."

"Shaped it just like a real bird," Mary confirms.

"Didn't let a thing go to waste," says Grandma.

"If you spilled Kool-Aid on the table, Deanie Wayne would suck it up," says Aunt Adele. We walk into the kitchen just as she presses her lips against the table and makes a loud sucking noise. The rest of my aunts laugh in a perfect chorus.

"Hi, everybody," I say from the kitchen doorway. "Sorry we're late."

"Look who it is!" Joy notices us first. Then everyone turns to greet us with warm and hearty hellos.

Eddie slings his arm around my shoulders and beams. He loves the attention my family lavishes on us much more than I do. It's always made me a little squirmy, as if I'm "special" in the pathetic sense and need more notice than anyone else.

"Great to see y'all!" Eddie booms, then takes a breath, as if preparing to say something more. I elbow him in the ribs, afraid he's going to blurt out our news in a fit of masculine pride among so many fecund women. "Ow," he mutters and rubs his side. I grin insipidly at everyone.

My grandmother rises from the table. "What'd you bring?" she asks.

I hand her one of Makiko's fig tarts, hoping it will make up for our tardiness. She peaks beneath the plastic wrap and looks pleased. "Sorry we're late," I say again, then pass around pecks on the cheeks to my aunts and cousins.

I see the back of Trina's head, turned around to talk to one of our other cousins behind her. She is the only other blond in the family, but hers comes from peroxide. Dark roots give her away. She struggles a bit to turn around in her chair, and then I see why. A firm round belly sticks out from beneath a tight Harley-Davidson tank top. Her hand fits snugly on the thigh of a weathered guy in a matching shirt sitting beside her. He looks at least ten years older than I am. I stare at both of them, completely dumbfounded. This is not what I had expected.

Eddie has much more composure than I do. He extends his hand to the guy. I pull myself together and lean down to hug Trina loosely. "So good to see you," I say and hope my face isn't giving away my horror that she's so young and so pregnant and that everybody seemed to know this but me. I feel a twinge of jealousy.

Trina smiles at the guy beside her. "Lemon, this is my boyfriend, Chuck."

"Nice to meet you, Chuck," I say.

He nods but doesn't crack a smile or extend his hand to me. I let it pass.

"So, now we can eat." My grandmother pulls two large frittatas out of the oven.

"You didn't have to wait on us," I say.

"Oh, you know what?" Trina pushes herself up to stand in that awkward swayback, bent-kneed pregnant woman way. She looks a good six, six-and-a-half months along. "Chuck and I can't stay."

"Trina," Aunt Adele says in a tight voice, "this brunch is for you."

"And it's so totally awesome and everything," says Trina. "But Chuck got tickets to a Lynyrd Skynyrd concert out at Jones Beach. Sort of a belated birthday present for me." She pats his arm. He doesn't flinch. "We told some friends we'd meet them out there early for a tailgating party."

Adele's face clouds over. She stares straight ahead. Everyone else busies themselves with nonsense tasks, straightening napkins, stirring potato salad, brushing lint away from clean clothes.

I grimace at Eddie. This is our fault. "I'm sorry," I say to my aunt. "I overslept. We didn't mean to be so late." Eddie puts his hand on my shoulder and squeezes gently.

Trina waves my apologies aside. "It isn't your fault, Lemon," she says. "Mom didn't tell me that this was a whole-day commitment." Then she holds her hand up beside her mouth and does an exaggerated whisper. "She still thinks I'm some little teenager."

My jaw drops. If anyone else in our family spoke so disrespectfully, they'd have my grandmother and a lineup of my aunts to contend with. But with Trina, everyone lets it pass.

"Is the party a pitch-in?" my grandmother asks. She jabs a big spoon into a bowl of fruit salad. "You could take some food with you."

Trina shakes her head no. "There'll be plenty of food out there. And Chuck's in charge of the barbecue. He's fierce on the grill."

Adele stares straight ahead, her face rigid with anger.

"Well, come by later if you want leftovers," my grandmother offers.

Trina and Chuck mumble their good-byes and slink away hand in hand. I stand by the window with Aunt Adele and watch them walk down the sidewalk toward a motorcycle. Trina lights a cigarette before slinging her leg over the bike. Adele's mouth is a straight, tight line. "They met in rehab," she says to me. It comes out a little sharp, high-pitched, pointed. "He's thirty-seven."

"Holy smokes," says my cousin Sophie. "Trina just turned twenty-one!"

"She says she's cleaned up her act," Adele tells us. We both watch the motorcycle speed off down the quiet tree-lined street. "Swears that she wants this baby."

I glance at Eddie. He's wedged himself in a corner by the door and watches everyone quietly.

Adele turns toward her sisters and holds out her hands. "How can I say anything? I was pregnant with Anthony when I was eighteen."

"You got married," Gladys says.

"They are getting married," says Adele. "At least, that's what she tells me."

This time Eddie shoots me a look that seems to say, See? I roll my eyes at him. As if I'm going to use Trina as my example of good choices in life.

"What's her rush?" Grandma asks.

"I thought marriage was a sacred institution to Catholics," I say.

"You Catholic all of the sudden?" she says pointedly. I drop it.

"And even if they don't get married," Adele goes on, "she's got us. We can help her."

Everyone is silent. What the hell is there to say? This is what women in my family do. They meet men, get pregnant, have babies, and make lives as mothers. Trina's not that different than the rest of them. And now, neither am I, apparently.

After a few seconds, Adele turns back toward the window and says dreamily, "You know, when I got pregnant with her, I thought I was going through menopause early. Which was fine with me. I figured, forty years old, I had my four kids. I'd get through my hot flashes before everyone else, then sit pretty with my estrogen pills for the rest of my life." She closes her eyes and thinks back. I watch my other aunts inch closer to her, nodding their heads, reaching out to comfort her.

"Then, with the morning sickness, I thought, God forbid, I had the stomach cancer." She opens her eyes and looks at each of her sisters. "Remember Uncle Elio with the stomach cancer?"

"Poor man couldn't keep anything down and wasted away to ninety-seven pounds," Mary tells us all.

"I kept telling myself to go to the doctor," says Adele. "But I couldn't face the possibility of cancer. Finally, I thought, wait a minute, I'm getting fat, not skinny, so it can't be stomach cancer."

"Thank God," says Joy.

"Knock wood." Gladys raps on the table.

"And then, I remember it so clearly. I was at the butcher's, buying veal. I was going to make *piccata*. And I'm standing there in front of the counter, looking at all the meat. I felt nauseous, dizzy, completely off-kilter and far away. All that pink naked meat. So exposed and defenseless. I almost wanted to cry for the meat. For the stupid meat."

My aunts laugh together, but my stomach tightens. I think about the pheasants. My first clue. I'm so much like all of them.

"That's when it hit me, like a ton of bricks. Just flattened me. I thought, I know this feeling. I've had this exact same feeling four times before. But with my other kids, I knew the minute I was pregnant."

"You just know," says Gladys. "Even with Sophie, here." She reaches out and runs her fingers through Sophie's soft black hair. "My first. I just knew."

"Me, too," says Joy. "I was puking ten seconds after I got pregnant with Teddy."

"But with Trina, it took me nearly two months to figure it out," says Adele with a laugh. "I walked out of the butcher's in a daze and called Dr. Pucci. Next day, he's like, Yeah, honey, you're going to be a mommy—again."

Everyone smiles fondly. I realize that my hand is resting on my belly. Slowly I move it before anyone notices.

"I don't know." Adele slumps back against the windowsill. "Maybe that was the problem. Maybe it's because I walked around for so long without knowing. Maybe I never bonded with her right."

Oh, great, I think, I've doomed myself to have a kid like Trina.

"No, no, no," says Joy.

"You can't blame yourself," Gladys tells Adele.

"You were just as good a mother to her as to your other four," says Mary.

I go stand with Eddie. He wraps his arms around my shoulders and holds me against his body. I need his reassurance now more than ever. If my aunts have come undone at the thought of Trina having a baby, what will they do when they find out I'm going to be a mother? Me, the least maternal of the entire brood?

"Listen to you all!" Grandma says. She opens the oven door and pulls out a rosy ham. "Blubbering about a baby." She sets the ham on the table. "I put up with every single one of you telling me you were pregnant when you were about her age, and none of you were exactly model citizens. Trina's a fighter. Like everyone in this family." She picks up a carving knife and brandishes it over the meat. "She'll be okay because she has us."

CHAPTER
SEVEN

After an hour of table conversation dissecting every detail of Trina's life, I've had enough. Trina and her baby, Trina and Chuck, Trina's wedding, Trina's hair. I'm more than sick of stupid pregnant Trina.

"I think I'll go down to see Aunt Livinia," I stand up from the kitchen table and announce.

The conversation lulls, and everyone looks at me like I've spoken Flemish.

Eddie stands up, too. "I'll go with you," he says. The man's a saint.

"Good," says my grandma without missing a beat. She grabs a plate and dollops a little bit of each brunch dish onto it. "Take her some food, will you?"

"How's she doing?" I ask.

"Oh, she's great," Grandma says. "Up dancing the Watusi till two, three o'clock in the morning. Throwing tea parties for all her friends." She stares at me. I stare back. "That woman has been sitting in the same chair for the past forty years, and you ask me how she's doing."

"I take it there's no change, then?" I say dryly.

"Eh," Grandma says with a shrug. "She's constipated, she tells me."

I take the plate from her and shake my head as my aunts giggle. Eddie and I head downstairs.

"Hi, Aunt Livvie," I call as we enter her dark musty apartment.

"In here, Poppy," she croaks. In the past few years, Livinia's mind has stayed firmly rooted in the past, when she lived on Staten Island with her sister Poppy.

Eddie and I make our way to the living room, where she's perched in her chair, crocheting. Doilies escape her fingers. Potholders. Tiny sweaters for nonexistent babies. That I thought this would be a better option than the kitchen table conversation upstairs certainly says a lot for my state of mind.

"It's Lemon," I say. "And Eddie. Grandma asked us to bring you down some food."

"Oh," says Livinia weakly. "I thought you were Poppy."

"Poppy's dead, honey," I remind her as I kiss her papery cheek. Eddie stands in the back of the room, rocking on his heels, trying not to touch anything in the crowded, dusty space. I set the covered dish on the end table next to a collection of her favorite photos. She seems not to notice.

Then she looks up from her crochet. "Oh, now," she says, as if she's just become aware of us. "Who's this nice young man here?"

"That's Eddie. Remember him? He's my boyfriend. You've met before."

"Are you two married?" she asks.

"No," I say. Jesus, my family is relentless. Even the senile have an agenda.

"Don't you want to marry our Lemon?" she asks Eddie.

"Sure," he says.

"Then what's the hold-up?" she demands.

Eddie laughs uncomfortably. "You'd have to ask her that."

"Oh," says Livinia. She picks at the plastic wrap over the plate of food. Her dry brittle fingers can't get a hold of it. "I've seen that on the *Montel Williams Show*. Everyone thinks it's the man, but sometimes it's the woman."

"Here," I say and lift the cover from her food. For an old bat, she sure is sharp. "Let me get you a fork."

"Nah," she says and turns away. "Not hungry."

I squint at a large photo on the end table. A baby girl with dark ringlets perched in a wooden high chair stares icily forward. The picture makes me queasy. I instinctively put my hand over my belly as if to protect my unborn child from the jinx of Livinia's dead-baby pictures.

Ever since I can remember, hanging all around Livinia's living room, propped up on every shelf, displayed over the mantel and on the end tables, have been dozens of grainy black-and-white photos of these blank-faced infants, dressed in fine lace christening gowns, posed on chairs, in carriages, sleeping in cribs. When I was a kid, I didn't believe my cousin Teddy that the babies in Livinia's pictures were really dead. Then I asked Aunt Gladys, and she said, "God rest their souls," and crossed herself.

"You sick?" Livinia motions at me with her crochet hook. "You're clutching your stomach like you don't feel well." I move my hand away. Aunt Livinia stares at me. She always was an odd bird. A little grin lurks on her lips. "Do you know what today is?"

"Wednesday," I say, thinking that she's merely confused.

"Today is the day that Tony left."

I'm startled by the clarity of her statement, although I have no idea if it's true. "Today?" I ask. "You sure?"

"July twenty-fifth," she says.

She's right about the date at least. It could be true. Perhaps it's the one piece of reality that she hangs on to. That and the *Montel Williams Show.*

"Ran off with the boss's wife," she says.

I've never heard this before. The family version is clean and tidy. One day Tony put his clothes in a paper sack, took the ferry to work, and never came back. Nobody knew why. Aunt Livinia was never right after that, so Little Great-Aunt Poppy, my grandmother's youngest sister, who had polio as a child and was my same height when I was ten, moved into the Staten Island house to take care of Livinia. After Poppy died, Livinia moved into the basement apartment at my grandmother's house with all her creepy baby pictures.

"Do you know why he left?" she asks, as if she is searching for the answer. As if after all these years, someone could finally explain to her.

"Well, Aunt Livvie," I say, trying my best to find some generic explanation, "some men just aren't cut out for marriage."

"He left me because of the babies."

"Did you offer to take down the pictures?" I ask. "They are a little—you know."

"She was pregnant," Aunt Livinia says.

I exchange glances with Eddie. He shrugs. "Who was pregnant?" I ask.

"You know who," she says and waits for me to get it.

"His boss's wife?"

"The mother-whore," she says with relish.

Eddie leans against the mantel and knocks over one of the pictures.

She looks up at it and gasps, "Poor babies."

"Sorry, sorry." Eddie fumbles to pick it up and replace it.

"See how much they were loved?" she asks him.

I roll my eyes. Here we go again with the stories about the

babies that no one loves. She's been saying these same things since I was a kid. When I was about eight, I asked my grandmother what happened to the babies.

"What babies?" she asked as she tucked me into bed.

"Livinia's babies," I said.

"She doesn't have any babies," she told me.

"Did she ever?"

"You ever meet her children?" She pulled the covers up tight against my body.

"I don't know." I kicked my feet and bent my knees up high to loosen the cover coffin my grandmother had constructed for me.

"Well, you haven't, because she doesn't have any."

"But why does she have those pictures?"

My grandmother held up her hand and looked away. "Filling your head," she muttered. "Never mind what Livinia has." She bent down and kissed me on the forehead.

"Did they die?"

"Who?"

"Like my mom and dad?"

"Hush."

"Did the babies get killed in a train wreck, too?" Those eerie ghostly children were the ones that invaded my dreams. Pressed their oddly peaceful little faces against the windows of my parents' plummeting train.

"Listen," Grandma said as she stroked my hair away from my face. "Your aunt Livinia is a very sad person."

"Sad like me?"

"You're not a sad person," Grandma informed me.

"I'm sad that my mom and dad died."

"That's different. You can be sad that your mom and dad are gone but still be a happy person. Aunt Livinia is sad about everything."

"I feel sad for her then."

Grandma patted my hand. "That's because you're a nice little girl." She stood slowly. Her knees creaked like old doors. "Nightie-night," she said as she turned off the light.

"Grandma," I whispered into the dark.

Grandma paused by the door with her hand on the knob.

"Did anyone take a picture of my mom and dad while they were dead?" I asked, but I knew the answer. Both their coffins were closed. My mother's empty. There was nothing to take a picture of.

"Heavens, no," said Grandma. She pulled the door closed behind her. "Now go to sleep."

I think that Livinia has lost the thread of the conversation. She seems engrossed in her handiwork again, endlessly drawing acrylic yarn from her wicker basket, looping it over and over her crochet hook in a pattern of flowers or stars. But I'm wrong.

She lifts her hook and points at the pictures on the mantel beside Eddie. "People used to love them," she says. "Nowadays they just have abortions."

"Did you see that on the Montel show, too?" I ask, then feel badly for being so mean to her.

She looks up suddenly. "Where's Poppy?" she asks.

Sometimes I wonder if her befuddlement is an act. The conversation gets tough, and she checks out. But her eyes have gone dull, and she seems genuinely confused. I squeeze her old soft hand. "She died, remember?"

"Oh," she says, small and sad. Tears fill up her eyes. "I forgot."

"I know," I say and lean down to hug her. She is tiny. Slight beneath her bulky cardigan sweater.

She reaches out unexpectedly and lays her frail hand against my belly, then looks up at me with that same sly smile on her face. "How far?" she asks.

I pull away. "What're you talking about, Livinia?" I try to

91

sound stern to shut her up, but inside I'm panicked. I look at Eddie. His eyes are wide. How could she know? She couldn't possibly know. She's just weird. Old and weird. What if she does know? If she's figured it out? Dread overtakes me. Not here, not now. Not with every single member of my extended family upstairs within earshot.

It's been this way my entire life. Anything that I didn't want my aunts to know, they'd find out. I'd get diarrhea, and they'd start a phone chain. For the next three weeks, every time I'd see one of them, no matter where I was (church, the grocery store, in the middle of the sidewalk) or who I was with (friends, Grandma, a boy I liked) they'd ask me how my diarrhea was. I can't take that prospect with this baby. Not yet anyway. If Livinia has figured it out, then it's all over. From this moment on this child will cease to belong to Eddie and me. For now and evermore this baby will be the property of the extended Calabria clan. Every decision I make, from what color socks to put on her feet to where to send her to school, will be scrutinized and endlessly discussed by my forty-seven closest relatives, and I will hear every last opinion on the subject. I look back at Livinia, ready to deny everything, but her eyes are gone again.

"Poor babies," she mutters. "Poor, poor babies."

I stand up quickly before she has a chance to become lucid. "We have to get going, Livvie," I say. "You want to come upstairs and say hello to everyone?"

She shakes her head.

"All rightie, then." I grab Eddie's hand and pull him toward the stairs.

"Nice to see you, ma'am," he says as we hightail it out of her morbid living room.

She raises her crochet hook at us, then goes back to her doilies as if we were never there.

CHAPTER
EIGHT

By the time we get back up to my grandmother's, most of my aunts and cousins have left. The lingerers are camped out in the living room, snacking on leftovers and watching the Mets lose again. Eddie joins them, but I venture into the kitchen, where my grandmother is rolling out dough.

"What's that for?" I ask.

"Noodles for the church bazaar," she says and cuts a thin rectangle of dough into long thin ribbons.

I dip an empty mixing bowl into the sink full of sudsy water and wash silently as I look out the window onto the backyard. My mother's pear tree is in full bloom. Little yellow and green pears hang heavy from the branches. "Did my mother want to get married?" I ask.

"Sure," says Grandma. "Why wouldn't she?"

"I don't know," I say without looking at her. "She seemed so different than every one else in the family. More of a free spirit."

"Yeah, well, people in her situation got married in those days." Grandma picks up the noodles, shakes the excess flour off, and lays them out to dry.

"It was the seventies," I point out.

"Not in this neighborhood."

"But do you think she wanted to get married or felt she had to get married?" I rinse the bowl under warm water and set it in the drying rack.

"What's the difference?"

"There's a huge difference."

Grandma eyes me suspiciously. "Why the sudden interest?" She starts on another piece of dough.

I shrug nonchalantly, or so I think. Anytime I've thought I was pulling something over on my grandmother, I've been wrong. She has an uncanny ability to ascertain the situation. Maybe she uses body language or telepathy. When I got back from Europe, she knew something had happened between Franny and me, but I wouldn't tell her what.

"She wasn't like Joy, Adele, Gladys, or Mary, was she?" I ask, hoping to sidetrack Grandma from watching me too closely.

"She was always different. Even as a kid. The other girls never wanted to be apart, but Norma would go off and climb the pear tree just to be alone. Or she'd play the piano for hours and hours, all by herself, getting lost in the music. She never had close friends or even boyfriends. I think plenty of neighborhood boys thought she was cute, but she intimidated them. She was aloof, strong, independent. Like you. Most girls weren't like that then. I always figured she'd be the one to break out and do something different. Move to Manhattan and never come back to see us." She looks at me but I don't take the bait. "But then she met Giovanni, and . . ." She trails off.

They met at a pool hall. Or that's the way my father liked to tell it. As if my mother were some hussy hanging around the pool sharks, looking for a good time. I never got tired of hearing my father tell the story.

He claimed he noticed her just as he was lining up a perfect cross-table eight-ball bounce off the sidewall into the corner pocket. He claimed there was a lot of money riding on that shot. That a couple of Irish guys from Bay Ridge had come to Carroll Gardens looking for trouble. Giovanni was ready to show them to the door, twenty dollars lighter. He always told it like it was a scene from *West Side Story*, as if everyone really did walk around with duck-butt haircuts and cigarette packets rolled up in their sleeves, snapping and singing menacing songs.

Then there was my mother. Standing in the doorway. Giving him her big brown-eyed Claudia Cardinale stare. Arms crossed, hip stuck out, watching him. He claimed that his heart skipped a beat when he saw her, causing his hands to shake, the cue to misfire, the eight ball to fly wildly across the table, bank hard to the right, actually bounce over the two remaining stripes, then off the table and under the jukebox as the cue ball rolled right up to the corner pocket, paused for just a moment, shuddered as if for dramatic effect, and then tipped past the edge, scratching, losing it all for the neighborhood boys, who never forgave him. But, my father always said it was worth it. Just to meet Norma Calabria in a pool hall.

My mother forever rolled her eyes and corrected him. "My sister Gladys introduced us in Fat Sal's pizzeria, attached to the pool hall. I might've stuck my head in once to get a look at him, but I never set foot in that lousy place."

My father would shrug and tilt his head as if to suggest that she had conveniently forgotten her sordid past.

"I was seeing this guy at the time," my mom would point out.

"A hood," my father would clarify. "A real tough guy who walked around in a leather jacket when it was eighty-five degrees outside and always had a toothpick between his lips."

For me, every man I ever saw in a leather jacket or with a

toothpick in his mouth became my mother's past. No matter what he looked like or how old he was, he could have been my father. I shivered at the thought of someone other than Giovanni tucking me in at night, singing me songs about the moon.

"A nice neighborhood kid. Mikey Tronoloni," my mother would interrupt. "Knew him since I was a baby. He wanted to get married, but I wasn't interested."

"Where would you be now?" my father would ask her. "In the Bronx. I tell you. You'd be living in the Bronx."

I would imagine myself living in the Bronx with my mother and Mikey Tronoloni in his leather jacket for a father.

She'd roll her eyes again. "But Gladys said she knew this guy, Giovanni. I said I'd meet him, maybe fix him up with my friend Sue."

"Sue, she says. Sue had a walleye. Never knew who Sue was talking to."

"Stop. You're awful. Sue was a very attractive girl. Real pretty. You'd hardly notice that eye. She ended up okay, Sue. Married an ophthalmologist. They live in Connecticut, you know."

"Connecticut, sheesh!" was always the response from my dad, which cracked me up. I grew up thinking Connecticut was where all the walleyed women lived, since I'd never met a walleyed woman in Brooklyn.

"So I met Giovanni. In the *pizzeria.*" My mother would emphasize the word. "Thought he was cute enough. Nice guy. Good manners."

"You were smitten. Admit it. Scooted over just enough so that when I slid in the booth, our legs touched."

"It was crowded. What'd you want me to do?"

"Ho-ho. You know what I wanted you to do."

"Giovanni, stop! You make it sound like I was some kind of loosey-goosey girl on the make."

The shrug. Again the tilt of the head. I wasn't sure what it meant, but I thought it was hilarious to see my father send my mother up.

"I found out he played the bass. Sometimes he'd come over, and we'd play music together."

"I knew the minute I heard her play the first three bars of 'Take the A Train' on her mother's old squeaky upright piano that this was the girl I would marry."

"So we dated for a while."

"Not that long," my father would say, with a wiggle of his bushy black eyebrows.

My mother would slap his arm. "And we decided to get married."

"Mikey Tronoloni threatened to cut my fingers off and feed them to me like cannoli."

"You exaggerate."

"I thought your mother was going to take him up on the offer."

"My mother always liked you. Likes you better than she likes me," my mother would say, and I'd laugh because sometimes it seemed true. My grandmother adored my father more than any of her other sons-in-law. I suspect she was thrilled when my mother announced that she would marry Giovanni.

It took me until I was nearly sixteen to figure out the math. I knew my parents were married in 1974. Same year that I was born. And I knew their wedding anniversary was January 10. My birthday is July 12. One day, looking at the Holy Name calendar on my grandmother's refrigerator I realized that those two dates were only six months apart.

My grandmother has finished two more batches of noodles while I've been lost in my memories, drying the same bowl over and over again.

"Do you think she wanted to have a baby?" I ask my grandmother. "I mean, me?"

Grandma lays down her last ball of dough. "You were the best thing that ever happened to your mother. I'd never seen her so happy. She hadn't even told me yet. I found her one day with her head over the toilet. 'You been drinking?' I asked. When she came up smiling, I knew. 'How far along are you?' I asked her. She just looked at me and kept on grinning. 'Does he know yet?' I asked. 'He wants to get married,' she told me."

I'm struck by how similarly my father and Eddie handled the same situation. I pick up the ball of dough from the counter and start to knead it. "What'd you say?" I try to picture my mother at twenty-three. I see her smirking on the courthouse steps, with my father laughing by her side.

"What could I say? They were in love," says my grandmother. "All the time playing their music together. Jazz wasn't even popular anymore. Everyone wanted disco and rock-n-roll. But those two didn't care. They loved the jazz. Talked about how they would play in clubs. How they'd travel across the country playing music. So what else could I say? I said I'd call the priest and see if there were any free days at the church, but of course they didn't want a church wedding. Just a quick ceremony at the courthouse."

Sometimes I suspect my grandmother revises history when it comes to my mother. I didn't know Norma that well, but looking back on what I did know about her, my grandmother's rosy picture of my mother's marriage hardly seems to fit.

Grandma wipes her hands on her apron and turns to me. "Why you asking me all of this now?"

"I don't know. Seeing Trina pregnant so young, I guess. Just made me curious about my mom."

She squints at me. Takes me in slowly. Am I giving it all

away? Do I want to? Maybe I do. She's seen this same look on each of her daughters' faces when they came to her with the news that they were unexpectedly pregnant. The look of excitement and terror. The look that says, Now everything is different.

"You thinking about marrying Eddie?" Grandma asks.

"No," I say honestly. "Why? Do you think I should?"

"What's it matter what I think?"

This is her game. The what's-it-matter-what-I-think strategy, when she knows perfectly well how badly it matters to me.

"You know, Lemon," Grandma says to me, "if you want to get married, that's okay."

"Who said anything about—" I start to say, but my grandmother is onto me. She puts her hands on her hips and simply waits.

"I'm not getting married," I say adamantly.

She stares at me with both eyebrows raised. Part of me wants to tell her. Wants to share it with her. Wants to see her reaction. I'm also scared. Scared of her expectations. Will my family think I'm awful when they find out I'm not planning to marry Eddie? That I intend to keep my restaurant, keep working crazy hours, keep pursuing what I want in life instead of completely devoting myself to this kid? Will they think I'm making the same mistakes as my mother? Or is that my fear for myself? My grandmother continues to wait. I'll have to tell her sooner or later. Maybe sooner is better. Give her more time to get used to the idea.

"But," I say, and then I stop. The words get caught, and I'm uncertain. How should I say it? There are no words big enough. You just have to blurt it out. *Blah blah blah blah pregnant blah blah baby blah.* There should be more to it than that. There should be dancing girls and juggling bears and horns and drums and majorettes. There should be a better way. A ritual. A dance. A special feast that says it all.

"I . . ." I start again and she waits. "We're . . ." That's not it either. I put the dough down. "I'm expecting," I say vaguely and quietly, my eyes averted.

"Expecting what?" she says, but I see the little laugh coming up on her face.

I look at her and roll my eyes. "I'm, you know . . ."

She doesn't budge.

I take a breath. "I'm pregnant, and Eddie wants to get married, but I'm freaking out because everything is changing so fast and the restaurant is barely making it and I don't know if I'll be able to handle it all when I have this kid so I just don't know what to do!"

Grandma claps her floured hands together and laughs through the white cloud. She laughs so hard, tears fill her eyes and her belly shakes.

"This is not the reaction I was hoping for," I say.

She doubles over and rests her hands on the counter while she catches her breath. I just stand there, waiting for her to finish.

"You done yet?" I ask.

She wipes the tears away, leaving streaks of flour on her face. "Finally caught up with you, didn't it?"

"What?"

"The ol' Calabria curse. The one you've been trying to outrun all your whole life."

"God!" I yell and nearly knock the dough off the counter. "This is why I don't tell this family anything. I was hoping for some support because I'm terrified! But I come here today, and Trina is as big as a house. Everybody's talking about Trina this and Trina that. But did anyone tell me? No! Nobody tells me anything."

"*You* never tell *us* anything, Lemon. You sat here all day with everyone and didn't say a word about being pregnant."

"Because I was afraid!" I blurt out. Then I realize that it feels good to admit it.

My grandmother scoffs. "Afraid of what?"

"Of what you'd all think. What you'd say."

"Since when has anything any of us thinks or says made a difference to you?"

"It does!" I insist. "It always has."

"Even if it does, you've always gone right ahead and done exactly what you've wanted."

"Just like my mother," I say.

"Yes," my grandmother answers. "You're a lot like her."

"I'm not giving up my restaurant," I tell her defiantly.

"Who says you should?"

"I know it's going to be really hard," I say. "With a kid and a business and the hours."

My grandmother rolls her eyes at me. "You think you're the only one who does anything hard in this family?"

This is how every argument with her goes. She has a way of turning everything big and important into something small and insignificant. "It's just that . . . I'm just so . . ." I fumble and mumble, then once again, like the pregnancy boob that I am, I'm bawling.

My grandmother opens her arms to me and pats me gently on the back. I calm down a little. Dab at my eyes with the corner of a dishtowel.

"I don't know what's wrong with me," I mutter into her shoulder.

"You're pregnant," my grandmother says simply. "That's all. Just pregnant."

"Hey," says Eddie from the doorway. He stands like a little

boy with his hands shoved deep into his pockets. "I thought we weren't telling anybody yet."

"Oh, well, the cat's out of the bag now," I tell him through a sniffle.

"Does this mean I can tell my parents?" he asks.

"Sure," I say and throw my hands up in exasperation. "What the hell! Tell everyone. Yell it from the rooftops. Take out an ad out in the *Times*. Lemon's pregnant! Ha. Ha. Ha."

My grandmother shakes her head at me. "Everything will be fine, Lemon," she says. "You have your whole family to help you."

I pull myself together and laugh a little. "That's what I'm afraid of."

EIGHT WEEKS

You are now an inch. Your mother's thumb tip. You are perfectly formed, with a head and dark spots for eyes, even the beginnings of soft eyelids. You have elbows and wrists that waggle your tiny webbed hands. Your feet paddle, froglike below. Inside, your organs are sketched to be filled in over the next week—heart, lungs, spleen, kidney; love, breath, anger, absolution.

You swim and somersault inside your mother, but still she cannot feel you. No matter how hard she concentrates. You are a matter of faith. She thinks of you as a girl. She doesn't know why. She considers it a gut instinct. She has a fifty-fifty chance of being right. And even though she will be perfectly happy if you are a son, she likes the idea of daughter. Someone to replace the missing link in her life of long-ago abandonment. But what she does not yet understand is, although you are inside her, although she is giving you life, although without her you are literally nothing, already you are your own person, and her life will be endless variations of letting you go.

CHAPTER
NINE

"Ellie Manelli," I say to the receptionist. "I'm a new patient, here to see Dr. Shin."

Once I started looking, I realized there are ob-gyn offices everywhere in my neighborhood. As well as armies of women with babies and strollers. I'd never noticed, but now it seems like everywhere I look, someone is either hugely pregnant or toting around an infant, like another accessory. I asked some friendly-looking new moms for recommendations and stuck my head in a few doctors' offices, then chose the East Village Women's Clinic, a few blocks away from Lemon. The waiting room is nice and simple. No annoying Anne Geddes baby-in-a-bee-costume photos or precious posters of fuzzy kittens. Just comfy chairs, good magazines, decent artwork on the walls, and two recommendations from happy mothers.

"Annual exam?" the receptionist asks without looking up from her computer screen.

Eddie puts his arm around my shoulders and squeezes. "No," he says with a huge, stupid grin on his face. "We're pregnant."

The receptionist stops typing long enough to look at him and blink.

"*I'm* pregnant," I clarify and jab my elbow into Eddie's ribs.

She hands me a clipboard with pink forms and a plastic cup. "Fill these out, then I need a urine sample." She looks at Eddie. "Hers, not yours."

He chuckles, takes the cup, and bounces across the waiting room to two empty chairs. I've yet to see Eddie get embarrassed about anything he's ever done or said. It's something that I love about him, even though his total lack of shame can mortify me at times.

"What's this *we* crap?" I say as I fill in all the standard info on the forms—name, address, phone, next of kin, social security number, family history.

"I'm part of this." He picks up a parenting magazine with a cherubic blue-eyed baby grinning from the cover.

"*We* might be having a baby," I tell him. "But *I'm* the one who's pregnant. *I'm* the one who'll get huge and fat and waddle around. *I'm* the one who has to give up booze and coffee and sushi and rare steaks. *I'll* be the one breast-feeding and having saggy boobs for the rest of my life. You'll be walking around handing out cigars and feeling like a virile stud for nine months."

"Yes," he concedes and grabs my hand. "But I'll have to put up with you, my dear."

I pull my hand away. "Sperm donor," I mutter.

"Sugar daddy, paying your bills," he says.

"Good point," I say and shut up. I know Eddie's only joking about the money, but part of me hates to be so financially dependent on him right now. That's one of the reasons I desperately want Lemon to start being profitable, so I don't feel forever indebted to Eddie for bankrolling me.

"So do I get to say *we're* pregnant, then?" he asks.

"When you pop a squealing ten-pound bowling ball out your ass—" I start to say. He looks at me with his eyebrows raised, a smirk lurking on his lips, and the words half formed. "Stop right there," I tell him. "Crapping and child birth have nothing in common."

He flips a page of the magazine indignantly. "Like I'd say that."

I laugh at him. "Like you wouldn't."

Dr. Shin is small and jittery, like a squirrel. She scurries into the room with my chart in front of her face and bangs into the portable sonogram machine. She pushes it away with her hip and continues reading my chart. She doesn't look like a doctor. Or at least any doctor I've ever seen. She wears an old orange-and-green flowered sundress under her open lab coat, no socks, and scuffed-up white Keds. Her hair is short, chopped right below her ears, with two plastic barrettes holding thick dark strands away from her round face.

"First, congratulations," she says in a singsong nasal accent. "The test is positive." She looks down at my chart. "Your last period was May sixteenth? So you're about eight weeks pregnant, right?"

"Pardon?" Eddie says.

Somehow, Eddie has lived in New York City for the better part of ten years, yet he still can barely distinguish any accent accept his own deep southern drawl.

"I'm not exactly sure," I say. "I was on the pill, and we weren't trying—"

"So this is a big surprise?" she says with a laugh.

"A what?" Eddie asks.

"Surprise," I say, emphasizing the *r*'s for his numb ears.

"Listen, I've been doing this for ten years," Dr. Shin says. "And every day I think it's more a mystery." She laughs again. "We don't understand anything."

"That's comforting," I say.

"Huh?" says Eddie.

"So we'll say May sixteenth was your last period, so you're due—" She pulls a small calendar out of her lab coat pocket. "Middle to end of February."

"February?" Eddie asks.

"Yes, February," I say. "For God's sake."

"February," he says dreamily and beams. "A Valentine's baby."

I want to smack him, or hug him, the sentimental drip.

"Now let's do the exam," says Dr. Shin. "Look inside, take some blood, then the sonogram. Maybe we'll see a heartbeat." She yanks the extension from the bottom of the exam table, then pulls the stirrups up.

"Do you want me to . . ." Eddie half stands and nods toward the door.

"No," says Dr. Shin. "You stay. A husband should know everything about his pregnant wife."

"We're not married," I tell her.

"Is he the father?" she asks.

"Huh?" says Eddie.

"Yes, he's the father," I admit.

"You want him in the delivery room?"

I look at Eddie. He's completely bewildered by our conversation. This is great, I think. I'll be in the middle of labor, panting and sweating and cursing, and I'll have to stop to translate Dr. Shin's Chinese-inflected English for Eddie's stubborn southern ears. "Yeah, he'll probably be there."

Dr. Shin holds up the cold metal duck lips. "Sit down. Relax," she says to Eddie.

He looks at me for a translation. "Stay," I command him, like he's a dog, then I hoist my feet into the godforsaken stirrups.

"You know about the female body?" Dr. Shin asks Eddie as she inserts the duck lips into my crotch.

"Do I know about it?" he asks uncertainly. She waits. He nods, then shakes his head. "Sort of. A little bit." He glances uneasily at a plastic uterus on the counter. "Enough to get her pregnant, I guess," he says with an awkward laugh.

Dr. Shin opens the clamp and sticks her hand inside me. "She has three holes, right?" She bends down and peers in.

"Did you say three?" Eddie asks, totally confused and slightly awed, as if he's either completely misunderstood or he's been missing out on some great opportunity all these years.

"Vagina," she says from somewhere close to mine. "You know that one." She grabs a swab from her tray and puts it in. "Urethra." She looks up from between my legs. "That's the pee-hole." She takes the swab out and releases the clamp. "And anus."

"What'd you know," says Eddie, squirming in his chair, clearly uncomfortable with someone talking candidly about my anus. I'm amazed that an ob-gyn would use the word *pee-hole*, let alone talk about my ass with my boyfriend. I'm not sure whether that makes her really cool or just plain odd.

Dr. Shin bullies the sonogram machine over toward the table. "You want natural childbirth?"

"I think natural," Eddie says.

I scowl at him. "I might want the drugs," I say.

"I'll tell you the best thing. You go into labor, you open a bottle of wine and start drinking," says Dr. Shin.

"Did you say a bottle of wine?" Eddie asks. I want to know the same thing.

"You go to the hospital too early and they tell you go home, or they make you stay and give you drugs. Which is better? At home together drinking good wine or in the hospital with an IV in your arm? You must relax. Wait. Save up your energy. Childbirth's hard work. So stay home. Have a nice time together.

Wait until you're eight centimeters dilated. Then you call me, and we meet."

Now I'm sure that she's just odd, but I run through the list of good wines in the restaurant stock anyway. I'll ask Eddie to pull out a good pinot grigio and stash it at home for the big night.

She fills a condom with some kind of cool blue lube, then rolls it over the ultrasound wand. "Let's say hello to the baby!"

She swishes the magic wand enthusiastically inside me, as if she's Glenda the Good Bitch in a lesbian porno flick called the *Wizard of Jizz.* Eddie stands by my side and holds my hand. We watch the scratchy black-and-white screen positioned between my knees.

Dr. Shin leans forward and squints at the screen, then she frowns and swashes the wand around more urgently. She makes a clicking sound with her tongue against her teeth, which irritates me. I don't want to be a pansy and cry with a quivering voice, "Is everything okay?" So I wait, forgetting to breathe, squeezing Eddie's hand.

"Do you have to pee?" she asks.

"Yeah, sort of," I say.

"See here? This big black blob. That's your bladder. Full. Always full when you're pregnant." She swishes the wand some more, then nods fervently and points to the screen with her ballpoint pen. "See this small black blob?" she asks.

Eddie and I peer more closely.

"That's your uterus."

It seems so small and ordinary. I expected something large and bright, pulsating like a disco ball, my tiny embryo shaking her groove thang to my amniotic beat. Or at least something cozier. An English drawing room with overstuffed wingback chairs covered in flowered chintz, where my wee babe would sit in front of a glowing fireplace.

"See this bright dot?" she asks.

I see a dot, but I'm not sure that's what she's pointing at.

"That's the embryo."

I squint, disbelieving—how could some dot, however bright, be my kid? In the books I've looked at, an eight-week embryo has form, substance, pizzazz. A kidney bean with great black eyes and tiny limbs. This dot looks like nothing. A speck. A blip. Hardly something to pin all our hopes and desires on.

"Now let's look for a heartbeat." She punches a few buttons, and the screen changes. The picture zooms in, and my insides look like a creepy aspic dish in an old cookbook. I see nothing but blobs and blurs and blotches, but it all makes sense to her, apparently. She *mmmms* and *aaaahs* as she searches around, then points her pen to what was the bright white dot. Suddenly it has more form. Shadows. "That's the embryo. And, if we're lucky . . . Hmmm," she says.

"What!" Eddie and I both jump.

"It's backward." She jabs her hand into my belly. "Let's see if we can make it turn."

I want to grab her arm and tell her to stop. She might hurt it. But the weird little alien inside me moves. I can't feel her, but I can see her, turning slowly on the screen. The form of a little body unravels. On top there's a giant weird head, and a tiny pulsating light appears at the center of the blob. Dr. Shin punches a button. Tiny blips moved across the bottom of the screen.

"There it is," she says proudly. She points to the blips. "That's the heartbeat."

Just as Eddie and I are gasping with delight, an itty-bitty foot appears beneath the curved body. Then, an arm! A tiny hand sticks up and waves at us from inside my uterus. Hello.

"Oh, my God," I whisper and reach out for the screen. I want to take this teensy being out and play with her. Dress her

up like an itty-bitty doll. Hold her up and show her off, shouting to the world, "See what I made?" Already, I am a pushy
overbearing mother, but I can't help it. My baby is so beautiful,
floating there inside me. She waves again.

"Hello," Eddie says with nothing short of awe. I blow a kiss
to the screen.

We walk out of the doctor's office into a fabulous morning. An
early haze has burned away, and it's become one of those perfect
summer days when everyone on the streets of Manhattan looks
gorgeous, rushing around in skimpy clothes under the bright
warm sun. I loop my arm in Eddie's and head toward the
restaurant. I still have plenty of time this morning to prep for
tonight's dinner, plus I need to go over the order sheets on my
desk, maybe even pay a few bills. If I'm lucky, I might get to
plan ahead for Sunday's brunch.

"I talked to my parents last night," Eddie tells me as we
walk. We stop at a corner and wait for the traffic to clear.

"Did you tell them about the baby yet?"

"You know, they really want to come for a visit," he says,
clearly evading my question.

"You didn't tell them, did you?" The light changes and we
step into the street.

"It'd be better to do it in person," he says.

"So fly down to Georgia, then."

"Would you come with me?"

I snort. "Yeah, right."

Eddie stops on the corner and lets go of my arm. "You never
go with me to Georgia, and you don't want my parents to come
up here."

"I've been to Georgia with you," I say indignantly.

"Once."

111

"Once was enough," I say. The trip wasn't all that bad. His family is perfectly nice. Maybe that was the problem. Everyone was so polite and welcoming that I was sure it was a ruse. I could imagine his family huddled in the butler's pantry while I was in the bathroom, whispering about all the ways I'm completely wrong for Eddie.

"Besides," I say. "Your mother doesn't even like me." His mother wasn't rude to me. Heavens, no—she is a southerner, after all. But all of her comments seemed vaguely judgmental, and I felt like I wasn't passing whatever tests she was giving me.

"That's not true," says Eddie. "She asks after you every time she calls."

"Hoping that you've come to your senses and dumped me." People step around us, bump our arms, give us dirty looks for blocking the sidewalk while we argue.

"You just don't understand southern women," says Eddie. "And anyway, she'd like you a lot better if you made an effort to see her every now and again."

"Aha! I was right. She doesn't like me."

"I said she'd like you *better*, meaning more than she likes you now, meaning she does like you now."

"Your family's nuts. Between your Aunt Eulabelle quizzing me on cuts of pork and your Uncle Jasper trying to get me liquored up on his special bourbon, not to mention all the stories of the glory days of the textile mill—"

Eddie smirks. "You're a fine one to talk."

"You're the one who's in love with my aunts."

"My mother's going to be the grandmother of this child, Lemon," Eddie says passionately.

"Why haven't you told her, then?"

"It would be better if we could tell her together," he says.

I poke him in the chest, and I laugh. "You're afraid to tell her that I'm knocked up."

"That's not true," he says, defensively.

"Scaredy-cat! Mama's boy!" I taunt.

"Stop," says Eddie, obviously not amused by me. He shifts from foot to foot. "Before I tell them—" he says. He scratches his neck and straightens his shirt. "I think that you should move in with me."

This does stop me. Shuts me up. I stand and stare at him under the clear blue sky. I almost laugh at the situation. Standing on the corner of First and First, taxis swerving around bikes, trucks rumbling over loose manhole covers, people pushing past us, this is where Eddie asks me to move in with him? He has an uncanny knack for terrible timing when it comes to proposing major life changes. But, he looks at me so sweetly, so tenderly, and also vulnerably, as if he's afraid of what I might say or do.

His uncertainty softens me, and I'm filled with the vision of our little critter growing inside me. I see Eddie and me in a bed together with this small person between us. I see walks in the park and lazy Sundays. Us on a picnic blanket watching the baby learn to smile, sit up, and crawl.

This past month, while I've walked around getting used to the idea of another being in my life, I've become sentimental and sappy. Overwhelmed with emotion at the sight of stumbling puppies and flowers growing up out of sidewalk cracks. I don't know what the hell is happening to me, but whatever it is, I realize at this moment that having a place separate from Eddie in the midst of all this confusion of urban life is just silly if we're going to have a kid, so I simply say, "Okay. I'll move in with you."

"Really?" he asks.

I nod.

He looks at me suspiciously. "Why?"

"You don't want me to?"

"You're never this easy."

"Must be the hormones," I say. "Enjoy it while you can."

He takes my arm, and we walk again. Eddie is buoyant, bouncing beside me like a little kid. "This is great, Lemon. You'll see. It'll be wonderful. We'll get settled, then my parents can come."

"Now you're pushing it," I tell him, but still I'm surprisingly calm and happy. Maybe I'm finally ready for all the changes in my life. Moving in with Eddie, having a kid, being a mom. Maybe I'll be able to handle it after all.

As we near the restaurant, I yawn. I've got that familiar late-morning heavy feeling. "I'm so sleepy all of a sudden."

"You should lie down, then," Eddie says. "I read an article in the doctor's office that says pregnant women should take naps. Especially in the first trimester."

"I don't have time for a nap," I say. "I have to work." As I say this and watch Eddie's reaction, the fears that I won't be able to handle everything start to creep back in.

"You should stop drinking coffee, too," Eddie tells me.

"I have one cup in the morning."

"Caffeine can lower birth weight."

"Okay." I let go of his arm. "I'll make it decaf."

"Decaf still has caffeine. Have you even read the books I bought?"

I think of the stack next to my bed, on top of all the old French cookbooks I devour like trashy romance novels. *What to Expect When You're Expecting. Birthing from Within. The Girlfriend's Guide to Pregnancy.* I've looked at them. Mostly at the pictures, and I end up wondering, Who in the hell are the women in these pages? Standing in flowing pink dresses and straw hats in the middle of wheat fields, staring dreamy-eyed into the distance with their hands cradling those monstrous bellies. Or little cartoon women, harried lines of consternation sprouting from their curly heads of hair as they wonder which is better to eat, potato chips or an apple. They're not me, that's for sure.

Eddie stands and waits for me to come to my senses, as if I'm one of those inane cartoon women who can't figure out the obvious best choice. Take a nap or work for sixteen hours straight? His zealousness makes me feel contrite for not taking more of an interest in my pregnancy so far, and once again, I'm terrified. Maybe he wants me to be one of those pansy-asses in the straw hat. Maybe those women make the best mothers. How would I know? That certainly wasn't my mom, but is she the example I want to follow?

Then I think of the heartbeat and the little arm waving to us from the sonogram screen. So fragile. So tiny. So completely reliant on me. Of course I want what's best for this little critter.

"And another thing," Eddie says. "You're going to have to hire someone to replace you for a while, so you should start looking now, because pretty soon you're going to have to stop working so many late shifts. It's not good for the baby."

"Oh, for Christ's sake," I snap. "I can second-guess myself all day when it comes to this kid—I don't need you to do it, too."

"I'm not second-guessing you, I'm looking out for our child."

"Well, Eddie, despite my obvious total lack of mothering instinct, the baby's doing just fine. The doctor said so."

"For now," Eddie says, and is about to start in on some other tirade, but I interrupt him.

"This is ridiculous! Women have been pregnant and having babies for a million years without all this no-caffeine crap. I'm not going to change my whole life—"

"But this is life-changing!" Eddie nearly yells. I walk away, but he doggedly runs beside me. "You're going to have to change your life," he says to me. "Starting now. You're carrying a child." He grabs my arm. "And it's partly mine. You have to think of that baby first."

"Jesus, Eddie!" I push his hands away. "You act like I'm the most horrible negligent mother already. It's not like I'm out shooting smack. I'm not even eating sushi. For God's sake, I bet your mother had her four-o'clock cocktail without fail through both of her pregnancies, and you guys turned out fine. My mother smoked the whole time she was carrying me around, and you're on me about drinking a cup of coffee and not taking a nap!"

"It was different then. They didn't know. Don't you think if they knew, they wouldn't have done those things?"

"Pregnancy's become so fucking precious all of a sudden!" I yell at him. "And yes, I have looked at those stupid books you've given me. Don't use an electric blanket. Don't eat goat cheese. Don't lie on your back or your stomach. Don't sneeze, don't move, don't breathe. But be sure to exercise, eat well, and get plenty of rest, and keep working but don't overdo it. It's a nightmare. I'm a healthy, reasonably young, and intelligent woman who can make my own choices about how to act."

"It isn't only your choice."

This stops me cold. I stand rooted to the sidewalk. "You think I'm going to be a terrible mother, don't you?"

"I just want you to take good care of yourself, that's all."

"I don't need this from you," I say as I stomp off toward the restaurant. "And if you're going to ride my ass about every decision I make, then you can forget about me moving in with you!" I yell over my shoulder.

CHAPTER
TEN

"That you, Lem?" Franny calls from the pantry when I huff into the kitchen. "It's about time you showed up. I'm not going to take inventory every week for you." She stops short when she sees me. I'm sweating from the furious walk from the doctor's to my restaurant and my hair is sticking to my face. "What the hell happened to you?"

"Eddie!" I fume. "He's such an asshole sometimes."

She chuckles. "What'd he do this time to piss you off?"

I haven't told Franny yet that I'm pregnant. I've tried to several times. Tried to find a way. I've thought of food metaphors: *Bun in the oven. A little something from the cabbage patch.* I've tried to hint around: *You know how I've been a real bitch lately?* And a few times I've nearly let crude remarks slip out of my mouth: *Guess who's up a pole?* But nothing has seemed right, and no moment has seemed appropriate.

"I have something I need to tell you," I say.

Franny puts her clipboard down and narrows her eyes at me suspiciously. "Oh, Christ. What now?"

"No, it's nothing bad," I assure her. I grab a pot and some olive oil to busy my hands. Then I put both of them down again and pick up a giant wooden spoon. The last time I told Franny that I thought I was pregnant, it ruined our friendship. Of course, this time is different, but I can't shake the feeling that she'll be angry with me.

"It's just that I'm sort of, you know, well, I'm—"

"What the hell is it, Lemon?" she asks impatiently.

"I'm pregnant!" I blurt.

Franny takes a step backward. She blinks at me a few times. "No way," she whispers.

I nod. "It's true."

"No fucking way," she says. She glances down at my belly, then back into my face. "Are you . . . Do you . . . I mean, is this what you want? Were you trying? Does Eddie know?"

"Yes. I mean no. I mean we weren't trying, but we're both happy. And it's okay. We just came from the doctor, and—"

But Franny's hardly listening. She's pacing the kitchen, shaking her head. "Oh, my God. You're pregnant. I can't believe it. What are we going to do? We can barely keep it together. And now you're going to have a kid!"

"How about a congratulations?"

"Oh, well, sorry," she snaps at me. "I forgot, the world revolves around Lemon."

"Shit," I mutter. I knew this was a horrible idea. I knew it would bring up bad feelings from the past, and Franny would get all freaked out. I drop to a stool and lay my head on the counter. "Between Eddie treating me like I'm some neglectful mother for coming in this morning and you being mad at me, I don't know what the hell I'm going to do."

Franny puts her hands on her hips. "What do you mean, he's treating you a like a neglectful mother?"

This is one of the things that's entirely infuriating and completely wonderful about Franny. She feels entitled to give the people closest to her hell anytime she pleases, but if anyone else mistreats one of her friends, then she's your most rabid defender.

"He wants me to take naps, for Christ's sake!" I say. "Thinks drinking one cup of coffee is going to make this baby deaf, dumb, and blind."

"So tell him to fuck off. It's your body."

"That's the thing," I say, and then it happens again. I'm crying. Suddenly. Without warning. My chest tightens. My chin quivers. My eyes fill with tears. I'm a blubberhead. "Oh Franny," I snivel. "I saw its little arm today. It waved at me."

Her face softens. She smiles brightly. "It has an arm already?"

"And a tiny little foot."

"A foot?" She nearly swoons.

"And a heartbeat."

Franny covers her mouth. "Oh, my God," she says reverently.

"At first, I told myself, It's my body, I can do what I want. But now, when I think about this baby. When I read about it. Its little arms, its little legs. That heart beating." I wipe my nose on a dishtowel. "It's not just me anymore, Franny. It's me plus this other thing. This other being. Not exactly a person. But something. Inside of me. Alive. And I feel like Eddie thinks I don't have a natural mothering instinct. It's like he's afraid I'm going to do something to hurt it. That somehow I'm careless. And, sometimes, I wonder if he's right."

"That's complete horse shit," Franny growls, and I love her for defending me so readily. "You'll make an amazing mom. Eddie knows that."

"Thanks," I say, and I feel terrible for complaining about her recently. She's always been a good friend to me when I needed her the most. "What really sucks is, five minutes before we had this fight, I agreed to move in with him. Now, there's no way."

Franny's mouth drops open, and she shakes her head at me. "He asked you to move in with him?"

I nod. "Actually, he wants to get married."

"And you said no?" Franny grabs the dishtowel from me and swats my arm with it. "You're such an asshole."

I grab the towel back from her. "I'm not going to marry him just because I'm pregnant."

"How about marrying him because he loves you and you love him and because he asked you? And because he's loaded!"

"That's a great reason," I say to Franny, but her comment stings. The last thing I'd ever do is marry Eddie for some kind of financial security.

"I was joking about the money part."

"Why do you care so much if I get married? Since when are you such a traditionalist anyway?"

"Since when do you have such a problem with marriage?"

I fidget on the stool. "It's sexist," I say.

"Bullshit, like you care."

I sit up straight and glare at her. "I am not a piece of property."

Franny rolls her eyes.

"Okay." I slump back down. "So maybe it's just not the right thing for me."

"Why not?" she asks.

"I don't know. God. Why's it matter?"

"It doesn't," says Franny. "But if you're going to take some grand stand against it, then you should at least have a good reason."

I stare at her dumbly. What is my problem? Is it Eddie? Am I unsure about him? No, I can easily imagine sitting across from

Eddie, drinking a good bottle of red wine, until we're both dod- dering old fools. But I can't picture myself in some silly frilly wedding dress, saying I do.

Before I can formulate an answer to Franny's question, the kitchen door swings open. Ernesto and Manuel walk in, chat- ting in Spanish. They look at us and immediately stop talking.

"Que pasa?" Ernesto says to Franny. "Everything okay?"

I give Franny a pleading please-don't-say-anything look.

"Burned soup," she says quickly.

"We can make more," Ernesto assures me with a pat on the back. Manuel nods. I love these guys.

"You up to this today?" Franny turns to me and asks. "It's going to be busy."

I haul myself up from the stool. "Don't you start, too," I warn. I walk to the stove and pour oil into a pot, then grab my knife and start sharpening. "I'm up for it."

But I'm not. By four-thirty I'm completely exhausted, and I have to lie down for a while, or I'll never make it through the night. I go into my office, shut the door, and lay my head on the cluttered desk to doze for a few minutes before the rest of the staff comes in. I'm woken soon after by Franny calling my name.

"In here," I say and try to look like I'm busy.

"Lying down on the job," she says when she catches me shuffling papers around. She snickers at her stupid joke.

"You're a riot," I say. "What'd you want?"

She shoves cooking catalogs and farm brochures off the chair opposite me and plops down. "Mona called."

"Don't tell me," I groan. "If she's calling in sick again—"

"Ear infection," Franny says.

I prop myself up on my elbows and hold my weary head.

"How the hell can an ear infection keep you from mixing drinks?"

"But she's dizzy," Franny says with fake concern. "It'll throw off her whole game."

"She might actually put the right amount of bourbon in a bourbon and soda," I say and lie back down.

"Don't give her credit for knowing what goes in one."

"We don't have time for this shit. How are we going to find another bartender?"

"Maybe someone will fall into our laps," Franny says.

"Like a big hunky French guy?"

"Named Luc," she adds.

"Do you think we can place an ad for one?"

"A hunky French guy? Sure, in the *Village Voice* personals. While we're at it, maybe we should think about hiring another sous-chef. Someone to cover when you're on maternity leave."

"Since when do we have maternity leave?"

"You can't just pop the kid out in the walk-in and be back at the stove fifteen minutes later. And you're certainly not going to push all the extra work off on me and Ernesto."

"I know," I whine, but stop when I hear the back door open and Xiao come into the kitchen calling, "Flowers here!"

"We're in the office, Xiao," I holler.

Xiao sticks her head through the open door. "Hi, hi, hi!" she sings. "Today I have most beautiful flowers. Gorgeous! Just gorgeous." She holds up two heavy bouquets of wildflowers. "More in van!" she says as she scuttles out the door again.

"She's so depressing," Franny says to me.

"Maybe she should consider Prozac."

Xiao comes back in with a bouquet of yellow roses in a vase.

"I didn't order roses, Xiao," I say.

She smiles sweetly. "Let's see. What this card here say?" She brings the flowers to me and hands me a tiny card with "Lemon" written in Eddie's perfect script.

"Did you have a little visitor today?" I ask Xiao.

"Someone very sad," she says and makes an exaggerated frown. "So I say, Mr. Eddie, roses make everything all better. Yellow roses for Miss Lemon, I think."

I inhale their pretty scent. "They're beautiful," I tell her. I pull the card out of the small envelope.

"Read it out loud," Franny commands. Xiao nods eagerly.

"Dear Lemon, Will you please live in sin with me and bear my bastard child? All my love, The Sperm Donor."

Franny and I crack up. "God, he loves you," she says.

"What's it mean?" Xiao asks.

Melanie walks in the door. "What's what mean?"

Ernesto comes out of the kitchen with a delivery confirmation for me to sign. "What're you guys talking about?"

Then Makiko sticks her head in the office. We all look at her. "What's going on?" she asks, immediately self-conscious.

"Lemon has something to tell us," Franny says sarcastically. Everyone looks from me to Franny to the flowers and back to me. Franny raises her eyebrows, expectantly.

I glower at her. I'm not sure I'm ready to tell. Part of me still feels protective of my pregnancy. I like having it all to myself. It can be a heady power trip to walk around secretly carrying another heartbeat, knowing that I'm growing a new human. Also, I worry that everyone will treat me differently if they know. It's already started with Eddie, and now with Franny. But another part of me wants to tell everyone, because every time I say it out loud, it seems more real to me, more certain, and that's exciting.

"Is it good news?" Mel asks eagerly.

"Okay, look," I say and hesitate. "It's not that big of a deal."

"Not a big deal," Franny says, mocking me.

"I mean, it's not going to change anything. At least for a while," I say.

"Oh, for God's sake, Lemon," Franny says. "Just tell them already."

"I'm pregnant," I announce.

Mel, Makiko, and Xiao all squeal and clap and laugh as they surround me with hugs and kisses. Ernesto stands back and grins. Only Franny sits off to the side with a smirk on her face. As I thank everyone for the well wishes, I eye Franny warily, hoping she's not taking my pregnancy as a personal affront.

CHAPTER
ELEVEN

A week later, I'm standing on the sidewalk in front of Lemon, watching two beefy movers carry my life in cardboard boxes down the stairs. Eddie insisted on paying them to pack my stuff, so I have no idea where anything is. Where are the chipped pink-flowered teacups with silver trim from Aunt Livinia's house? Little Great-Aunt Poppy's favorite iron skillet? The faded blue flannel sheets Aunt Adele gave me when I first moved in here? And the lace curtains I took from Grandma's living room when she bought new drapes? My battered cookbooks? My scuffed-up shoes? My mother's fake pearls and my father's old LPs?

My life has been a collection of hand-me-downs and second bests, Dumpster finds, and gifts from my aunts. Nothing in my apartment has ever cost over thirty dollars. I've prided myself on that thrift and lack of domestic interest my entire adult life. I've had more important things to consider than matching the soap dish to the shower curtain. Now as I watch them load my stuff and I imagine it in Eddie's place, I realize that everything I own is pure crap.

Franny comes out of the restaurant. The smell of garlic and

chilies follows her and fills the muggy afternoon air. "This is so weird," she says.

"Why?" I ask.

"You're moving to Brooklyn. To Park Slope, for God's sake," she says, then laughs derisively. "All those pregnancy hormones must've taken over your brain and turned you into some weird Stepford mother-to-be."

"Thanks, Fran," I say.

"You're welcome. What're you going to do with two places? A city home in Manhattan and a country home in Brooklyn. How very bourgeois of you."

"I don't know if I'll keep this one," I tell her. Even after I agreed to move in with Eddie, I insisted that I wanted to keep my apartment. I argued that it would be a good place to rest and occasionally sleep while I'm working. Maybe even a place for him to be with the baby if she's still breast-feeding when I go back to work. I don't think he really bought my argument, but he agreed anyway, probably for fear that I'd back out of the whole deal if he protested.

Now, as I watch my world being systematically disassembled, I realize that I don't want it like that. I'll miss my little hovel with its crooked moldings and loud steam heat. The grimy windows and mildewed tub. My mismatched chairs and dusty books. Everything familiar, with its own story that only I know. At the same time, I realize that it's time to move on. Make a clean break and fully embrace the new version of my life. The one where Eddie and I grow up a little and put this kid's welfare above our own interests. If I have this apartment, then I'll have an excuse not to go to Brooklyn. I'll work too long, too late. If I'm going to do this right, then I have to start compromising.

"You want it?" I ask Franny. "The apartment? I'll sublet it to you, or turn over the lease."

"No way," she says. "You'll hate my guts in seven months after this kid pops out and you've gone loco pushing a stroller with all the lesbians and rich pseudo-lefties in Park Slope."

I cringe, imagining myself as one of the fresh-faced moms in cargo pants and comfortable shoes who meander down the wide clean sidewalks, pushing squalling babies in Maclaren strollers, pulling happy trotting dogs beneath a canopy of old London plane trees. "You're probably right," I tell Franny.

I watch a mover carry down three boxes bound to his back with a long blue and white strap. He slides them into the truck.

"But come on," I say. "This place would be awful for a baby. There's no room for a crib. I'd have to lug the stroller up five flights. And two seconds after she learns to crawl, she'll either have her finger in a light socket or fall out the window."

Another mover yells down to me from the fifth floor. "You want the couch to stay or go?"

"You want the couch?" I ask Franny.

"Are you serious about this?"

I nod. "Sure. Why not? I don't need it. You live in a crap hole and have to take the train an hour to get here every day. Why don't you just take it?"

"Are you going to resent it?" Franny asks.

The guy above us waits.

I shake my head no, then ask her, "What's it going to be?"

"Hell, yes!" she yells. "Sign me up!"

"Do you want the other furniture, too?"

"As long as it'll match my milk crates and futon."

"Leave all the big stuff," I yell up to the movers.

Franny runs back into the restaurant, yelling, "Wait until I tell Ernesto!" over her shoulder. I laugh at her, but feel glad that I'm the one making her happy instead of pissing her off, like I seem to do a lot these days.

127

"I think that's all," the guy yells. "You want to take a look?"

I shake my head no. I don't want to see my place so desolate. I want to remember it how it was. When Eddie comes downstairs, I hold out my hand. "Can I have your keys to my place, please?"

"Why?" he asks. "Where are yours?"

"I made a decision," I tell him. "I'm giving this place to Franny."

Eddie does a quick double take. "But I thought you wanted—"

I shake my head. "I don't want two places."

"Since when?"

"Since now," I say.

He extracts the keys from his pocket and holds them out to me. "Is that really what you want?" I nod and take the keys from him. "You're awesome, Lemon," he says and hugs me tight.

The movers slide the van door closed. "Prospect Park West and Carroll?" the driver asks.

"Yep. I'll meet you there," says Eddie. He turns to me. "You sure you don't want to come?"

I point to the restaurant. "Too much to do."

"Come home early," he says.

I roll my eyes.

He kisses my cheek. "Okay, so see you when you get there. Love you."

"I love you, too," I mumble as I watch the truck creep through a congested intersection toward Brooklyn, where I'll start my life over again.

TEN WEEKS

Oh, baby, what a world you will come into. For now, you nest inside your mother, so naive, with your hands flexed over your tiny pulsing heart as if praying. What favors do you request from God? Your fingers and toes are pronounced, definitive, and real, with touch pads on the ends for you to explore all sharp edges and soft surfaces of the planet.

In profile, you look vaguely human now, with an oversize noggin, evident ears, and a bump of a nose over that tiny slit mouth where taste and tooth buds form. Your tail is gone. Reabsorbed, making you more person than fish. You move, jerky involuntary motions with your limbs. Or, are you really waving to your mother?

You are a girl, as your mother has suspected. Not that anyone can tell yet. But deep inside it's been determined, and already you carry the eggs of another generation, making your mother a temporary nesting doll, carrying her future grandchildren. Your grandmother carried half of your genetic material for a short time. Do you remember? Your mother is bookended by the two of you. Mother, daughter. She is forever both now.

CHAPTER
TWELVE

I've been a Sloper for a week, and I already desperately miss the squalor and inconvenience of the East Village. Here there is no never-ending din of humanity, no slurry of garbage in the gutters. All the people appear well fed, clean-scrubbed, and happy in their comfy lives. Even the loonies who sit on park benches ask politely for change instead of skulking through the streets, yelling at the voices in their heads.

Of course, I still go back to the East Village every day. Half an hour on the F train from Seventh Avenue in Brooklyn to Second Avenue across the river. I'm constantly late. Every morning is a mad rush to find the simplest things in the chaos of our communal space. Boxes from my apartment still line the walls of the bedroom and the hall in Eddie's apartment. I rummage through them every day, looking for something to wear to work.

This morning in one box I uncover a wool sweater, a pair of running shorts, and two framed pictures. In one picture, my grandmother stands in front of a giant fir tree beside Little Great-Aunt Poppy outside Aunt Livinia's old Staten Island house. Aunt Poppy comes up to my grandmother's waist, and she leans on the garden gate, but they have the same broad smile. In the other picture, my mother and her sisters pose by a dock somewhere. My mother stands off to the side, looking coolly ahead while the rest of my aunts sling their arms around one another and mug for the camera. I set the photos on Eddie's dresser, promising myself I'll find a place to hang them soon.

In another box I find my Crock-Pot and a salad spinner, but no clothes. In the hallway, I find a bag of shoes below a set of martini glasses and a wooden bowl. Inside the bag are a lone cooking clog and a pair of Greek sandals from my month in Crete, where I learned to grill anchovies and make a killer *tzatziki* at a little cantina by the beach. As I look at those sandals, I remember Spiro, the waiter there, who liked to slurp ouzo from my belly button. At least he never lit it on fire. I toss the sandals back in the box and give up. I pick up the clothes I wore yesterday and dress quickly.

In the kitchen, I pull open half-empty drawers, looking for herbal tea bags. Each drawer holds a hodgepodge of weird utensils. A tea ball but no tea, a grapefruit knife, an old corkscrew. Cheese grater, mismatched chopsticks. Meat thermometer. "Do we have tea?" I yell to Eddie.

"Above the stove," he yells back from his office, where I hear the clacking of his computer keys.

"Who keeps tea above the stove?"

He comes out of his office, carrying a mug of steaming coffee. The aroma taunts me.

"It's so uncool to drink coffee in front of me," I tell him as I plop a bag of Tummy Mint into a lukewarm cup of water. He holds the coffee behind his back, as if that will help.

"I got a lead on a new white truffle oil from the Piedmont," Eddie tells me.

"Great," I say, but I'm more interested in slathering butter and jam on a piece of bread, hoping to quell the gnawing nausea in my stomach.

"You sure you're still okay with me going on this trip?" he asks.

"Of course." I take a huge bite of the bread. The sticky sweet strawberry jam is wonderful in my mouth. "Why wouldn't I be?"

"I feel bad leaving you."

"I'm not an invalid."

"I wish you'd come with me."

"Stop," I say as I cram the rest of the bread in my mouth, then rush out of the kitchen in search of my bag.

"I also got an e-mail from my mom," Eddie says after me.

I know what's coming. We've still never resolved the issue of a visit from his parents, and I don't feel like another fight right now. I'm too tired. Too harried. Like so many things in my life, I'm following the path of least resistance. I figure it's good training for motherhood. Pick your battles, and all that.

"They want to know if they can come the week before I leave."

"Fine," I yell from the living room, where I find a pair of jeans slung across a chair, but not my bag or my shoes.

"Did you say 'fine'?" Eddie asks from the doorway.

"Sure," I say. "Whatever. I'm late."

"I was also thinking," Eddie says slowly, as if testing the water, sticking one toe in at a time, looking for piranhas, "that maybe we could have a party, so my family can meet your family."

I trot through the apartment, peeking under furniture and behind doors for my lost bag. "You're really pushing it."

"You don't have to do a thing. Just close the restaurant one night, and I'll arrange everything."

"Close the restaurant?" I ask as I drop down on all fours and sweep my hand below the bed. I find running shoes. Then I think, What's it matter? Close the restaurant? Open the restaurant? *Blah blah blah.* So I say, "Fine."

"Did you say 'fine' again?" Eddie asks.

"Sure, whatever." I rush past him into the hall. "As long as you arrange it, and I don't have to do anything but show up." My bag is miraculously hanging by the front door.

Eddie grabs my arm and pulls me back for a kiss before I leave. "Thanks, Lemon. Thanks for agreeing. This is going to be so much fun."

"You have a strange sense of fun, Eddie." I peck him on the cheek and hurry out the door.

It doesn't take long for my aunts to descend once they learn that the Kilbys are due in town and that our apartment is still a wreck. Three days later, while I'm basting a leg of lamb at Lemon, Melanie sticks her head into the kitchen and says, "Eddie's on line one."

"I'll call him back," I say as I slowly brush juices over the browning meat. The lamb smells amazingly good, and I could sink my teeth in right to the bone. Lately all I've wanted to eat is meat, rich and hearty stews, dripping greasy burgers.

"He says he really needs to talk to you now."

"Christ," I mutter as I shove the lamb back in the oven and lick the juices from my fingers.

In the dining room, Xiao hums happily as she makes small arrangements of dahlias for each table. "Good morning, Lemon!" she sings to me. I wave as I pick up the phone.

"Hey," I say. "I'm swamped."

"Listen," says Eddie. He sounds slightly panicked. "I tried to tell them that they should talk to you first—"

"Who?" I thumb through the reservation book. The next two nights are booked up nearly solid. I let Franny plan the menu for the rest of the week to avoid any tension in the kitchen. And this morning, I paid off all the vendors, leaving us broke.

"But they just showed up, and—"

I hear familiar voices in the background at Eddie's. I close the reservation book. "Oh, my God," I say when I hear Aunt Mary exclaim, "Isn't this bay window darling!"

Aunt Joy, or maybe it's Aunt Adele, says, "Some lace curtains would look great."

"And a valance," another adds.

"What are they doing there!" I nearly yell into the phone. I begin to pace. They've done this to me over and over since I was a kid. Before every important event in my life, they've swooped in and taken over. They'd make all the decisions without asking me what I wanted. My first communion dress, wallpaper for my bedroom, what songs to play at my piano recitals, what food to have at my high school graduation party. I tried to put an end to their micromanagement of my life when I left Brooklyn for the first time and ran away to Europe. Since I've been back in New York, my strategy has been not to have important events, keep everything low-key so they don't have a chance to interfere. No one in my family even knew I had a restaurant until I sent out invitations for the opening night.

Now, I can imagine my aunts planning this assault for weeks. I'm back on their turf. Fair game again. I knew this would happen. Since Grandma told them that I'm pregnant and living in Brooklyn with Eddie, I've carefully avoided them, not wanting to unleash the constant barrage of advice, tips, how-tos, and other commentary on how I, like my mother, have no clue about the right way to be domestic. Now they've descended upon our house, no doubt armed with Martha Stewart magazines and bolts of chintz, ready to make my life presentable so that Eddie's parents will believe that I'll be the perfect mother.

"They want to unpack your stuff," Eddie says.

"Eddie," one of them yells, "which closet will be Lemon's?"

"Who is that?" I demand. "Is it Aunt Joy? Put her on the phone!"

"Either one is fine," he hollers away from the phone. "Just throw my stuff on the bed."

"Eddie!" I snarl. "Eddie, listen to me!" I say as sternly as I can, hoping to awaken some fighter instinct in him.

I hear something heavy bang, then Eddie says, "Let me help you with that."

"Don't help them!" I screech. "You have to stop them. Let me talk to one of them."

"Hang on," Eddie says to me. He puts the phone down, and I hear his footsteps across the room. Their muffled voices are unclear, but I think I make out the words, "In the corner," and "That lamp doesn't match."

"Eddie!" I shout into the phone again. "Eddie, get back here!"

He comes back slightly breathless. "Look, Lem." I hear defeat in his voice. "I know this upsets you, but I think we should let them do what they want."

"Do you know what will happen? Do you understand? We'll end up surrounded by rattan baskets and fake ivy and bad reproduction Victorian prints in gold frames. And they'll never leave. They'll be there for weeks. When they finally do leave, they'll come back every chance they get, because then they'll feel entitled, justified. They're like wild dogs, only they rearrange furniture. You have to stop them now, because after this kid comes, it'll just get worse."

"Good God!" Aunt Mary shrieks. "I thought Mother got rid of these ages ago."

"Hey! Hey!" I say into the phone. I know that she's found my grandmother's old lace curtains. "You tell them not to throw anything away. Not one single thing."

"You said yourself that we should just get rid of most of this junk," Eddie says to me.

"So now my stuff is junk?"

"Your words."

"I never said 'junk.'"

Eddie switches gears. "You're too busy as it is. You're dead tired when you come home. And I'm leaving for Italy. My parents are coming. At least this way things will get done."

They've already got him. Brainwashed him. Swayed my poor little Eddie over to their side. "Christ," I mutter.

"You're going to have to start accepting help from people, Lemon. Especially from your family."

"Help is one thing. Completely taking over my life is another."

"It's just stuff," Eddie says.

I can smell the lamb. I need to finish basting it. I have to find a replacement for Mona again tonight. The lights on the phone are blinking. People are calling for reservations, and I'm tying up the lines trying to negotiate through Eddie with my crazy aunts, who are hell-bent on making my life respectable before the Kilbys blow into town. I stop and think, Is it worth the struggle?

"You don't need these," I hear one of my aunts say. "You'll get new ones for your wedding."

"Wedding!" I yell. "You tell her there is no wedding!"

"I'll start a trash pile," says another one.

"Oh, look!" one of them coos. "Lemon's baby pictures."

136

"Let's find some of Eddie and hang them up together," another one answers.

That's when I give in. What's the use? It's already gone too far, and Eddie is helpless. I can't do anything from here, and I can't abandon the restaurant right now. Even if I did, it would take me at least half an hour on the subway to get home. By that time the place will be unrecognizable.

"Fine, fine, fine," I mutter into the phone. I'll draw the line somewhere else. "It's not worth it. Let them do whatever they want," I say.

"You won't regret it," Eddie tells me.

"I might," I say. "But I'll get over it."

When I get home at one that morning, four large black trash bags and a huge stack of broken-down cardboard boxes neatly tied with twine squat on the sidewalk near the curb. I have the urge to rip open each bag and see what parts of my past have been purged without my permission. But I don't. I walk past it all. Up the steps, searching for my keys at the bottom of my bag. I'm too exhausted to undo any of my aunts' handiwork right now anyway. And Eddie's right. It's just stuff. Stuff I don't have the time or energy to deal with when I have plenty of other things to worry about. Like the crappy review in a new lifestyle magazine, calling my food pretentious and my space twee. The fact that I'm still not turning a profit despite all the dinners we're cooking. Franny's growing hostility about my declining productivity. And what the hell I'm going to do about finding a bartender to replace the ever-evasive Mona.

Inside the apartment, everything has been rearranged. One of my old quilts is slung over the back of Eddie's sofa, which is now in front of the bay window, itself covered with new lace curtains. My old green-shaded library lamps are on the end tables that used to be in my grandmother's living room. His coffee table holds a stack of my cooking magazines, and an old samovar that I found behind a Russian restaurant is nestled nicely on a plant stand in the corner. Some of Eddie's books have been cleared out to make room for my father's LP collection. A photo of my mom and dad sits on the mantel next to our baby pictures and a small basket filled with potpourri. I stand in the middle of the room, shake my head, and laugh.

"Lem?" Eddie calls from the bedroom. He emerges, befuddled in his boxer shorts and T-shirt.

I hold my arms out for him. "You look like a hostage that's just been released."

He shakes his head and rubs his eyes. "They were great."

"Stockholm syndrome," I say. I hug and kiss him.

"Don't you think they did a nice job?"

"Yeah," I admit. "The place does look nice. Warm, cozy. Like a real home. Suitable for a child."

"They say they're not done yet."

"What next?"

"The nursery."

"We have a nursery?" I ask.

"Apparently my office."

I shake my head. "We're going to have to draw the line."

"Fine," says Eddie as he heads back toward the bedroom, scratching his stomach as he goes. "Just as long as you're here doing the drawing. They scare me."

In bed we lie side by side. I read because even though I'm exhausted, I'm too wound up to sleep. I thumb through cookbooks, trying to figure out how to use the overabundance of Parma figs we ended up with this week.

Eddie rolls over and curls into me. He slings an arm across my belly. "My mom called today."

"Mm-hmm." I think through the cheeses in the walk-in. How much gorgonzola do we have?

"She's excited about coming this weekend."

"Good," I say, thinking more about a salad with figs and gorgonzola and a warm bacon dressing than Eddie's mom.

"Maybe when they get here, we could make a nice dinner and tell them about the baby."

I drop the cookbook to my lap. "You still haven't told her?" He shrugs, helpless. "God, Eddie. Stop being such a wimp. Just tell her I'm bearing your bastard child and get it over with already."

"It doesn't have to be that way," he says.

"What way?" I go back to my cookbook. Figs wrapped in bacon? Fig ice cream? Fig and melon appetizer?

"Some people get married when they have children, Lemon."

"So what?" I say. I know I sound like a petulant idiot, but I don't care. This conversation has gotten old fast.

"Give me one good reason why you won't marry me," Eddie demands.

I put the book down and look him straight in the eye. "You're fat, stupid, ugly, and lazy."

He smirks. "Just the guy for you, then."

I laugh. This is why I love Eddie. He'll only take so much of my shit. I go back to my book, thinking that maybe this little tiff is over. Maybe Eddie will drop it so that I can get my work done and go to sleep. But I'm wrong.

"Are you unsure about me? About us?" he asks.

This is worse. "I swear, Eddie. You're more like a girl than I am."

He looks at me sadly. "Maybe we should go to a therapist."

I bark a little laugh.

"I'm being serious. We need to think ahead about our lives. Because it's not just our lives anymore. It's our kid's life, too."

"You want me to see a shrink so she can talk me into getting married? I have four aunts, fifteen cousins, and a grandmother who will happily do that for free. Anyway, what makes you think being married is the best thing for us or for this kid?"

"I never said—"

"Plenty of married people have worse relationships than we do."

"You're not listening—"

"Being married isn't magically going to change everything. I'm not suddenly going to be some woman who sits at home knitting fucking baby booties all day. I'm not going to close my restaurant and devote myself full-time to cleaning up poop and anticipating your every whim and desire."

"I've never expected you to be like that."

"Why do you want to get married so badly, then?" I ask.

"I'm an old fart curmudgeon, Lemon," he says. "Underneath it all, I like traditions. I want a big wedding down in Georgia with all our family and friends there. I want a preacher and a flower girl and a band and a cake. I want to see you in a big white dress. I want a honeymoon."

"For God's sake, Eddie. You sound like a fifteen-year-old girl. Should I get you a subscription to *Modern Bride* magazine?"

"You don't have a good reason not to marry me."

I pause. Take a breath. Try to find some reverence for the situation. I try to think seriously about why I'm so afraid to say yes. Slowly, I admit, "I don't want to be like every other woman in my family who got married because she was pregnant, then gave up her entire life."

"Not every woman in your family is like that."

"Name one."

"Your great-aunt Anne Marie."

"She's a nun."

"So?"

"Not your mom."

"She's dead." I sit back against the pillows and stare straight ahead.

"Are you afraid you'll be like her?"

"What was she like?" I ask, daring him to try to understand who my mother was when even I have no idea.

"All I asked was for us to tell my parents together," Eddie says.

"Marriage is stupid," I say, quickly reverting back to my default position so I don't have to think about why I'm so opposed.

"That's mature."

"It's just some dumb ceremony and a stupid piece of paper that proves nothing. And I won't marry you just because you're afraid to tell your mother that I'm pregnant."

"Okay, fine. Let's just drop it," says Eddie. He scoots over to his side of the bed and opens a book called *The Expectant Father*.

"Now you're mad," I say.

He flips the pages of his book crisply. "No, I'm not."

"Fine, neither am I." I grab one of my baby books and open it to a random page. A man supports a naked woman in a squat as she grimaces. Jesus, I think. I want machines and tubes and drugs when this thing comes out.

Eddie sighs. "I don't want to fight with you."

"Then don't."

He reaches for my hand. "Come on," he coaxes.

I flip the page. A blue squealing creature covered in goo stares up from the book. "For crap sake," I say and show Eddie the picture.

He smiles weirdly. "Are you scared?"

"Terrified," I admit.

"Me, too."

I close the book and lay my head on his shoulder. "Can you please just tell them?" I ask.

"We'll call them from the delivery room."

"I'm already completely overwhelmed." I hate to admit it, so I add, "Maybe I'm a wussy."

"You're not a wussy," Eddie assures me. "You're tough, and you've put up with a lot of crap lately."

"But I can't do anything else right now," I say. "You have to take care of this one on your own."

"Okay," he says and kisses my hair. "Don't worry. I'll take care of it. They'll know before they get here."

"Thank you," I say, and I close my eyes. At least that's something I won't have to worry about. One small thing off my plate, which has felt more and more full lately. I don't know how I'm going to balance everything once this baby comes. Obviously some things are going to have to change.

CHAPTER
THIRTEEN

'Scilla and Bucky arrive on Friday morning in their dark red Cadillac. They pull up in front of Eddie's brownstone, tooting and waving out the windows like the king and queen of the pet parade. Their two miniature schnauzers, Rhett and Miss Scarlett, scamper around the backseat, yapping and jumping, pressing their serious faces against the windows, leaving giant smudgy nose marks on the glass.

Eddie and I sit on the stoop. As I watch them, half the gene pool of my child, my stomach feels like tripe stew. Eddie clutches my hand in his, most likely to keep me from fleeing.

'Scilla opens her car door and bursts out onto the curb in a great flash of magenta. Skirts twirl, jackets flare, a scarf flutters out behind her. "Hello, Brooklyn!" she hollers. "Georgia has arrived."

Eddie stands and laughs. "Good morning, Mother!" he calls down to her. "You look as fresh and pretty as spring tulips."

'Scilla strikes a quick pose, and I see Eddie's fine, delicate features in her face. She reaches for the back door, where Rhett and Scarlett scratch soundlessly at the window. She opens the door and releases her minions from hell. The dogs tumble out onto the sidewalk, yipping and yapping in tight circles around 'Scilla's legs. "Yes, yes, I know, I know!" she tells the dogs. "It's your big brother! You are so excited to see him!"

One of the dogs, Rhett or Scarlett—who the hell can tell them apart?—drags its ass across the cement. The other one drops a giant turd in the middle of the sidewalk. 'Scilla claps her hands and howls with delight.

I stay on the stoop and look on in horror as Eddie descends with his arms wide open. I imagine the scene in less than eight hours when Eddie's family and mine mingle at Lemon, trying to find a common language over champagne cocktails and trays of paté. I'm certain it'll be like watching a perverse nature special— the giant whooping cranes of Rhodesia encountering the feisty pygmy chimps of Borneo for the first time. Will they line up on either side of the room and size each other up? Circle one another, deciphering who's the predator, who's the prey? Will an all-out battle ensue for control of the canapés? All as a precursor for who will control this child's destiny. Or will they peacefully coexist, discovering some astounding symbiosis, like rhinos and oxpecker tick birds, that will fascinate scientists for years to come?

Eddie takes his mother in a sweet embrace. She clings to him like a beetle on a stick. I know I'm supposed to be happy that he has a good relationship with his mother, but frankly I find their affection a bit creepy.

At the curb, the car rocks back and forth as Bucky unfolds himself from the front seat. He's a large man with a giant head the size and shape of a pumpkin. His perpetually flushed cheeks give his shock of white hair a pinkish tinge. And, as always, he's impeccably dressed in pressed khaki pants, a stiff button-down oxford shirt, and shiny leather loafers.

"Well, there you are!" he shouts and raises an enormous hand once he's free from the leather interior of the car.

"Thought we'd never get here. Traffic on that Verrazano Bridge is a son of a bitch, I tell ya, a real son of a bitch!"

Then he laughs, loud and hilarious, with his head thrown back and all his yellowing teeth showing. Eddie and 'Scilla join in the vast amusement while I wonder, would anyone notice if I simply slipped out the back? Shimmied down a drain spout. Snuck through the finely manicured gardens of Park Slope and slunk off to some anonymous bar on Fourth Avenue, where I could sip one coveted glass of crisp white wine very, very slowly. Of course, I haven't moved at all. I'm too afraid, lest I draw attention to myself, but Bucky has spotted me anyway.

"Lemon!" he roars as he reaches the bottom of the stoop. "Come on down here and give us a hug, girl!"

Before I can make a move, the schnauzers zip up the steps and snap at my toes with their angry little mouths. Perhaps if I lie down and play dead, they'll ignore me. Bucky mounts the steps after them and lurches toward me with his arms wide open. I glance down at Eddie, who watches with one arm around his mother's waist and a look of pure amusement on his face. I'll grind him up and feed him to the dogs for putting me through this.

Bucky reaches me in three giant strides, lifts me off the stairs, and envelops me in a smothering hug. My face smooshes into his shoulder, which reeks of some spicy aftershave. I sling my arms over his broad back but can't reach my hands together. He lifts me a few inches off the steps with an extra squeeze. The dogs nip at my exposed ankles.

"Great to see you, Lemon! Great to see you!"

I am back on the ground, with Bucky's enormous mitt of a hand pressed against my belly. Then he leans down and yells into my navel, "Hello there, future grandchild! I'm your grand-daddy Bucky!"

"Well, Lemon, honey. I should say, you're hardly showing at all!" says 'Scilla, as she and Eddie walk up the steps together, still with their arms intertwined around each other's waists. "What are you now, four, five months?"

Eddie throws his head back and laughs long and hard. "Hell, mama, she's just ten weeks."

"Oh, well, honey." She reaches out and pinches my side. "It'll all come off when you start breast-feeding. I was the skinniest I'd ever been when I was nursing my boys. It's a beautiful thing," she assures me. "A beautiful thing."

I assume Eddie sees the wrath coming up on my face, because he quickly suggests we all go inside.

"You owe me big-time," I whisper in his ear. "My family is nothing compared to this."

After their luggage is stowed in the office/guest room/future nursery and 'Scilla has freshened up, we all sit politely on Eddie's Pottery Barn beige couch and chairs covered with my mismatched moth-worn quilts and throws. My green-shaded library lamps look hideously out of place mingling with his fake Frank Lloyd Wright floor lamps. Despite my aunts' best efforts, I see now that our apartment is a decorator's worst nightmare. I can't imagine what Eddie's mother must think. Her house is full of themes: the Orchid Room, the Yachter's Club, the Book Nook.

I offer tea and coffee and a tray of pastries that Makiko made, hoping to distract 'Scilla from scrutinizing too closely. She settles herself in the middle of the sofa with Eddie on one side and the dogs on the other. She looks mighty happy, sipping her coffee and nibbling on an almond cherry scone.

"Lemon," she says in her breathy whisper, "these pastries are certainly yummy, darling. So light. Do you use lard?"

"Lard?" I ask.

"My grandmother swore by lard, and she made the flakiest pie crust you could ever imagine. Do you remember MeeMaw's pies, Eddie?"

Eddie nods. I think, MeeMaw? Could I allow my child to say that silly word?

"They were great," Eddie says. "Lemon's grandmother makes a durn good pie herself."

Immediately upon talking to any member of his family, Eddie's vowels expand and his vocabulary shortens. Words like *durn* and *heckfire* slip out of his mouth. Sometimes I think it's all an act. As if any Princeton grad would say such things. But now I worry that they really do talk like that in Georgia, and that it'll be hereditary.

"Well, I for one cannot wait to eat at your restaurant tonight. Eddie tells me it's magnificent," 'Scilla raves. "And that *Gourmet* article. I showed half of Georgia. You must be the toast of the town!"

"Well, I wouldn't say—"

"She's modest!" Bucky shouts.

"No, it's just that—"

"Never met a modest New Yorker!" Bucky cracks himself up. Guffs and huffs at his own joke.

'Scilla crushes up some of the cheese Danish in her palm and holds it out to the dogs. They snuffle at her hand. I wince at the sight of Makiko's hard labor going down Rhett's gullet.

"Poor babies must be starving," coos 'Scilla. "They both have Ménière's disease, you know. Makes them carsick. I don't feed them when we travel. Just give them a little bit of Dramamine before we set out and it does them a world of good. They sit in the back like little angels. Not ever a peep. But by now they must be famished. And it's time for their medicine!" she announces gleefully.

Out of her purse she extracts a large Ziploc bag full of pill bottles and packets. "Rhett has to take Prozac for his nerves," she tells me. "Zantac for his stomach and Centrum for the trots from the mix of Prozac and Zantac. Poor little thing is just a bundle of nerves. And I've noticed lately that he stumbles when he pees." She counts out each pill and makes a neat pile next to the pastry platter.

"The staggering three-legged piss, I like to call it," Bucky chimes in and then guffaws again until his face is as red and puffy as a roasted tomato.

'Scilla smooshes the mustachioed pup against her chest and nuzzles his ear. "Poor baby. I'm just sure he has a brain tumor. What else could it be?"

"All the meds?" I offer, thinking that I will never let her near this baby. Eddie shoots me a wearied look. He learned a long time ago not to mess with his mother's Munchausen syndrome by proxy for her dogs. Probably for fear that she will turn her medical obsession on him and insist that he be tested for West Nile virus and syphilis at the slightest cough.

"Oh, I don't think so," she says. "He's disoriented. He ran into the door the other day, and sometimes he snaps at me, as if he has no idea who I am. The tumor might be pressing against his optic nerve."

Bucky takes a slurp of his coffee. "I'm not paying for goddamned brain surgery for that dog," he grumbles, but finishes with a burble of laughter. "Damn thing has already cost us ten grand. Can you believe that? Ten grand for a dog!" Again the laugh.

"Bucky!" 'Scilla says and clasps Rhett closer to her body. The dog looks on, glassy-eyed and defeated. "Rhett has given us the best years of his life, and you wouldn't care for him in his declining years?"

Bucky looks at Eddie and works himself up into a rumble of laughs. "Eddie, son, if I'm ever in as bad a shape as that there dog, just shoot me! Okay, son! Just put the gun to my head and—"

"Oh, well, now you're just being asinine," 'Scilla says. She releases her death grip on the dog and pats his head fondly. "Don't worry, Rhetty, Daddy loves you. He's just too macho to admit it in front of Lemon." She turns to me. "You'll see, Lemon. Bucky is an absolute cuddle bear with his grandson. Broke down and wept, just wept, at the christening." She stops a moment and cocks her head. "You are planning to christen the baby, now, aren't you? Catholics do that, right?"

"I'm not really a practicing Catholic," I tell her.

"Oh, well, then, whew, what a relief. We can do it down at our church with Pastor John Craig." She leans over, elbows on her knees and reaches toward me. "You'll love him, Lemon. He's a real nice guy. Very modern interpretation of the Bible. Married Eddie's brother. Wish you could've been there. Such a lovely service." She winks at me.

I look at Eddie, totally appalled, but he's oblivious. Just nodding along with whatever the woman says. "Well," I say and stand up. "I have to get going. All that food for the big party isn't going to prep itself!"

"But I thought Franny and Ernesto—" Eddie says.

"Oh, they'll be there," I say. "But I can't expect them to do everything without me. Not yet, anyway." I trot out the room, wondering how I will make it through another three days of this.

CHAPTER
FOURTEEN

There's really nothing for me to do at the restaurant. Franny and Ernesto have everything under control, like I knew they would, especially since I'm paying them time-and-a-half. I use the extra hour to sit in my office and grapple with the books, trying to figure out why I struggle to pay bills every month.

Am I spending too much on the food? How can I skimp on that? That's what makes us who we are. Maybe I have too many people on staff. But I already feel pared down to the bone. I couldn't ask my staff to work any more than they already do. Maybe the rent's too high. I could've looked for a less established neighborhood, but then I wouldn't have as much business. Or maybe it's the little things. All the extraneous stuff I never thought about, like insurance and electric bills and the constant replacement of broken dishes.

I wonder how other, successful, people balance the business side of things with the craft of being a chef. Obviously, I've got the chef part down. The food is great, people flock here for it, laud me with praise, but those are the least of my worries, and everything else about running this place remains a mystery to me. I probably should've managed a restaurant before I got into this. I've never been one to plan ahead much, though. I see a hoop I like, and I light my hair on fire and jump through. Eddie keeps suggesting that I hire a manager, which is a great idea, if I had enough money to pay someone else.

By the time Franny raps on the door to tell me that the guests are arriving, I've worked myself into a tizzy. Numbers swim in front of my eyes, and I have no better idea where we're at financially than I did an hour ago. I'm relieved to shut down the computer and ignore the problems for another day.

I freshen up in the staff bathroom. Somehow, despite my aching head and tired eyes, I look good. My skin glows pink, my hair is shiny. I attribute it to the prenatal vitamins and a day of not standing over a hot stove. I pull on a loose yellow silk sundress that Eddie brought me from Italy last summer. It fits a little snug around my middle. I think of 'Scilla pinching my side. She touches me tonight, and I'll stab her with a fish fork.

"Watch out now, Lemon." Eddie's father stands much too close to me as he points across the room to his wife, holding court in the midst of my aunts. "'Scilla can talk the balls off a brass monkey." He spews a whiskey-scented whistle with every "s" until a fine mist of his alcohol-flecked spit dampens the side of my face and tickles the hollow of my right ear.

"And that one there, Penelope Jardin, in the hat?"

I follow his finger to a large-hipped woman wearing what appears to be a Harry & David fruit basket on her head. Some relation of Eddie's who has a pied-à-terre overlooking the MoMA.

"She looks harmless enough, but she's shrewd. Married to a real bastard." He stops and looks at me, eyebrows raised. I grimace, having no idea what he wants from me. "My cousin Richard!" he nearly screams in my ear, then claps me on the back and sends me pitching forward.

"A real Johnny at the rat hole, if you know what I mean!" He rumbles a deep throaty laugh and catches me by the elbow. Hauls me back up to stand by his side, nearly spilling my third tonic and bitters down the front of my dress.

I need to escape this man. He takes up so much space! His gut nudges at my hip, his elbow niggles at my side. He's a toucher, a squeezer, a slapper-of-backs. He massages my shoulders and chucks me on the chin, grabs my knees and elbows me until I feel like he's antagonizing me into taking a swing. As if he's saying, Let's see what you've got, Yankee. I'm about ready to show him when Lyla skirts by with a tray full of champagne. I reach out for a glass, desperate for anything to take the edge off the night, but she smacks my hand away. "Not good for the baby," she reminds me.

"I'd give my left tit for one of those," I grumble to her.

She glances down at my chest and says, "Honey, with the size of those things, you could get a whole damn bottle."

Buck delicately swipes a flute from the tray for himself. Despite his girth, he's an elegant and graceful man in a perfectly tailored suit and buffed fingernails. Before I can protest and demand some booze, Lyla scuttles off to give away my champagne to all the ungrateful louts in my family who've never been to my restaurant before tonight, and I'm left standing prisoner to Eddie's father, stone-cold sober.

Eddie catches my eye from across the room and grins at me. I plead with my eyes to be rescued. He tosses his head back and laughs as if amused by my creepy cousin James (the author of many graphic novels about a tribe of omnisexual chimp-women with double genitals), who corners Eddie to talk "olive oil" at every family event. I suspect James has lurid notions for Eddie's oil. Serves Eddie right, being cornered by the weirdo.

'Scilla has entertained my aunts for the better part of the cocktail hour. Huge peals of laughter erupt from their circle.

I'm sure she's regaling them with stories from her glamorous girlhood filled with debutante balls and summers on the coast with MeeMaw. My aunts eat it up, as if they're reading a Jackie Collins novel. I can't imagine what stories my family is telling 'Scilla in exchange. Tales of pool-hall brawls, pregnant girls, and steamy summer nights at Coney Island?

I imagine my mother in this situation. Wisecracking and sly, back up against the bar, cigarette in hand. How much would I give to stand beside her and listen to her take a few pokes at these genteel southerners mingling with our sprawling Brooklyn clan? I wonder what she'd think of my life. This restaurant. Eddie. I think my father would've approved. He told me over and over again when I was a kid to do what makes me happy.

Am I happy? I look around at everyone who cares enough to be here tonight. My grandmother, looking gorgeous in her dark red pantsuit, holding court by the bar with a glass of Chianti. My uncles, sitting in the back, talking sports and politics and horse racing. Many of my cousins, who've driven from all over Brooklyn and Jersey, leaving their little urchins behind with babysitters in order to celebrate with us. As much as I complain about my family, I know these people love me and would go to great lengths to see me happy. So yes, despite all my grumbling and grousing, I am happy.

The tinkling bells above the front door draw my attention away from watching my family while nodding mindlessly at Bucky's inane stories. I crane my neck to see who's coming in and catch sight of Trina and Chuck. She's huge, pushing her belly in front of herself like a shopping cart. Apparently, she's fully embraced impending motherhood, giving up her usual biker-chick gear for an oversize Winnie-the-Pooh T-shirt over lavender leggings. She's even let her hair fade back to its natural dirty brown. Chuck, on the other hand, still looks like he recently escaped from prison.

All of my aunts rush to Trina's side, leaving 'Scilla free to glide across the room toward us, white skirts rippling behind her like unfurling sails. She holds a full martini glass daintily between her middle finger and thumb but doesn't spill a drop as she sidesteps the swaggering drunks I call my family, who are dead set on getting every last drop out of Mona at the bar.

I wilt under Eddie's father's five-hundredth poke to my ribs. "Here comes trouble," he chortles in my ear. "'Scilla, darlin','" he says, then swoops out his arm to catch his wife in a practiced embrace.

"Lemon, dear! This place is simply exquisite!" The woman makes grand, sweeping statements about everything in her path, as if her brain constantly churns out marketing copy. She lays her free hand across Bucky's belly and pats him fondly. "I can't get over it. It's so quaint and eclectic! Don't you think so, Bucky?"

"Just like our Lemon, here," he says and wraps his arm around my shoulders, jostling me to the depths of his armpit and bending me forward so that I come face to face with Eddie's mother across his giant gut. She scrunches up her nose as she pats my cheek, like I'm one of her insipid dogs.

As abruptly as he grabbed me, Eddie's father lets me go and sticks out his hand to welcome his cousin Richard, married to the woman in the fruited hat. "Richard!" Bucky hollers as they warmly greet one another. "Have you met the mother-to-be yet?" They turn to me but I'm long gone. Latched onto the elbow of Franny as she scurries toward the kitchen.

"Kill me now, Franny," I beg when we're behind the swinging door. "Shove me in the oven and turn it up to broil. I can't take it anymore."

"Such violent language from the pregnant lady!" Franny pulls an oven mitt over her hand. "It's like some fucked-up reality show gone wrong out there." She opens the warming oven and pokes at the duck breasts with a fork. "The Clampetts meet the Sopranos."

"I won't make it through dinner. Maybe I could claim a sudden illness. Preeclampsia. Early labor."

"Schade!" Franny spits in her best Jewish grandmother voice. "That you should talk that way of your unborn." She plucks a fingerful of salt from a cellar on the counter and tosses it over my shoulder. "Now spit three times before you curse yourself."

"Sorry, sorry. I repent," I say.

"Serves you right. Knocked-up hussy."

"You're enjoying my pain, aren't you?"

Franny bastes the duck breasts. "Oh, more than you can possibly imagine." She cackles with delight. Ernesto joins in while he carefully dresses salad greens on old flowered dessert plates that I got at a flea market years ago.

"Just you two wait." I shove yellow pear tomatoes from the salads into my mouth. "When your families are dancing the *hora* to some mariachi band, I'll be laughing my ass off."

Kirsten pushes through the doors. Her eyes are wide, and a nervous smile plays on her lips. "Lemon, one of your cousins asked me for my phone number. His name is James. What should I tell him?"

"Run, Kirsten!" I say. "Run for your life!"

"Lemon!" My aunt Joy comes in on the tails of Lyla. "There you are." She bustles into the room, grabbing for my arms. "What are you doing in the kitchen? This is your party. You're the hostess. We're all about ready to sit down. Aren't we, Franny?" She has her claws into my skin, pulling me back toward the dining room. I want to grab onto the lip of the counter and refuse to let go, hold on tight until my legs are straight out behind me, as if a giant wind is trying to carry me away.

"That's right," says Franny, pushing me toward the door. "We're going to start the salads. Now get out there and host!"

I throw a tomato at her as Joy drags me out the door.

•   •   •

Eddie and I sit at the head of the front table, with Bucky and 'Scilla to our right and my grandmother to my left. Radiating out from us are my aunts and their families. Eddie's poor second cousin in the fruit hat has been surrounded by my aunt Joy's extended family, including my cousin Teddy's two teenage boys, who fight over the bread basket and flick figs at one another.

"I understand that you're quite the cook," 'Scilla says to my grandmother over the salad. "Is that where Lemon learned her trade?"

My grandmother holds up a forkful of baby greens. "I don't cook fancy like this."

"Eddie has raved about your home-cooked Italian food. I'm surprised that Lemon doesn't have more of that kind of thing on the menu," says 'Scilla. Somehow she makes it sound like an insult that I don't have Grandma Calabria's Home-Cooked Pasta Sauce for sale at the front of the house.

"She learned to cook gourmet food in Europe," my grandmother says with the slightest hint of pride. This is the first time I've heard her talk about my time abroad as something good. "Went from country to country, cooking for different chefs. Came home with recipes for things that I'd never heard of. That's what makes Lemon such a special restaurant."

"Now I've been wondering about something since the first time we met you," booms Bucky. His voice echoes around the room and quiets the tables near us. "You named your restaurant after yourself, but how did you get the name Lemon?"

My Aunt Adele leans over from the next table and says, "She looked like a lemon when she was born."

"She really did," Aunt Joy adds from the other side. "All puckered up." She scrunches her face in a very unflattering way.

"With blond fuzz sticking straight up all over her head," Aunt Mary calls from across the room.

"We'd never seen a blond baby with so much hair," Gladys yells from her table at the back.

"Dark-haired babies, sure. Remember my Vincent?" asks Adele. She points to her son, whose hairline starts right above his eyebrows, which meet like a hedge across his nose.

"He looked like a chimp," says Grandma.

"Still does," says Adele and slaps him playfully on the back of his furry skull.

"You know," 'Scilla says, "I'm just realizing that I don't even know your given name, Lemon. No one's ever told me."

"Ellie," Grandma tells her.

"Short for Eleanor?" asks 'Scilla.

"Just Ellie," Grandma says.

"That's gorgeous!" says 'Scilla. "Why don't you go by that, dear?"

"Ellie Manelli?" I ask. "Sounds like a joke."

Grandma looks up from her salad. "What do you mean, a joke?"

"I sound like a defunct pop band."

My aunts have all risen from their chairs to encircle my table.

"Your father gave you that name," Adele scolds me.

"When she was born, we all called her Lemon," Gladys explains. "But her mother said we had to think up a proper name."

"So her dad wrapped her up in a blanket and danced around with her in his arms, singing," Joy says.

I've heard this story many times before, but like anyone hearing the story of herself, I never tire of it. I put my fork down and listen to my aunt Mary sing my name, "Lemon Manelli, Lemon Manelli, Lemon Manelli."

"But he got all confused," says Adele.

Joy and Gladys lean across Bucky's shoulders and sing, "Lemon Manelli, Lemon Manelli. Lemon-elli. Lemon-elli Manelli, Ellie Manelli."

"Then he just stopped and lifted her up and shouted, 'Ellie Manelli!'" Mary tells us. Everyone chuckles appreciatively.

"Was he drunk?" I ask, meaning it as a joke.

Grandma rubs a piece of bread around the bottom of her salad plate, sopping up all the olive oil. "Probably," she says with a shrug. "Giovanni liked his booze."

"What?" I say. "Are you telling me my father was actually drunk when I was born?"

"Men drank then," says Grandma and looks to Bucky for confirmation. He grins and nods. "They weren't allowed in the hospital, so they went down to the social clubs and got tight until they got the call that everything was okay. Then they'd stumble into the hospital, weepy-eyed and stinking, carrying crushed bouquets of carnations, blubbering about how they were the happiest men alive. That's just how we did things then. Giovanni was no exception."

I glance around at my aunts. "So my father decided to name me while he was drunk, and not one of you said anything?"

"Eh," says Grandma with a shrug. "We thought it was cute."

"Were you *all* drunk?" I ask.

"It's possible," Joy says, and everyone, including Eddie's parents, cracks up.

"Where the hell was my mother in all this?" I whine.

"What'd you mean, where was she?" Grandma asks. "She was right there. She'd just had a baby, for Christ's sake. Where do you think she was? Out dancing?"

"I don't know at this point. Apparently when I was born, every adult around me was rip-roaring wasted, so I suppose it's possible that my mother was out dancing while you were all naming me." No one reacts to my accusations. "Didn't she protest?" I ask.

Grandma shakes her head and laughs. "Nah. Once Giovanni got her to laughing, she'd agree to anything."

"That's probably how she ended up with me in the first place," I say.

My aunts all look at one another and mutter, "That's probably true."

"Could be."

"That's how it usually happened."

"Well," I say. "I'll tell you one thing. This kid is getting a proper name."

"And what about the baby's last name?" 'Scilla asks. She leans forward eagerly. Now I see where this has all been leading.

Eddie perks up. "Kilby," he says, as if it's a given.

"Says who?" I ask. Everyone, including me, looks at Eddie and waits.

"I suppose we could hyphenate," he offers.

"Manelli-Kilby?" 'Scilla says skeptically.

"What's wrong with Manelli?" I say.

As Eddie opens his mouth to protest, a little squeal goes up from the table beside us. Trina stands with her hands pressed against her belly and her mouth open. "Oh, my gawd," she says. "The baby is kicking!" She lifts up her Pooh shirt to reveal her enormous belly with its dark hairline down the middle. "Can you see that?" A little ball punches out from her gut. She gasps and laughs, and my aunts rush to her side to put their hands on the next Calabria addition.

I could be mad at Trina for yanking the spotlight away from me during my party, but truthfully, I'm glad the attention has shifted. This whole thing is exhausting me. I reach out and touch Eddie's hand.

"Manelli my ass," he says to me playfully.

"She's as much mine as she is yours," I answer.

He leans in close to me. "You're just trying to stick it to my mother," he says into my ear.

"We'll see," I say, but I kiss his neck. All I want to do is go home, get in bed, and spend the last few hours before Eddie leaves on his trip curled up in his arms.

"Isn't this great?" he asks me, pointing toward his mother in the middle of my aunts, fawning over Trina.

I know how important it is for him to see my family and his family coexisting. He's a sucker for stuff like that. As part of my ongoing effort to be a better girlfriend to Eddie, I squeeze his hand and say, "Yes, it's great. I'm glad you organized this party. Thank you."

"You're welcome." He wraps his arm around me and laughs. "It's nice of you to lie."

"Any time," I say and lay my head against his shoulder. As I watch my aunts, my grandmother, and 'Scilla, I realize how much love our child will have in this world, and I know for the first time that having this kid is absolutely the right thing for me to do. I only wish my mother could be here, too. I have no idea if she would've been a better grandmother than she was a mother, but I would've liked the chance to find out. I also realize that I have no idea what kind of mother I'll be, but I'll have plenty of help, probably more than I want. That's a nice problem to have. I press Eddie's hand firmly against my belly. "She's going to have a great life," I tell him. "And we're going to be just fine."

TWELVE WEEKS

Congratulations, you are now a fetus. Lucky you. No longer an embryo, half-formed blob. But don't let it go to your grotesquely large head. Half your weight comes from your noggin, where your ears have migrated from your neck to the sides of your face. You're looking mighty human these days.

Now you have nail beds and the beginnings of bones and spontaneous twitching from your minuscule muscles. You can squint, open your mouth, and move your separate fingers and toes. Your intestines are tucked nicely into your abdomen. Hairs sprout across your body. Tiny genitalia announce your sex to the world, and your pituitary gland is switched on. You no longer fit so nicely beneath your mother's belly button. You are beginning to protrude and announce yourself in the primordial line of hair drawn down her taut belly. She often finds her hand resting there, touching the idea of you inside of her.

Despite your gradual showing, you remain largely an abstraction to your mother. As if you are someone that she once knew and holds now only in memory. Or a character in a book. Or a famous person she glimpses on the street and finds vaguely familiar. Sometimes it frightens her to think of your reality. Of how completely you will be inserted into her life. And yet she loves you dearly, no matter how afraid she is.

CHAPTER
FIFTEEN

Eddie's gone. Left Monday morning on the heels of his parents, who offered to stay and keep me company while he's away. This after a long weekend of cheery, not-so-subtle hints about how much nicer, easier, and better our lives would be if we moved to Georgia, where Eddie could have a steady job and our child would get a decent education. I politely declined all offers of assistance and secretly threatened to jump off the Brooklyn Bridge if Eddie didn't get Bucky and 'Scilla out of our place soon.

Eddie was the perfect peacekeeper and never lost his composure, with either his parents or me. On the morning of their departure, he dutifully ushered them out the door, packed the dogs into the Caddy, and sent them on their way home with a crate of olive oil and vinegar and promises for another visit soon.

Now it's time for me to get serious again about Lemon. The past three months have been pure chaos, and I feel like I've abandoned my restaurant. I have to get everything in order so that when this baby comes, things will run smoothly. With

Eddie gone for two weeks, I can throw myself into work, come home as late as I want, and not feel guilty.

Despite my intention to work like a dog while Eddie's away, I did promise that I'd read the latest crop of pregnancy books he bought. I never thought I'd want to read about every gory detail of fetal development. Women have been having babies for a million years, and nobody needed to know exactly when the fingernails form on a fetus. But the further I get into this pregnancy, the more fascinated I become with what's going on inside me.

As I ride the train to and from work, I look at the books. I trace on colorful diagrams the path of this embryo that has lodged between my hipbones. First a blob, then a sea monkey, eventually a viable fetus. I have hemorrhoids, constipation, and engorged breasts to look forward to. All of this is labeled the Miracle of Childbirth, but I'm skeptical. Most of it sounds like hell.

In fact, the more I learn, the more vulnerable I feel. For the first time in my life, I stand on the subway platform full of trepidation. What if someone pushes me? Accidentally or on purpose? And I go careening out of control to the lip of the platform, then windmill my arms and tumble just as the train comes charging into the station? Even when I sit on the bench, I imagine a group of high-school-age delinquents bullying their way down the stairs. They spy me. Alone, because I've come early to avoid rush hour. I'm an easy mark in my cooking clogs and heavy bag of pregnancy books. They surround me, taunt me, throw jabs at me, punch me in the gut, leave me half dead on the platform.

Or what if I eat the wrong thing? The books are full of lists of things a pregnant woman can't have. They've done an excellent job of naming all my favorite foods. Soft unpasteurized cheese, rare meat, liver, raw fish, booze. Even if I stay away from all of those off-limit foods, I could get a hold of something bad. The cream cheese on my bagel could turn rancid; then my baby will end up three-legged and with gills.

Today as I sit in my seat and read about the best exercise for women in my condition (as if), the doors of the train open, and I look up. A woman steps on board, but something is terribly wrong with her. She has no arms. Not even stubs. Nothing. Just two empty sleeves hanging from her shoulders. Her back is twisted, and she walks with a limp. I stare stupidly. Can't stop looking at her. How did she make it through the turnstile? Hell, how has she made it through life? And for God's sake, what happened to her arms? Was there a horrible accident? Did she get thrown in front of a train or beaten bloody by a gang of juvenile marauders? Did she eat rancid cheese?

I stare at her. Watch her find a seat. Thank God she has a seat! How could she stand on a moving subway without holding on to a pole? Do people always give her a seat? What if they didn't? What if she fell? Could she get up? I stare because I am a horrible person. I stare because I am sickened. Was she born this way? Some tragic congenital birth defect? Did her mother eat rancid cheese? Drink too much coffee? Work too many long hours? I look away, hold my breath, wanting not to inhale any bad luck from this poor soul.

I'm sure that I've cursed myself with these horrid thoughts. Cursed the growing baby inside of me. My baby will have no arms now. This is, of course, entirely stupid, since I've seen my baby's arms on the ultrasound. But it doesn't matter. The woman with no arms is an omen in my mind. A harbinger of all the things I've done in my life that will be visited upon the innocent head of my child, who will pay dearly for my mistakes.

I try to shake myself out of this stupor. Since when did I start reasoning like a midcentury Appalachian woman afraid of the evil eye? I can't help it, though.

I force myself to look up at her again. I resolve this instant to be a better person. A better mother. The woman is looking blandly at me. I try to smile. Try to breathe. She blinks at me indifferently, then turns her attention to the Dr. Zizmor dermatology ad above my head. I shudder and go back to my book, wondering if I could handle a child who came out so deformed.

I put my hand on my belly. Touch the presence of my child. *You will be all right,* I tell her, and then I know it's true. No matter if she has no arms or a cleft palate or a hole in her tiny heart, she will be all right because I will love her as I already do. Nothing will change that, but please, I pray to some murky, invisible God, despite everything I do wrong, please let my daughter be okay.

CHAPTER
SIXTEEN

It's Thursday, and we've already plated more dinners since Monday than we usually do in a whole week. That's not even considering the full house we had at last Sunday's brunch. I've been here since seven-forty-five this morning going over the books, checking stock, ordering for next week, and struggling to pay overdue bills. Makiko came in at eight to get a jump start on her lemon wine mousse with raspberry sauce. Franny and Ernesto closed last night, so they sauntered in around noon today and started prepping. Everyone is tired and grouchy and a little bit snippy with each other. Franny's pissed at me for planning the specials without her input. I'm ticked at Ernesto for accepting a crate of heirloom tomatoes that are as hard and green as Granny Smith apples. Makiko's mad that Franny used all the whole cream in a leek and potato soup.

By the time our first diners arrive, I'm already dead tired, achy, and my stomach hurts. Probably because I haven't eaten anything decent all day. Just grabbed bites of bread and bits of chicken or stuck my finger in soups and batters. Eddie would be appalled.

At least everyone else has pulled it together. All around me, they are poised and ready for the night. Franny raises a gleaming butcher knife above a silver trout. Ernesto dunks a hook-end ladle in the giant stockpot of soup. Makiko puts the finishing touches on forty individual chocolate pudding cakes, and Manuel hauls a bag of fresh baguettes from the delivery entrance. Kirsten is halfway in the kitchen door, Lyla halfway out. Hopefully, my staff can carry me through this night, like they've been carrying me every other night for the past twelve weeks.

An order comes in. "Lamb, roasted chestnuts, braised chard on one," I shout out to the kitchen. "Where's my filet for twelve?"

"Up," says Franny and slides the plate my way.

I garnish it with sprigs of quick-fried lemon thyme and send it out. I'm slowly getting into the groove. Forgetting about how my body feels as the multitasking frenzy of the kitchen takes over. Ernesto dances around me with thick cuts of sizzling filet mignon. I dunk a batch of cumin-dusted Vidalia onion rings into the deep fryer. Franny whisks up a fresh batch of bleu cheese sauce. We put it all together on one gorgeous plate with mashed celeriac and asparagus spears.

Despite my grousing, I love the easy chaos among us. The way everything outside this kitchen ceases to exist for the hours while we cook. No matter how I feel when I walk into the restaurant, by the time Franny, Ernesto, and I hit our stride and turn out a plate like the bleu-cheese-smothered filet with onion rings, I'm happy.

My euphoria is short-lived, though. In an hour we get slammed, and I'm quickly in the weeds.

"Where's the *poulet* for five?" Franny asks. She's got a plate ready and waiting. The other orders for the table are in the window.

"Sorry," I mutter. "Got it." I grab a plate that's too hot and send the chicken careening to the floor. "Motherfucker!" I yell. Manuel is already at my feet, scooping up the lost chicken, and

Ernesto has another one out of the warming oven and onto the grill in a matter of seconds.

"Sorry, sorry," I mumble as I dunk my hand in ice water. "Where's three?" I search frantically for the ticket with my free hand.

"Out," says Franny.

"But whose trout is this?" I stare bewildered at the bacon-wrapped fillet left in the window.

Franny is behind me with a tray of miniature crab cakes. "Don't know. Maybe table four. The soup's just going out now." She scoots ramekins of green tomato mint chutney to the salad prep area, then is back at her station, saucing another trout.

"Shit," I say to myself and try to pull it together. I haven't felt this lost and incompetent since I worked in a high-volume tourist trap in the Alps where I didn't speak a word of German and the chef had a penchant for pinching my ass every time he walked by.

"Why don't we switch?" Ernesto says when he sees me standing utterly confused.

"I can do it," I tell him, but it comes out bitchy and I immediately feel badly. "Sorry. I'm just—"

"It's okay," he says and goes back to prepping salads and soups.

We have no time for my nonsense. It was stupid for me to say I'd work the grill tonight, but I was trying to make up for all the shifts I've missed lately.

"Lamb's up," Franny calls.

The kitchen doors swing open, and Mona carries in a bowl of bouillabaisse. "Hey, guys," she chirps.

"Who's at the bar?" I bark at her as I try to catch up on the orders.

She looks over her shoulder. "Uh, nobody right now, I guess."

"You can't leave the bar when we're getting slammed like this!" I yell and try to remember—which order was next, the scallops or the veal?

She shoves the bouillabaisse in front of me. "I just—"

"Get the hell back out there!" I yell.

"But the guy eating at the bar wanted trout, and you sent out this fish soup stuff." She drops the bowl by my grill and slops broth onto the counter.

"You ordered bouillabaisse!" I insist. I flutter through the tickets discarded behind me to find hers.

"We don't have time for this," Franny says. She swipes the bowl from my station and hands it off to Manuel. "Just get the trout for her."

"Thank you, Franny," Mona says as if they are best friends in the whole world. Then she gives me an insipid grin as she plucks the trout from the window.

"Christ," I mutter. My hand is killing me. It's bright red, and already a blister is filling with water on my palm. My head is pounding and my belly aching. Clearly I need a break. I hand my tongs to Ernesto, and without a word, he takes over the grill.

My body feels as if I've been hit by a truck and dragged for a few miles over potholes and dead animal carcasses. And of course, I have to piss like a racehorse. The peeing never ends. So far, pregnancy seems to be mostly about the peeing. That, and this constant churning in my stomach, plus a new ache down deep in my gut.

In the tiny staff bathroom, I splash cold water on my face and press a damp towel into my tired eyes. I catch my reflection in the mirror. I have a slightly greenish tinge. I thought pregnant women were supposed to glow. Maybe later, when I'm huge and fat and waddle around. How will I maneuver through our tiny kitchen with a giant belly? The books say I should have an energy surge in my second trimester. It better get here soon, or I'll be flat out on a pallet in the walk-in.

I sit on the toilet and close my eyes. It feels wonderful to be off my feet. I could fall asleep just like this. Pants around my ankles, elbows on my knees, head cradled in my hands. It's the most comfortable position in the world now. Just a few minutes, I think to myself. Just a few tiny moments of rest before I go back out there.

When I open my eyes and reach for the toilet paper, I see it. There, in my panties. Some dark spots. I immediately think of meat drippings, and for the slightest moment in my delirium I wonder how I managed to spill gravy in my underwear. Then I snap out of my stupidity and realize that it's not gravy, it's blood. Like the first drops of a period, those brownish splotches. That's not supposed to be there, says my brain, but my body is much quicker on the uptake. My heart has sped up, and my breath has become shallow without me realizing it. I'm in panic mode, but I'm stuck. There is gravy in my underwear. What should I do?

Think! I command myself. Think! What do the books say? I haven't read anything about this. All the books talk about the wonderful changes in your body. The amazing route of your baby's development. And anyway, I mostly look at pictures and think about how weird those alien fetuses look inside the womb. I think of myself as an oven. A stupid useless oven that has one job, to bake the bread. Stay closed and warm and bake the bread. But something has gone wrong. I have a leak.

Move! I tell myself. Get up and get help. But from whom? Franny? What would I say? It might be nothing. I could be totally overreacting. What time is it in Italy? Eddie would tell me to go to the doctor's office right now. I look at my watch. It's not even seven. I know Dr. Shin works late some days. I could call her. Run over there. Calm down, I tell myself. It's okay. It's just a little bit of blood. I get up and wash my hands carefully. Am I in pain? I close my eyes and try to feel my body. It's what Eddie told me to do when I first realized I might be pregnant. Hello? Hello? I silently call to my wee babe. Are you okay?

Please be okay, I beg. I'm sorry. I'm sorry. I'm sorry for everything I've done wrong. Please please please be okay. I'll be a better mom. I'll take naps. I really won't drink coffee anymore. Not even decaf. And I'll read all the books. Cover to cover. Just be okay.

I have to leave. I need to get off my feet. That much seems apparent. Even to me. The woman who has no idea why her body does what it does. I wish I were a yogi now. One of those bendy, twisty people who could put herself in a tiny box and breathe at the rate of a hibernating snake. Then I would know, really know, what's happening to me, instead of panicking like this. The armless woman from the train pops into my mind. No! I beg God or whoever's listening. Please, please no. I hurry into the kitchen.

Franny glances up at me. "What's wrong?" she asks as she garnishes two plates of scallops.

"I can't do this," I say, but I can't finish my sentence and tell her why. "Can you guys get by without me?"

"Of course we can get by," Franny snaps. "We've been getting by for weeks now." Her eyes go immediately to my belly, then she shakes her head as if I'm simply using pregnancy as an excuse to get out of work.

I don't have time to deal with her grudges, as if my pregnancy has been designed to make her life harder. "I have to go," I say. "Right now."

"What's wrong with Lemon?" Ernesto asks as I slip out the back.

"Who knows," says Franny angrily.

172

From the alley, I hear the door open behind me, and I turn around, expecting to find Franny, ready to give me hell about leaving early, but it's Makiko. She stands with her arms crossed tightly against her body and hurries to catch up with me.

"Are you okay?" she asks.

"I'll be all right," I tell her, but my words are uncertain.

"I think something's wrong," she says. She reaches out and puts her small hand on my upper arm.

I want to tell Makiko. Want to voice all my deepest fears right now, but it feels like blasphemy to say it out loud. As if I'll jinx whatever's the matter and make it worse. So I simply say, "I'll be fine," and hurry away.

"Call if you need anything," she yells after me.

When I'm around the corner, I pull out my cell phone and dial Dr. Shin's number. I try to explain the situation to the receptionist quietly and calmly. I use the words "abnormal" and "spotting" as if speaking in some quasi-medical jargon will prompt her into action. She seems bored by my description.

"Do you want to see the doctor?" she asks.

"Yes!" I say. "Of course. I'm bleeding. I'm not supposed to bleed. I'm just a few blocks away. Can I talk to her?"

"She's in with a patient." I hear her flip pages. "She could see you Wednesday."

"Next week! You're not listening to me!" Then I lose it. I whimper into the phone. "I have to see her right now," I plead.

"You'd have to hurry. She's getting ready to leave," the receptionist says.

"I can be there in two minutes." I speed up.

"I'll ask her to wait," she says and hangs up the phone.

CHAPTER
SEVENTEEN

Dr. Shin is behind the desk with her coat on when I walk in. She looks up and frowns at me. "You have an appointment?" she asks.

"I just called. She told me I could come in." I point to the receptionist, who gives me an indifferent stare.

"Oh, no," says Dr. Shin. She looks at the appointment book on the desk. "No, no. She made a mistake. I have to go to the hospital now."

"But I just called. I'm bleeding. I have cramps. She said you could see me."

Dr. Shin juts her head forward like a turtle. "What do you mean, bleeding?"

"It just started," I say and force myself to stay calm. To explain the facts. No emotion.

"How much?" she asks.

"Spots. Dark spots."

"Spotting's not abnormal," she says. "You probably just bumped your cervix." She gathers her things. "Did you have sex today?"

"No," I say.

"Or you could have a little food poisoning that upset your stomach." She turns away and puts a chart in her bag. This can't happen. She can't leave. She has to see me.

"But what if I—" I choke. Sputter. The words fail.

"What if what?" she asks.

"I shouldn't be bleeding."

"I know what you're afraid of." She waves her hand dismissively. "Every woman thinks she's going to have a miscarriage."

"Can't you just look?"

"If you're going to lose it, you're going to lose it. Nothing we can do."

She must see the horrified look on my face, because she stops collecting her stuff and leans against the desk. "How far are you?"

"Twelve weeks."

"Did we see a heartbeat?"

I think of the little blips. I think of the foot. The arm. The hand waving to me. I nod furiously.

"Then you don't need to worry. There's an eighty percent chance that you won't lose it."

I stare, dumbfounded. What am I, a thunderstorm?

"It's very rare to lose it after we see a heartbeat," she says. "Sometimes women bleed. We don't know why. It's not abnormal. There's a good chance everything is fine. Anyway, if it's not, there's nothing I can do. It's your body's way. Nature," she says and tries to sound cheery. "So, go home. Relax. Enjoy this time. You're pregnant. Be happy. Lots of women can't even get pregnant."

"But—" I sputter some more. She cannot dismiss me like this. She puts her charts in a briefcase. She gathers her keys. "Stop!" I demand.

Her face goes stony. "You're not listening to what I'm saying," she says sternly. "You're okay. And if not, I can't do anything. It's too early. You're only twelve weeks. It's still normal to lose it. Some women do. Maybe thirty percent of first pregnancies end in the first twelve weeks."

"But, wait a minute. You just said that I'm probably fine."

"Right. You're probably fine, but if not, it wouldn't be abnormal."

I don't understand this at all. I feel weak and dizzy.

She softens her voice. "I'm telling you, you're most likely fine. Go home and rest if you want. Take it easy. Calm your mind down. Stop stressing. It's not good for the baby."

She walks around from the behind the desk. I want to grab her arm and force her to stop. I want to slap her silly.

"Your body will take care of itself," she says, as if she's being comforting. "That's what it's designed to do."

I stand in her way and don't let her pass. "I want to see the baby," I tell her. "I need to know for certain that it's okay."

"I can't tell you that for certain."

"Please," I say and grab her arm. "Please."

Clearly irritated, but probably fearing that I'll follow her down the street if she doesn't agree, she turns around and heads toward an exam room. "Come on," she says and I follow.

I know the routine. In the bathroom off the exam room, I strip from the waist down and cover myself with a scratchy gown. That slow trickle from between my legs has continued and become a brighter red blotch in my underwear. The cramps are worse. Everything's in knots. *Go away*, I implore, as if this problem were a disobedient dog.

In the exam room, Dr. Shin has pushed the ultrasound machine beside the table. She waits for me with the wand in one hand, looking more like she wants to clobber me with it than scan my insides. I ignore her as I climb on board and hoist my legs into the stirrups. Without a word, she puts the wand inside me, and I hold my breath as I watch the screen, as if I'll know what to look for. As if my baby will either be dancing the cancan and holding up a banner proclaiming her safety or there will be a funeral procession complete with a tiny hearse progressing through my womb.

"The cervix is closed," Dr. Shin says matter-of-factly. "But it looks a little tender, swollen."

"Is that why I'm bleeding?" I ask her.

She shrugs. "Hard to say." She moves the wand around.

I see blobs go by, but nothing that looks like my wee babe. Where could she have gone? Disappeared just like that? Vanished to the bottom of a murky brown river, never to be seen again? I remember Eddie's teary eyes when he brought me the pregnancy test to show me the line. How my grandmother laughed so hard she cried when I told her I was pregnant. Franny's bright and happy face in the restaurant kitchen when I said I'd seen the baby's heartbeat. Makiko and Mel and Xiao hugging and kissing me in the office. All of my aunts at Eddie's apartment, making a nest for this kid. Bucky and 'Scilla touching my belly and grinning. *You can't leave us,* I silently tell my baby. *We all love you so much already.* I'll give up the restaurant, marry Eddie, be a stay-at-home mom, move to Georgia. Do anything. Just please stay here with me.

Dr. Shin points to the screen. "There it is," she says. I see the familiar white dot pulsate in the middle of a tiny gray glob. "Just like I said."

I don't know what to do. Should I smile? Laugh? Ha-ha-ha! False alarm! Stand up and shake the doctor's hand? Slap her heartily on the back? Looks like I won't lose this baby after all. Whew! What a scare! You gave us such a scare, kiddo! The only thing I can do is cry at the sight of that beating heart.

Dr. Shin pulls the wand out of me and slags off the splotchy condom. "See, like I said, every woman thinks she's going to miscarry." She sounds like she's chastising me for being as silly as every other woman who fears the worst. "Now you go home. Rest."

Despite the beating heart and her tone, I'm still not convinced everything is fine. "Bed rest?" I ask. I've heard of those weak-wombed women who are driven to their beds, flat on their backs for months, as the only way to save their babies. I'll do it, if that's what it takes.

"No. No," she says dismissively. "I don't believe in bed rest this early. If this baby isn't going to make it, there's nothing you can do. You should live your life like normal. That's the best thing for you and this baby."

"But how will I know? If I'm going to lose it, I mean?"

She sighs, exasperated. She's had enough of me. "If the bleeding gets heavy, like a period, or if you have a lot of cramping, then you can call me." She picks up her bag from the chair by the door. "Otherwise, you're fine," she says emphatically as she leaves.

Outside of the doctor's office, I stand on the sidewalk and stare stupidly at the ground. What's happened to me? Where did that fearless woman I always intended to be go? Why am I so afraid that something's wrong? I'm still bleeding and my belly aches, but Dr. Shin says that I'm fine. That I should go ahead and live my life like normal. What she doesn't get is, my normal life is completely inconducive to motherhood. And therein lies the rub. If something's wrong, then I've likely caused it, only I don't know what I'm doing wrong. She tells me to act normal, but what if that's precisely the problem?

I try to find solace in her assurance. The heartbeat was there.

My cervix is closed. Eighty percent chance. I'm always in the ninety-ninth percentile, I remind myself. The ninety-ninth percentile of winners. On standardized tests. On physical fitness exams. Of the hundred people who will open a New York restaurant, mine will be the one that makes it. With 80 percent odds, I won't be a part of the lousy 20 percent of people who will get the raw deal. So clearly, I'm fine.

In fact, I should probably go back to work. It's the logical thing to do. Only I can't. I can't face another three hours of standing up over a hot grill worried about this baby. Ernesto and Franny will be fine. I'll make it up to them later. I turn toward the subway and head home.

CHAPTER
EIGHTEEN

When I get home, I'm exhausted, but I can't sleep quite yet. Every time I close my eyes, I think about the constant dribble and persistent ache below my belly button. I turn on the light and find my books beside the bed.

I don't read the thin chapters called "Pregnancy Loss," because that's a stupid title. As if some negligent mother has misplaced her pregnancy, like an errant set of keys. As if she could look between couch cushions or inside her overcoat pockets, and well, there it is! That darn embryo. Always getting lost.

Instead, I look at development charts. I study what my baby is supposed to look like. She should be two-and-a-half inches long, the size of my thumb and perfectly formed. With her grape-seed lungs and minuscule fingers she could play a tiny oboe as she somersaults inside of me. I put my hand down below my belly button and concentrate quietly, but I still can't feel her, no matter how hard I try.

From the beginning, I've been amazed at how separate and independent my child is from me, but I'm not from her. I want to know everything. If she's in distress, I want to console her. Take her pain for my own. Maybe if I put more thought and energy into being pregnant, rather than grousing about all the ways it's changing my life for the worse, then I would be able to feel her. I would know why my body is leaking and whether she's going to be okay. I'd never once thought of losing this baby. It seems so stupid now. Of course that was always a possibility. Why didn't anyone tell me?

I open up the books again, and I look at the small sections on miscarriage. What a stupid word, I think. Miscarriage, as if you drop it. As if it falls out of a carriage because you are sloppy and inattentive. The books tell me not to worry. That every woman thinks she might miscarry, but most won't. What about the women who do? They must feel foolish.

I read on. Make myself take in all the words. I need to know *What to Expect When I'm Expecting the Worst*. The books tell me the symptoms of miscarriage are bleeding, cramping, and the passing of tissue, as if I'm gestating a box of Kleenex. There are threatened miscarriages, inevitable miscarriages, missed miscarriages, incomplete miscarriages, and habitual miscarriages. So many kinds to chose from! Yet everything is inconclusive. Uncertain. If you bleed, you might miscarry, but then again, you might not. If you cramp, you could be losing it, but then again, everything could be okay. Why can't they give it to me straight? Does no one know, or am I just presumed too dense to understand, with all the pregnancy hormones coursing through my system? Have I become the ol' hysterical woman à la Freud?

Now I've worked myself into another tizzy, and I know I'll never sleep, so I find the phone in the living room and dial Eddie's cell number. I have no idea what time it is in Italy, but at the moment I don't care. I'm scared. I'm uncertain. I'm alone, and I need the comfort of his voice, even if everything is okay, as Dr. Shin assures me. He answers on the fourth ring. Behind him are loud voices, clanging dishes, and the cacophony of a live band.

"Lem? That you?" he shouts into the phone.

"Can you go someplace quiet?" I yell back. "I need to talk to you."

"Hang on, darling." He covers the phone and says something to someone in his atrocious southern-inflected Italian. "I'm going outside," he tells me. I hear a door open, swing shut, the party noise recede, then he is walking on gravel. I imagine him alone, in the country, and I wish I were there, too.

"Where are you?" I ask.

He laughs. "I'm at a wedding. Can you believe it? I've been going to this farm outside Cerignola in Puglia to talk to a guy about importing his sun-dried *lampascioni* and eggplant. I think I'm close to a deal with him, but he's been a little cagey. Then yesterday he invited me to his daughter's wedding. It's a trip. You'd love it. The food, Lemon. Oh my God. The lamb. Spit-roasted with fresh rosemary and mint. I wish you were here."

"Eddie," I say abruptly. I need him to shut up. I need him to listen. I need him to intuit simply from the timbre of my voice that something is wrong.

"Yeah, babe. What's going on? Everything okay?"

"No." I wish that I could text-message my worries to him, because I don't know how to say them out loud. "It's not." A door opens behind him, and the noise from the party spills over into the phone just as I say, "I'm bleeding."

"Ciao! Ciao!" he yells to someone. They yell back. I'm ready to hang up. I can't compete with the revelry. It was stupid to even call. What do I expect Eddie to do for me? "What's that, darling? You're what?"

"I'm bleeding!" I say, and it comes out wavering, wobbly, my words teetering near hysteria.

182

"Did you cut yourself?"

"For Christ's sake, Eddie!"

"Wait. Wait. Let me go over here." I hear the crunch of gravel under his feet again. In my mind, I see him on some bucolic farm, rolling green grass hills, stone buildings, a setting sun. If I were there with him, maybe none of this would be happening. "Now tell me what's going on," he says.

I take a breath. I'll start from the beginning. Tell him everything. Purge all the worry from my brain. "I worked all day, then I got really tired about four o'clock."

"I've been telling you to take it easy, darling. You push yourself way too hard."

"Goddammit, Eddie. Would you please listen to me?"

"Jesus, Lem," he says. "You seem upset."

I drop the phone to my lap. I can't take it. Maybe he's drunk or the connection's bad, or maybe he's just an idiot. I hear him calling my name through the receiver. I put the phone to my ear again. "I think I'm losing this baby," I tell him as simply as I can.

He is silent.

"I'm bleeding. I saw the doctor."

"For Christ's sake, Lemon!" I hear the gravel crunching under his feet as he begins to pace. Where's he going? Home toward me?

"What'd she say?" he asks. "Are you in the hospital? Do I need to come home?"

Now I feel like a fool. I've completely overstated the situation just to get his attention. I hate to be such a drama queen. So needy and clingy. The books say not to worry. Dr. Shin says not to worry, and here I am, scaring Eddie half to death when he's so far away.

"She says I'm okay," I quickly tell him. "There's an eighty

percent chance that everything is fine." I repeat the odds dutifully, hoping that I'll believe in them if I say them enough.

"Eighty percent?" he says with a relieved sigh. "That's pretty
good. You scared the shit out of me."

"I'm sorry," I say and wonder why I'm apologizing. He's the
one who isn't listening. "I'm scared, Eddie."

"You're probably just working too hard. Why don't you take
a couple of days off?"

I'm silent. This is not the comfort that I need.

"Lem? You still there? Can you hear me?"

"I can hear you," I say stonily.

We're both silent for several seconds. "Do you need me to
come home?" Eddie asks, but I hear the implication in his
voice. That I would need him to come home because I can't
take care of myself.

"No," I say. I feel silly now. As silly as I did when I forced
Dr. Shin to look inside me. "Don't be ridiculous."

"I can if you want."

"I'm sure it's all fine. You should get back to your wedding."
I mean this to come out sarcastic, but my tone is lost over the
long satellite distance carrying my small voice.

"You're sure that you're okay?"

"Yes," I say. "I'm sure."

"Good. Then get some sleep. Relax," Eddie says. "I'll call
you tomorrow and see how you're feeling."

That's it, I think? That's all I get. Eddie's words feel like
another pat on the head. "Fine," I say and hang up abruptly.

Should I call someone else? Who would take my fears seriously? My grandmother? One of my aunts? Franny or Makiko?
But maybe the problem isn't everyone else. Maybe it's me. If my
doctor and my boyfriend aren't worried, then I shouldn't be
either. If I'd listen to them, trust them, relax, go to sleep, stop all

this nonsense, then perhaps everything truly would be all right.

I push the books aside and fluff my pillows, smooth the sheets. I'm just fine, I tell myself, taking on the same conciliatory tone with myself that Dr. Shin and Eddie have taken. A little achy. A little nauseous. But so what? That's pregnancy, right? Why get all freaked out by what's probably normal? I resolve to sleep. To rest. To build up my energy for tomorrow, when everything will be different. I close my eyes, and I breathe slowly and carefully. With each inhale, I tell my baby girl that we will be okay.

I must've slept, because at some point in the night, I wake up with a low deep cramp, as if I need the toilet. Dr. Shin said it could be food poisoning, but I've hardly eaten anything today. Maybe that's the problem. Eddie's right. I'd feel better if I took better care of myself. I could get up and eat, but we have nothing here. I roll over, and the cramp goes away.

Again I doze. This time I dream of a farm and people dancing while I sit in the background on a large, round egg. I'm happy, but I worry that the egg will crack from all the noise of the party. The egg begins to rumble, shimmy, shake, vibrate beneath me. Those vibrations turn to pounding, then to throbbing between my legs. I wake up and blink around the room. The light of a full moon pours into the window, but I'm not sure where I am. Where's the party and the egg that I was sitting on?

As I slowly come back into myself, I forget about everything that's happened recently. I forget that my restaurant worries me. That I live with Eddie, but he's gone. That I'm pregnant and afraid my baby is in trouble. I remember me, but only me. The me of months ago, with no second heartbeat inside. The person with limitless possibilities in my life and everything wide open in front of me.

I remember this feeling from another time in my life. A child's version of this same optimism about the world. I was looking forward to my small six-year-old day. My aunts had promised to take my cousins and me to see *Herbie the Love Bug* in the theater, and when we got home, they promised, my parents would be back.

When I came downstairs that morning, my aunts were all there, sitting around the kitchen table. Their eyes were red and swollen. Mounds of wadded tissues covered the countertops. The radio was on, but someone quickly flicked it off. Aunt Mary pulled me into her lap.

"Your mom and dad might be late," she told me simply as she stroked my hair.

I hated for my hair to be touched, so I squirmed away. "Why?" I asked.

Everyone was quiet. I thought maybe they hadn't heard me. I started to ask again, but Aunt Joy cut me off. "There was an accident, honey," she said.

It's not that I was a particularly savvy six-year-old, but I knew something else was up. There are no Mata Haris in my family. Subtlety is not our strong suit. Something in the moaning and averted eyes and constant crossing of themselves led me to believe my aunts weren't telling me the whole story that morning.

Later, while I was supposed to be napping in my grandmother's bed, I slipped down the hall and slithered beneath the dining room table, where I could see my aunts and grandmother watching television in the living room. On the screen was a river that looked like chocolate milk right after you stir it up, with white frothy bubbles around the edges. I thought of my mother's chocolate milk. She didn't skimp on the Quik powder like every other grown-up I knew. She'd let the excess chocolate sink to the bottom of the glass so that at the end of drinking there would be the most delectable sludge to slurp up. I imagined the river, sweet and chocolatey like that.

I don't remember what the newscasters were saying. Probably things like "rescue efforts continue" and "tragedy" and "worst train accident in New Jersey history." I remember a crane lifting bent and twisted train cars out of the murky water as if they were toys fished from a muddy stream. I didn't put together my parents' "accident" with the mess on the screen. An accident was a small thing. Spilling milk. Bumping my cousins with my bike. Oops, sorry, accident.

Then divers brought up a body wrapped in a black rubber sheet. As the crane lifted it, an arm slipped out, and my grandmother stood up abruptly and turned off the TV.

"Enough," she said. "They should let her be. Norma always did love the water."

I wondered what she meant by that. Who was this Norma that supposedly loved the water? Couldn't have been my mother. I had no fond memories of building sand castles and running in the frothy waves with her. And the only water I'd ever seen in Brooklyn was a stinking canal where my cousin Teddy claimed dead bodies surfaced every once in a while. So the Norma my grandmother must have been talking about was some other Norma that I never knew. One that was somewhere inside that awful picture on TV, while my mother was on her way home to me.

But it was my mother who was left at the bottom of the river after my father's body was fished out. Grandfather Manelli was a World War II veteran who believed deeply in dead heroes and recovery missions, so he approved when my father was brought up from the depths. When the state called off the search without finding Norma, I think Grandma Calabria was relieved.

Grandmother Manelli thought it a sin to leave my mother down in the river, and she made no secret of it. At the funeral, she sat on her perch, the martyred mother with her four daughters circling her. "No body for the priest to bless," she muttered. "No eternal resting place next to her husband," she moaned and spat while eyeing my Grandmother Calabria on the other side of the church, as if it were her fault.

Now from my bed, in a cloudy, half-delirious vision, I see my mother beside me. She's in her red dress, coming in from a late-night gig. She reaches out her hand to stroke the hair away from my face. Then a sudden strong ache deep in my belly hits me, and I curl onto my side. My mother's gone, long gone, I remember, so I call out for my grandmother. I ask her to come and help me because I'm sick. My voice echoes back to me, and I realize that I'm not at her house either. I'm home alone, and something horrible is happening. Another flash of pain, and I push myself out of bed.

In the bathroom, when I lower my panties, I see the bright red stain of blood. Not the small dark spots or slow trickle of before, but the mark of something worse. Something far more profound. Then I feel a slip inside of me. A glob. A blob. What's falling from my body? Some kind of clot, a clump. Is this what the books mean by tissue? A torrent of blood and bright pink liquid as thin and powerful as pee comes out of me, and I moan.

When it stops, I rummage in the drawers for a pad. I put it in and stand up. I have to get to the phone. Call Eddie. Call Dr. Shin. Ask someone for help. As I walk, I break into a shivering sweat. A dark cloud covers my eyes, and I know I'm going down. I fall, gently crumple, everything dark and shadowy. I catch myself on all fours, lower myself, and roll into a ball. I think I'm dying. The baby and I are dying. Here. Alone.

But I don't die. Of course not. This is not my death tonight. My vision clears, and I haul myself onto the bed. The phone is beside the pillow. I dial Eddie's number. It takes several seconds of scratchy white noise before the call goes through, then I hear his familiar voice telling me to leave a message.

"Goddammit!" I yell into the phone and hang up. Where could he be? What the hell time is it in Italy? Why didn't he answer? He's still at that wedding while I writhe on our bed. I dial his number again. Again his voice mail. I try to say something. Try to form a sentence, but I don't know what to say. How to say it. After several seconds I growl into the phone, "Where the fuck are you when I need you?"

Why am I calling him anyway? He can't do anything. I hang up and call Dr. Shin. I don't care what time it is. A sleepy man at her answering service picks up. He asks me if this is an emergency, and I tell him that it is. He takes my number and assures me that Dr. Shin will call me back. I hang up and fear that I'll never hear from her. But seconds later, the phone rings. It's her.

I try to explain exactly what's happening, but I can't talk right. "Something's very wrong," I say in some strange slurry language, my tongue thick with unwanted words. I can barely talk or breathe because I'm crying.

"Ellie!" Dr. Shin says sharply. "You must calm down." I hear the tiredness in her voice. The slow draw of her annoyed words. "I already told you, some women bleed during pregnancy. There's a heartbeat. Most likely you're fine. I want you to go back to bed. Put your feet up and get some sleep."

"I can't," I tell her. "I'm afraid."

"Is your husband there with you?" she asks. "Let me talk to him."

"I'm alone," I say, and then I think, Why? Why am I alone?

"You must stop panicking," she says sternly.

"Please make it stop?" I beg.

"I can't," she says softly. "And you don't want me to. If you're going to lose it, it's because it's no good. It means something is wrong with that fetus. All you can do right now is go back to bed. Put your feet up. Try to sleep."

I snap into a moment of lucidity when she tells me this. All my fear and concern morphs into outrage. I spew at her, "Are you fucking serious? This is your advice? I'm bleeding and cramping, maybe losing this baby in the middle of the fucking night, and you tell me to put my fucking feet up? What the hell kind of doctor are you?" I'm pissed. Livid. If she were here, I'd whack her with my pregnancy books.

She sighs wearily. "Ellie," she says full of pity. I hate to hear my name, especially in that scolding tone. As quickly as I was angry and ready to fight with her, I am chastised. I've become her nightmare patient. Who am I to tell her that her advice is bad? She's the doctor. Seen it all a thousand times before. I'm just some lousy sniveling woman who has no idea what the hell my body is doing.

"If I send you to the hospital," Dr. shin explains to me, "they won't be able to do anything for you. Sometimes women bleed, heavily, and we don't always know why. Sometimes everything is fine. It's too early to tell, and it's too early in the pregnancy to try to save it if something's wrong. So the best thing for you to do is wait and see. I'll call you in a few hours to check on you. Do you understand?"

I tell her that I understand, but I don't understand how this could be happening to me. I've read the books. Followed the directions. Consulted with my doctor. Spoken to the father of my child. I did what they told me. Put my feet up and tried to relax. None of this has helped. I think of calling Eddie again or my grandmother, maybe Franny, but I'm tired of explaining a situation that no one can do anything about. So I tell myself that I will be okay, and I close my eyes.

I know I've done everything I can do, yet nothing could prepare me for this full-moon night, when gravity loosens the fetus slowly dying in my body. I feel it let go from deep inside of me. I bolt upright and scramble from the bed, thinking I can save it if I move quickly enough. If I'm in the bathroom. If I can make it to the phone. But it plummets in a sickening slide from between my soft labia to land between my legs in a quivering mess. I gasp and call out to God, but I know that this is the end.

I take tiny mincing steps, doubled over, my body racked with huge aching sobs. I walk like an elderly woman with slow unsure steps toward the bathroom. I feel ancient because at this moment there's more death in me than there is life. In the soft moonlight filtering through the bathroom windows, I slowly lower my pajama bottoms with my eyes half closed because I do not want to see what has come loose from my body. It feels gigantic, and I'm afraid.

I sit on the toilet, squinting in the half dark, and carefully remove what's fallen. I hold it up with both hands, cradled in my underwear, as if I'm offering it to an angry God. And I keen, a sound so desperate and sad that it surprises even me.

In my hands is death. A tiny orb has fallen out of me, like a gelatinous comet trailing its own life support system. The books said the fetus was two inches. My thumb. The pictures made it seem as if the baby floated happily around inside of me like an alien astronaut (with its outsized noggin and paddle arms) attached to me by a long thin cord. But no. That isn't it at all. All kinds of extraneous material held everything in place. What I see lying bloody in my hands would have been my child, and it is huge.

Nowhere in that mess do I see the body of my baby, because she is packed inside a yellow orb. A spaceship built for one. Time traveling through a wormhole between my legs. Part of me wants to touch the quivering glob. Break it open with my fingernail like a soft egg and expose my daughter to the world. I want to see her, just once. Hold her minuscule hand and look into her eyes. But it seems profane to disturb her cocoon, so I don't touch it.

I want to create some sort of shroud from gauzy fabric and carve a box from fragrant wood. Carry her out to the woods. Alone. Just the two of us, to bury what I've lost. Or slide her tiny form into the sea to join my mother. This can't be the way it will end for us. Me wracked and wailing on the toilet. Her wrapped in wads of toilet paper. I have no fabric or a box. I have nothing to offer her. What else can I do? I lay her remains gently in the trashcan and close my eyes to spare myself the sight of my failure.

CHAPTER
NINETEEN

When I'm clean, when I'm empty, when some sort of ratio-nality kicks back in and I've taken care of myself, I crawl into bed. The first call I make is to Dr. Shin.

"The worst is over," she tells me after I explain what happened.

"What now?" I ask, and I'm surprised by how calm and rea-sonable my voice is.

"You'll bleed for a while. Like a bad period. Some cramping. You can take painkillers if you need to. Any over-the-counter thing is fine. Doesn't matter."

"Don't I at least deserve Vicodin or OxyContin?" I ask, trying in vain to find some humor. Then again, maybe I'm not kidding.

"You shouldn't need something that strong," she says.

"Should I come in to see you?"

"Call me when the bleeding tapers off. About a week or so, and we'll take a look inside. Make sure everything passed. But you're young and healthy. You'll do fine."

"Do I need to stay in bed or anything?" I sound desperate as I seek some kind of guidance about how to act and what to do because I feel so lost.

"You can do whatever you feel up to, really," she says and I want to ask, waterskiing, equestrian sports? "But," she adds quickly, "nothing vaginal until I see you."

Nothing vaginal! What's she think I'm going to do? Stick a banana up there? Shoot Ping-Pong balls across the room? I just lost my baby, for Christ's sake.

"So, are you okay?" Her voice is all tenderness and caring now. Too little too late, I think, but I tell her that I'm all right and that I understand what to do, even though I still can't comprehend why or how this has happened.

The next call I make is to Eddie. "You have to be there," I say aloud to the ringing phone.

"Lem?" he answers sleepily. "That you?"

I sit, confused. I don't know what to say.

"Lem? Darling? You there?"

"Eddie," I whisper.

"I can barely hear you, honey. Can you speak up?"

"Eddie, I lost it." My voice sounds tiny. Vanquished across the miles in the sky.

"Lost what?" he says with a little laugh. "Are you dreaming?"

"The baby," I tell him. "I lost the baby. It's gone."

He's silent except for his breathing. In and out, a little ragged and uncertain. "What'd you mean, it's gone?"

I can't answer him. I can't talk anymore. I lie with the phone beside my head, and I cry, quietly.

"I don't understand, Lemon. You have to explain this to me. Where'd it go?" His voice grows frantic, creeping up and up. "Where are you? What the hell happened?" His words hit me like little slaps, and I cry harder.

"It died," I choke. "It came out." Those words. So simple. So tiny and small. What I thought the thing alive inside of me was once, but I was wrong. It was huge and complicated in death. These little words can't convey.

"No. Wait," he says. Demands. "This can't be right. You must be wrong. The doctor said you were fine. You just told me that you were fine an hour ago. Are you at the hospital? Are you with the doctor? Put the doctor on the phone. Put the doctor on the phone now, Lemon."

"Stop," I say. "Stop yelling at me."

He takes a breath. Regroups himself and says more calmly, "Tell me where you are."

"I'm at home. I'm alone."

"What do you mean, you're alone?" he explodes. "Why aren't you at the hospital? Call nine-one-one. Do something!"

I'm exhausted now. I want everything to be done. I want to close my eyes and sleep. "There's nothing else I can do," I tell him simply.

He's quiet. I imagine him in some old hotel, his room over-looking a quiet piazza where the same moon is high in the sky. I want to touch him. Feel him beside me. Have his arms around my poor sad body.

"I'm sorry," I whisper to him.

"Why did this happen?" Eddie asks. "What did you do?"

His voice breaks, and he cries. Rough whimpers crackle on the line. But I can't tell him what I did. Can't explain how I crawled beneath the moon as I felt our child fall from inside of me. Can't tell him what I saw in my hands and how I wrapped her up and threw her away.

"I told you to take better care of yourself!" Eddie yelps.

Now I understand his question. He means, What did I do wrong? What did I do to cause this? I lie there, stunned, listening to his words, taking in his anger. I ask myself, What *did* I do wrong? The answer is very clear. Everything. I've done nothing right. From my smug self-assurance that being pregnant would be a snap for me because it's the one thing every Manelli and

Calabria woman before me has done with ease, to my begrudging acceptance of my family's joy. My refusal to listen to Eddie and my stubborn certainty that I could have it all—restaurant, Eddie, this kid. I've been greedy. I've been selfish. Hardly the characteristics of a good mother. I've backed myself into a corner so that here, alone, in this bed with nothing left, I've gotten just what I deserved.

I steel myself against Eddie's harsh sobs. Against his words. If I let them in, I will shrivel. "I'm so sorry," I say one last time and hang up the phone.

I wake to the phone ringing. My eyes are gummy and thick. My hands clumsy. I fumble to find the phone somewhere, lost in the pillows beneath my head. I'm confused. Did I sleep? How long? The phone continues to ring urgently. I assume it's Eddie, but I don't want to talk to him again. I can't take any more of his anger tonight. It stops, and I'm relieved, but then it starts again. If I don't answer, he'll call all night. I'll never sleep. On the third round of rings, I pick up, ready to tell him not to call anymore.

"Lemon! Oh, my God, honey."

It's one of my aunts. I hear the others in the background, giving directions and planning my rescue. I have no idea which one is talking to me, but it doesn't matter. Just the sound of that familiar voice cracks whatever thin protective coating I had armored myself with after Eddie's words. If I thought I would lie here alone, I was wrong.

"We're coming!" my aunt says.

"Please hurry," I tell her.

I have no idea how they know. It wouldn't surprise me it they felt some cosmic rift pull each of them out of a deep sleep, yanking them toward me. I don't care how they figured it out.

They're coming, and I am grateful. Not two minutes after I've hung up the phone, the buzzer rings. Rings and rings. I imagine them in a huddle on the stoop, leaning on the bell, ready to break down the door if I don't answer promptly.

I walk slowly through the dark hall to the foyer and buzz them in. Like a gaggle of wild geese, they flock up the stairs to me and explode through the door. I am embraced, patted, kissed, and cried on. Told to sit on the couch and not to move. They fill the apartment. Rush from room to room, turning on lights. They bring me water, tissues, soda crackers, and a blanket. I'm befuddled, bovine in my acceptance, and deeply appreciative. When I walk back toward the bedroom to find my shoes and some clothes, I see splotches of blood on the floorboards, on the bathroom tile. Joy and Adele usher me out of the hall.

"Don't worry," Mary tells me. She holds a wet rag and a bucket of steaming water that smells like pine. "We'll take care of everything."

Gladys hands Joy a bag of my clothes, my shoes are put on my feet, a coat is thrown around my shoulders. When they are ready, they shuffle me off, in the center of their foursome, moving steadily as one, leading me out the door, down the stairs and into the waiting car, idling by the curb. I see my Aunt Mary toss a bag of trash into the cans by the building, and I wail. *That was her!* I want to tell them, but I can't. Adele pulls my head down into her lap.

"It's okay," she whispers to me. "You're with us now."

CHAPTER
TWENTY

My grandmother stands sentinel at the door with her arms outstretched, ready to enfold me. In her nightgown, she seems smaller than I remember. Older. Almost frail. This is a new one on her, I think, and feel badly for causing her any more grief and worry. My aunts walk me up the stairs. Grandma reaches out for me. "You'll be just fine," she says firmly into my ear.

I've heard these words many times from her. When I was a child, it sounded like a command. And I listened as if I had no choice. I willed myself to be fine through every bump and scrape and emotional bruise. But this time I hear it differently. She needs me to be okay.

My aunts hover behind me, but my grandmother shakes her head. "She needs to sleep. So do you. Go on home now," she tells them. They shoo like stray dogs, and I'm relieved.

Grandma carries my bag up the stairs and deposits me in my old room. "I put on fresh sheets," she says as she pulls back the familiar yellow and green flower-basket quilt. This small act of love, the simplest thing, is what breaks me. She hangs on to me, holds me upright as I cry, and walks me to the bed. "It's going to be okay," she tells me. "We'll get you through this."

As soon as I get beneath the clean, cool covers, I pass out and sleep heavily with no dreams.

I wake late the next morning, confused for a moment to find myself in my old bedroom on the second floor of my grandmother's house. Sun slips through the blinds, and the room is stifling hot. The distant sounds of kids playing at the small park a few blocks from my grandmother's float through the screen. I inhale the heady fragrance of my childhood—a mixture of starchy noodles, pungent garlic, laundry detergent, mock orange, and must. When my head clears, I remember why I'm here and what I lost last night.

I stare at an old water stain on the ceiling, trying to figure out what the hell I'm supposed to do. How I'll get through a day. I hear the familiar sounds of my grandmother moving across creaking floors below, and I wonder how she did it. How she got up every day after my mother died. Why she didn't lie down and die, too. Because she had me, I suppose.

What do I have? Eddie? He's gone. On the other side of the ocean. Blaming me for what's happened. There's Lemon. I can't even begin to think about that. I want to burrow beneath the covers and stay here forever, where it's warm and it smells nice and I don't have to face anyone. I stay in bed for as long as I can. Hours maybe. I fall in and out of sleep. Turn my pillow over and over to find the cool side. I refuse to get up until I have to pee so badly it hurts. I try to ignore it. Will it away. But this is reality. I have to get up.

Out of the cozy cocoon of my bed, I feel disgusting, dirty, and polluted. In the bathroom, I undress and look at myself in the mirror. My body looks the same as it did yesterday and the day before. My breasts are still heavy and swollen, my nipples darker and larger than normal. My belly protrudes a little more than usual, yet I'm not pregnant anymore. I was. Now I'm not. And I have no baby to show for it.

Strange, how quickly I grew attached to that little primordial tadpole. The beginnings of my family. Lost now. Gone. Nature's way of telling me it was no good. The earlier the better. A natural part of pregnancy. And all that crap my aunts said to me last night in the car, trying to console me, to console themselves. I listened, but nothing helped. What they don't understand is, I wanted *that* baby, no matter what the problem.

I climb into the shower, hoping to wash all the memories of last night away. As soon as the water hits my head, I start to cry. I let go of what I've been saving up since I first opened my eyes this morning. As I move through the motions of washing my hair, my face, scrubbing my body, I sob, letting the rush of water drown out my sounds as blood circles pink down the drain. All that potential gone.

Once I'm clean and dressed and done crying, I feel better. I don't want to get back in the bed. I want some normalcy, some simple thing to take my mind off what's happened. I want to walk down the stairs and find my old life waiting for me, complete with my aunts driving me crazy, Eddie smiling, and the restaurant my only worry. Instead, I find my grandmother in the kitchen, working a crossword puzzle. In the center of the table is a huge bouquet of yellow roses. They fill the room with their seductive scent. I lift the small card and see Eddie's name at the bottom. "All my love," is the inscription. As if that were enough.

"He called," Grandma says. "Early this morning. You needed to sleep, so I didn't wake you."

"Thanks," I say. My grandmother's complete practicality served me well in this situation.

"He's on a flight. He should be here tonight."

"Really?" I ask.

"You sound surprised."

I shrug. "He didn't have to rush back." I say this, but it's a lie. Of course I expected him to come home, but then again, after last night, I wasn't sure that he'd ever come back.

Grandma looks at me, her eyes large through her reading glasses. "You know he's the one who called last night, don't you? Called me, then Adele and Joy, Mary and Gladys. He wanted to make sure you were okay. That you had someone with you."

"No," I say as I play with the soft silky petals of the roses. "He wanted to make sure someone was keeping an eye on me because he thinks I'm irresponsible."

My grandmother frowns at me, but she lets my comment go. "His mother called here this morning, too."

"Did you talk to her?"

"No, I hung up on her. Of course I talked to her."

"What'd she want?"

My grandmother takes off her glasses and gazes at me like I'm slightly demented. "She wanted to make sure that you're okay."

"What'd you tell her?"

She sighs and shakes her head. "I told her that you were asleep."

"I wonder what Eddie told her," I mutter as I slide into a chair across from Grandma.

She's clearly had enough of my cynicism. She pushes back from the table. "How about some breakfast?"

"I'll just have tea."

"You need to get your strength up. I'll make you some bacon and eggs."

I stay at the table, obediently, as she lays strips of bacon in a skillet and whips up eggs with milk.

"Scrambled eggs were the first thing you taught me to cook," I tell her.

"They're easy. Hard to ruin." Then she smiles. "You loved cooking. Loved being in the kitchen since you were little."

"Especially at Little Great-Aunt Poppy's house." Poppy had a special stool to allow her to reach the stove. It was the perfect size for me when I was a kid. Every time Grandma and I went to Staten Island to visit Poppy and Livinia, I'd beg to stand on the stool and learn something new. She taught me to make my first meatballs, ravioli, and black raspberry pie.

"When did Poppy move in with Livinia?" I ask.

"I don't know," Grandma says as she flips the bacon. 'Fifty-two, 'fifty-three. Somewhere thereabouts."

"Livinia told me that Uncle Tony ran away with his boss's wife, and that she was pregnant."

"Who was pregnant?" Grandma slips two pieces of wheat bread into the toaster slots.

"His mistress."

"Hmm," snorts my grandmother.

"Do you think that's true?"

She shrugs. Removes each piece of crispy bacon to a paper towel, then pours the hot grease into an empty coffee can.

"What happened to Livinia?" I ask. "Why'd she fall apart so badly?"

"She was always fragile." Grandma pours the egg batter over the remaining grease and stirs. "Everything hit her hardest. When our mother died, she didn't get out of bed for a month. Everyone else had to make all the arrangements. Figure out how to take care of Papa. I think Tony couldn't take it. Not that I blame him."

"You're so harsh," I tell her.

The eggs firm up. The toast pops. My grandmother puts

everything on a chipped blue plate. "Everyone's got problems," she says as she sets the food in front of me. I've heard this refrain many times before. "Take Poppy. Crippled when she was a baby. Never married. Had to live with my parents, then take care of Livinia."

"She was the happiest person I knew," I say.

Grandma pours steaming water from the teakettle into the egg pan. "I don't know if she was all that happy, but she got by without complaining."

"I never heard a negative thing come out of her mouth." I nibble at the toast, then take a bite of the eggs and realize that I'm ravenous.

"Yeah, well, you were her favorite. She was always happy to see you."

As if in tribute to Poppy, Grandma sets a jar of black raspberry jam, Poppy's specialty, beside me.

"You know what's weird?" I ask as I cover my toast with the sticky black jam. "I remember being so much more sad at Poppy's funeral than at my parents'."

"You were too young to understand what was happening at your parents' funeral."

She's right, of course. Up until that point, funerals had been fun for my cousins and me. The only people who died were old distant relatives. We took great disgusted pleasure in daring each other to touch the dead's clammy wrinkled skin. They felt like crayons to me, cold and waxy. I got a secret thrill from coloring in those days, imagining I was gripping the finger of some poor lost soul.

My parents' funeral was different. I knew I was supposed to be sad, but mostly I was confused. The only clear memory I have is asking Grandmother Manelli if my mother would go to heaven, since there was no body for the priest to bless.

"That's for our Lord Jesus Christ to decide," she told me in a vaguely threatening way.

I liked the idea of Jesus diving down in the water to talk to my mother. She'd be sitting on a rock in her favorite red dress, smoking a skinny cigarette, with fish swimming through her hair. "Norma," he'd say in his nice voice. "Would you like to come up to Heaven?" And she'd say, "No, thanks, Jesus. I'm happy here. I always did like the water."

Aunt Poppy's funeral, though, I remember clearly. I was thirteen, awkward, angry, and I felt her death acutely. No one else seemed all that sad. She had outlived everyone's expectation by dying in her fifties. But for me, Poppy's death highlighted the sum total of my abandonment. She was the one adult in my life who I didn't have to share with any other children. Although my grandmother and my aunts were always around when I needed them, I never had their full attention. Poppy, though, lavished care on me. Listened to me. Talked to me about the world. Once she was gone, I felt I had no one who loved just me.

"So." My grandmother interrupts my memories. "What are you going to do today?"

I finish my toast and push my plate away. "First, I have to call Franny and check on the restaurant."

"Don't rush yourself," she says as she collects my dirty dishes.

"You sound like Eddie."

"It's true," she says. "You don't have to be in a hurry now."

"That's fine advice from the woman who hasn't slowed down in eighty years."

She shrugs and dunks my dishes in the sink. "Suit yourself," she says. "You always do."

From the living room, I call Franny's apartment. I get her voice mail. "Not home. Leave a message." I hang up and call the restaurant.

Melanie answers and asks me to hold. I suppose that's a good sign. She must be taking reservations on another line. I listen to the canned Coltrane loop and try to remember what was going on at the restaurant when I left. It seems like days ago, although it was just last night. What did we have in the walk-in that needs to be cooked tonight? How many tables are booked? What did I plan for specials? I have no idea. It's as if all memory of Lemon has faded and been replaced by this giant black blob in my head.

"Hey, Lem," Mel says when she comes back on. "You coming in soon?" she asks brightly. Clueless.

"No," I say, and then I pause. What should I tell her? How could I explain? I can't even bring myself to say it. "I'm not feeling well."

"You sick?"

"Yeah," I say, uncertainly. "Is Franny there?"

"Hang on. I'll find her. Feel better," she tells me cheerily.

"Lemon," Franny whispers anxiously.

"Hey, Franny," I say, but my voice falters.

I hear a door close and a chair squeak. I imagine that she's in the office. "I heard what happened. Eddie called this morning."

"Eddie called you, too?" I ask. I'm befuddled by this. Who else did he call while I slept? Who else knows what happened?

"Where are you?" she asks.

"I'm at my grandmother's. What's going on there?"

"Everything's under control."

"I won't be gone too long."

"Oh, Christ, Lemon," Franny says. I hear the squeak of the door and someone saying her name. Franny puts her hand over the mouthpiece. I can't make out what she's saying.

"What are you telling people?" I ask.

"What do you want me to say?"

"Just tell them I'm sick."

"Okay," she says. I hear the office door squeak open again and a muddled voice in the background, then Franny asks me, "Did you order skate wings for tonight?"

"Skate wings?" I repeat. Skate wings? I can't even remember what a skate wing is. "I don't know."

"Okay, whatever. Don't worry about it. We'll take care of it. You feel better. I gotta go."

Franny hangs up, and I listen to the dial tone, infuriated. That's all she has to say to me right now? She hopes I'll feel better? Why didn't she call me if Eddie called her? And skate wings? Who gives a flying fuck about skate wings?

I spend my day lying on the couch, watching confessional TV, game shows, and reruns of sitcoms. I'm perfectly content to wallow in the ordinary pleasures of American life. In fact, I think I've been missing out. All these years, busting my ass to prove that I wouldn't be like everyone else in my family. I'd be the successful one. The one who got out of Brooklyn and made something of herself. But now I'm perfectly content to plant myself in front of the television and lap up canned laughter and ads for processed food.

Between shows I drop into a drugged sleep filled with blurry dreams of me on the floor beneath the moon, Eddie standing over me, my aunts with buckets of cleaning fluid. Sometimes I dream of the restaurant. I see meat, raw and bloody, and know that I can't cook it. I panic because there is a full house out front, and I have nothing to serve them. I see Franny, angry at me, wielding a knife.

In the late evening, I wake up with my stomach gnawing and in knots. I smell tomato sauce, rich and aromatic from simmering for hours. When I was a kid, this smell was the cue for my cousins and me to line up, single file, by the stove, for "juice sandwiches." My grandmother dipped pieces of Wonder Bread into the sauce and sprinkled them with parmesan cheese. Later, we would practice twirling spaghetti on our forks and slurping the noodles, purposefully jerking our heads back to smack ourselves in the foreheads with a long string of sauce-coated pasta. This is the life I had imagined for my own child. Not now.

As I head for the kitchen, I see a shadow by the hall. "Grandma?" I ask.

"Poor Lemon," croaks Aunt Livinia. She shuffles toward me. I turn on the light. She is tiny and wrinkled, a hunchbacked old gnome, lost in her baggy black clothes.

"What are you doing up here?" I ask.

She reaches up and lays her soft hand against my cheek. Her eyes fill with tears. "Poor baby," she whispers through a little sob. "Poor, poor baby, Lemon. It's so sad."

"I'm okay," I tell her, but her tears make me choke up, too.

"They loved you so much," she says. "They didn't mean to go away like that."

"Who are you talking about?"

"Norma and Giovanni," she says.

I gently take her wrist and lower her hand away from my face. "They died a long time ago, Aunt Livinia."

"Norma loves that piano," she says and points a gnarled finger to the old upright in the corner.

"Yes," I say. "She played beautifully."

Aunt Livinia stands and stares at me. Then she looks around the room, clearly uncertain where she is.

"You want me to help you back to your apartment?"

"Poppy's making a pie," she tells me.

"Uh-huh," I say as I lead her slowly to the steps.

My grandmother comes out of the kitchen, wiping her hands on a dishtowel.

"Poppy's making a pie," Livinia repeats to my grandmother.

"Oh, really?" Grandma says. "What kind?"

"Black raspberry," Livinia says with an eager smile. "She picked the berries behind my house."

"That's right," says my grandmother.

I think it's cruel of her to lead Livinia on like this. "Poppy's dead," I say. "Remember?"

"Oh," Livinia sounds disappointed. "Are we still having pie?"

"I'll bake you a nice peach pie," says Grandma as she helps Livinia downstairs.

In the kitchen, a huge wicker basket covered in cellophane and topped with a giant yellow bow sits in the center of the table. Inside are pears and apples, cheese logs and sausage, cookies, chocolates, and tins of crackers. I can't imagine who would send such a thing. My family would certainly turn to food to assuage grief, but in the form of giant homemade lasagnas and casseroles. No one else but Franny knows I'm here, and fruit baskets aren't her style. I open the card and see, "You're in our prayers. Much Love, 'Scilla & Bucky." Of course.

"Wasn't that nice?" my grandmother asks when she comes into the kitchen. She lifts the lid off the saucepot and releases the intoxicating fragrance of the tomato sauce into the muggy air.

"I guess so," I say. I swipe a piece of bread from a plate on the counter and dip it in the pot.

She smacks my hand away. "Don't you appreciate it? It must've cost a fortune."

"You don't know 'Scilla," I say and blow on the dripping bread. "She's probably down in Georgia right now bemoaning to all her socialite friends how this little Italian slut from Brooklyn lost her baby boy's only heir."

"Ellie Manelli," my grandmother says sharply. She raps the wooden spoon against the side of the pot and turns to scowl at me.

"Sorry," I say sheepishly. Even now she reduces me to a child when she uses my real name.

"Eddie's mother is trying to reach out to you."

"The fruit basket is very nice," I say. "I'll send her a thank-you note."

My grandmother shakes her head at me. She knows when I'm full of shit. "I know you're hurting inside, but you can't take it out on everyone around you, or you'll end up alone and bitter."

I think of Livinia downstairs in her apartment, surrounded by the dead baby pictures, yelling at the TV. For the first time, her life doesn't seem so bad to me. I could imagine holing up, running away, retreating into myself, where no one could expect anything or blame me for what goes wrong. But I don't tell my grandmother this.

"How about some dinner?" she asks as a peace offering.

I nod my head. "Smells delicious," I say and sit at the table in my old spot.

When Eddie comes, I'm dead asleep in front of the TV. He squats beside me and gently strokes the back of my hair. "Sweetheart," he says. "Lem. Wake up."

I open my eyes to see him staring at me, smiling, holding out his arms. In my near delirium, I forget that I'm furious with him. For being gone. For blaming me. For thinking that a simple bouquet of roses was enough to smooth over everything he missed. But before I can think about what I'm doing, I'm sitting up, reaching out, losing myself in his hug, happy to have him near me now.

I see my grandmother in the doorway. She stands with her robe wrapped tightly around her body. She nods her approval, and I think the worst is truly over. He's home now, and he's not mad at me. I'm so relieved to have his love that when he says, "Come on," and pulls me to my feet, I go willingly.

CHAPTER
TWENTY-ONE

Eddie and I don't talk as the cab winds its way through the back streets of Brooklyn from Carroll Gardens to Park Slope. Everything we have to say is too intimate, too sacred, to blurt out in front of the stranger driving the car. Instead, I rest my head on Eddie's shoulder. He wraps his arms around me. Maybe this is all I needed. To see him, touch him, breathe the same air as him in order to forgive him for being gone and for blaming me. Besides, being happy to be with him is so much easier than being furious.

When the cab pulls up in front of our apartment building, I see the trashcans out by the curb. I sit with my face against the car window. Eddie waits for me to get out, but I can't because I know what's packed away somewhere deep inside those plastic barrels. I'm afraid that if I get out of the car, I'll claw through the trash. The banana peels and coffee grounds, the plastic bags of dog crap and old soda bottles, the newspapers, used Kleenex, and cartons of moldy take-out food. I'll want to find her. To tell her one more time how sorry I am. How badly I feel for abandoning her like that.

Eddie reaches across me and opens the door. "Come on," he says and gives me a little nudge. "Let's go inside."

As the cab pulls away, I stand on the curb, and I say, "I didn't mean to."

"Didn't mean to what?" Eddie asks softly, gently, in the voice of someone coaxing a very slow child to form simple sentences.

"Get rid of it like that," I tell him.

"Get rid of what?"

"The baby," I nearly whisper. "I didn't know what else to do."

He's quiet for a moment, then he says, "I don't understand, Lem."

I want to tell Eddie everything that happened so that he'll understand and help me find some solace. "The trashcans," is what I say.

"What about them?" He yawns. Bored by my grief already?

"Never mind," I say and turn away. I won't be able to explain it.

"Come on. Let's go in." He takes me by the elbow, and I dutifully follow.

In our bed neither of us sleeps. I want to talk to Eddie, find our way back to normal—but I don't know what to say. Finally, out of the silence, he asks me quietly, "What was it like?"

I think back to myself on the floor, looking up at the moon. Feeling that baby drop from deep inside of me. Plummet. The memory makes me dizzy. Queasy. My breath is shallow and unsteady. Maybe this is when I'll tell Eddie everything. Put the burden on both our shoulders, let him take a bit from me so that I can stop feeling so encumbered.

"I got a book," he tells me before I can put all of my thoughts into words. "In Milan. I found an English bookstore before I caught my plane. I read about it." He hesitates. "About miscarriage. The book said it's like a heavy menstrual cycle with lots of cramping."

I almost laugh, hearing him talk about it in such sterile terms. Then I remember holding her in my hands. Wanting to understand who she was, who she would've been.

"Was it like that?" he asks.

"Yes," I lie. "Like that."

"Must've been hard." He rolls to his back and puts his hands behind his head. Stares up at the patterns of light on the ceiling from passing cars outside. "You know, it's weird," he tells me.

And I think, *weird?* This is *weird* to you?

"The whole time you were pregnant was sort of abstract for me. It was more like an idea. I was excited about it, but it didn't seem all that real. But for you. Wow. It was so real."

I want to punch him as hard as I can for such an insulting understatement.

"I'm glad you had your aunts and your grandmother with you."

"I was alone," I tell him. I grip the sheets in my fist and twist.

"That's why I called them."

"And you were mad at me for that." I feel it all again. Lying here with the phone against my head, listening to Eddie yell at me. "You told me I should be at the hospital. With the doctor. Said that I was stubborn and didn't listen to you."

He rolls toward me and reaches out for my hand. I keep my fingers tight around the covers. "I was just upset and frustrated that I couldn't help you," Eddie says.

"Maybe you were right."

"About what?"

"Maybe it was my fault."

"The book said not to blame yourself."

"You do," I say quietly with hostility.

"I don't blame you."

"If you don't blame me, who's left to blame?" I ask. "The baby? Should we be mad at her for leaving me?"

"It wasn't a baby, Lemon."

"What was it then?" I ask, confused.

"A *fetus,*" he tells me in that same sterile tone he used for the words *menstrual cycle.*

I look at him with disgust. "Maybe to you," I say. "But to me it was a baby."

He shakes his head, pats my hand, and rolls to his back again with a sigh. "We're going to have to get past this, Lemon," he tells me. "We're going to have to let it go."

That's enough. That's all I need to rip the covers off my body and scream, "I lost a baby, and you want me to fucking forget about it! You have no idea what I went through. No idea what I saw. You weren't here!"

"You're the one who told me to go!" he yells back. I'm startled. Eddie's never yelled at me before. "You're the one who said we had to live our lives," he says. "And see what happened?"

I explode. I'm shaking and spewing sounds that I don't recognize. My body is in revolt. I want to vomit. To erupt. I can't be near him anymore. I stumble away from the bedroom, down the hall, banging into walls. I have no idea where I'm going. Everything I thought we had, all the love and forgiveness, was a sham. He still thinks it was my fault, and I still believe him.

In the living room, I fall down, crouch on the floor, and claw at the rug because I have no place else to go. I hear my words echoing around the room. "I miss my baby so much, I want my baby back," I chant like some creepy doo-wop song.

Knowing what I'm saying breaks my heart all over again, because I remember just how much I had wanted that baby and how much I've lost.

Then I hear the bed squeak and Eddie rise with a small groan. Like a feral animal caught inside, I scurry across the floor in the dark. I want to hide from him. I don't want to talk to him or listen to what he has to say. His footsteps advance, slow and plodding, down the hall. I consider closets. Consider fleeing out the front door. He's nearly in the room, and I shuffle into a corner, as if I'll become invisible in a smaller space.

He turns on a light, finds me huddled behind the chair, and comes to me with outstretched arms. "Lemon. Come on. I'm sorry. This is a horrible way to start. Come back to bed so we can talk."

"No," I say and shake my head frantically as I curl into a ball, trying my best to shrink. "I'm going to stay right here."

He squats down beside me and touches my shoulder. "Please come back." He finds my arms, pulls me by the wrist, holds me against his chest. I stay rigid, huffing into his shirt because I'll be damned if I'm going to cry or carry on in front of him anymore. "At least get up off the floor." He stands and pulls on my arm. "This is crazy."

"Go away," I say.

He stops trying. Sighs. Slumps down beside me, defeated. "I'm tired, Lem. Exhausted. I haven't slept in a few days."

"Poor baby," I say.

He sets his jaw. He's fuming now. This makes me happy. I want to anger him. I want him to hurt as badly as I do.

"Can we please just get some sleep and discuss this in the morning?"

"There's nothing to discuss," I snap.

"Fine," he says. He pushes himself up off the floor. Stands

above me and reaches out his hand one more time. "Come on," he says. "Please."

"No," I say firmly.

He turns away. I am buoyant. He's going. My anchor. I simultaneously hate him for leaving me right now and feel satisfied as I watch his figure retreat into the hall. I want to spit at him. Tell him to never come back. I want to dissolve into my aching body so that I don't have to feel any of this pain anymore. And then, just when he's about to disappear into the bedroom, I panic. I can't be left alone again. I open my mouth and yell, "I'm sorry, Eddie! Please don't leave."

He turns around. I see his shoulders slump. I see how tired he is of me. I scramble to my feet and stumble toward him.

"I'm just being stupid," I say. "I shouldn't have gotten so upset. I'll be all right. I promise." My words come out like machine-gun fire.

He allows me into a hug. Wraps his weary arms around my shoulders. "Calm down," he says. "You're hysterical."

"You're right," I tell him. "This is stupid. I should be over it by now. It was just a baby. Not even a real baby. A *fetus*. People lose them all the time. It's nothing. I can handle it. I'm sorry to be such a mess."

I hear myself say it all, and I cringe with every word until my stomach squeezes and I think that I might throw up. Who's this woman apologizing for my grief? Who's this woman blaming me for something beyond my control? I would never do that. Women from the 1950s who were unfulfilled and hid behind the identity of their husbands would say such things. Mrs. Bud Simmons from 15 Nutmeg Lane in a shirtwaist dress and Betty Crocker apron would do that.

But at this moment apologizing and accepting every ounce of blame is the only solution I can see. Because if Eddie is angry with me for losing our child, then I have to make things right. I need him to go on loving me enough to take me back into his bed where I so desperately want to be because I'm tired and I can't stand the thought of being alone for another minute. So I blather on, apologizing for everything, and hating myself more with every word I say.

Finally he hugs me so tightly that I lose my breath and whispers, "Shhhh." I relax against his chest and cry quietly, wondering when I was reduced to this sniveling stereotype of a woman. The kind I promised never to be.

"Come to bed," he says. "It'll be okay in the morning."

I follow him obediently, trying to believe in his words.

In the morning, the phone rings. I don't answer for fear that it's one of my aunts. I can't face assuring them that I'm fine right now. But Eddie brings me the phone and whispers, "It's Makiko."

My first thought is that something is wrong at the restaurant. Franny has gone mad. Makiko can't take it anymore, and she's quitting. The whole place burned down while I was away. I'm not sure that I want to know, but I can't not talk to Makiko. I push myself up and brush the hair out of my face. I try to find a normal voice. "Hey, Makiko. What's up?"

"I'm sorry to call you at home, Lemon," she says. "But Franny won't tell me what's going on, and I'm worried. Are you okay?"

"Oh." I falter. I don't know how to answer. On the one hand, I asked Franny not to tell anyone what happened, so I guess I should be grateful that Makiko doesn't know. On the other hand, Makiko's the only one thoughtful enough to call and check up on me anyway. Franny hasn't called me once since I called her. "I'm not so good," I admit to Makiko and realize how comforting it is to divulge that truth.

217

"Is there anything I can do for you?"

I don't what it is, the anonymity of the phone, the easy timbre of her voice, or just the fact that she's the first person who's asked me what she can do for me rather than telling me how to feel better. For whatever reason, I break down then, and I confide everything to her. I tell her about the spotting and how Dr. Shin dismissed me like some hysterical female whose uterus has gone running amok inside her body. I tell her about losing it while I was alone and how my aunts rescued me and took me to my grandmother's house until Eddie came to get me. I leave out the gory details and the fight with Eddie last night. And I don't admit how much I'm hurt by the fact that it's Makiko calling me instead of Franny.

"I'm so sorry, Lemon." I hear the tears in her voice. "I want to help you. Tell me what I can do."

"I wish there was something," I say sadly. "But I just need some time, I think."

She's quiet for a few seconds. "If you think of something. If you want to talk some more. Or just cry. Maybe take a walk or have some tea. I don't know. Just anything. Whatever you need. Please call me."

"I will." I should say good-bye now. Our conversation is over, but I don't want to let Makiko go. We both breathe into the phone. "How's everything at the restaurant?" I ask. It feels good to focus on something other than me for a moment.

"Everything is fine," she says. "Just the same. Please don't worry about that. Just take care of yourself."

When I hang up, Eddie brings me a cup of tea with lots of milk and sugar. "You doing okay?"

"Will you check on things at Lemon for me?" I ask.

He sits on the edge of the bed. We don't touch. "Can't we just focus on this for now?" he asks.

"Last night you told me I had to get over *this.*"

"That's not what I said."

"Yes, you did," I insist without giving him a chance to explain his side of things.

He draws a long breath in through his nose and lets it out slowly. The sound of exasperation. "I don't think rushing right back into work is the answer."

"*I'm* not rushing back in. I asked *you* to check on it."

"Can we at least wait until you get the okay from your doctor before you start dealing with the restaurant again?"

How artfully he avoids the issue. "She said I could do whatever I feel up to," I tell him.

"You have a tendency to overdo it, Lemon." His tone is rankled, as if he's arguing with a stubborn teenager and trying not to lose his temper.

I know that I'm pushing him again and that if I don't watch it, I'll push him away like I did last night. "Fine. I won't go in or ask you to check up," I say. Not because I think that's the best idea, but because I'm trying. Trying to get over what happened. Trying to show him that I can listen, compromise, and take good care of myself. I'm also trying to remember what it feels like to be happy with Eddie. Free and easy without this smog of my sadness hanging over our heads.

He pats my leg and leaves the tea on the nightstand. "You want some breakfast?" he asks me brightly. "I could go get us bagels."

"Okay," I say, indifferently.

As soon as I hear him walk out the door, I pick up the phone and consider calling Franny. She'll tell me if everything has gone to hell. I hold the phone in my hand, but I don't dial. Then it occurs to me that I don't want to talk to Franny. She's the one who should be calling me. I set the phone down again and bury my head in the pillows. Of course, I could call somebody else. Melanie or Ernesto. But maybe Eddie's right. Maybe I don't really want to know how things are going at Lemon because if things aren't going well, I'd be useless anyhow.

Eddie tries very hard to do everything right while I'm home for the next few days. "How you doing, Lemon?" he asks every time I walk through a room. "How're you feeling?"

I answer each enquiry with "Fine" because I don't think he really wants to know. I don't tell him that I still cry every time I take a shower. Or share with him how much I bleed. It's amazing how much blood I can lose without dying. Ropy red nodules fall from my body. What's next? A shoe? An old tire? Jimmy Hoffa? Nothing would surprise me. I can't imagine what it's like not to bleed anymore. And I'm afraid of when the blood dries up, because then it will all be over, she'll really be gone, and I'll have to move on. So as long as I'm functioning, putting one foot in front of another, then Eddie assumes everything is okay, and that's fine with me.

His mother calls daily, and so far, I've successfully avoided talking to her. Eddie passes her messages along to me such as, "Keep your chin up" and "Look on the bright side." Every time he blurts out another useless platitude, I want to kick him in the balls.

His method for helping me is getting me out of the house. He takes me to do normal things like shop for groceries. This morning he suggests we eat breakfast at the diner near the park. I go along with his plan. Get up, get dressed, walk outside. Pretend that all's well in the world, even though I'd really like to be back in bed, alone.

As soon as we walk into the restaurant, I regret it. Twin boys, no older than three, sit at the counter, spinning on the stools.

They wear striped T-shirts and matching pants and little tennis shoes with lights in the heels. They spin and squeal while their mother cajoles them to take bites of their scrambled eggs. In a booth, a mother nurses a newborn. Her face is placid, serene, as if she's smoked a joint. An older woman sits across from her, gazing at the daughter and granddaughter with doe eyes, pure love.

Eddie sees the distress on my face. "Let's eat outside," he says as if we would do it just for fun, even though he hates to eat outside. I nod and follow him out the door.

We sip cups of strong black coffee beneath the red-striped awning as we watch people mill by on their way to and from the park. It's a gorgeous late summer day with the sun already high and bright at ten A.M. A group of girls bounce by on their way to the subway. They're all in tank tops and jeans and flip-flops. They laugh and wear funky sunglasses. Who are they, I wonder? They look so young. Surely they're out of high school. Are they in college? I think of myself at that indeterminate age that I now define merely as young or at least younger than me.

I never had that loose-limbed carefree gait. That confident walk as if nothing in the world had ever been sad. And I'll never look like they look now. I'm already worn, battered down, and I think, this is what it means to be an adult. To carry sadness with you that will never go away. That's what makes us slowly shrivel up and get old.

I slump over the table and stare into my coffee. "God," I say. "I feel like such a big fat blob."

"You look great to me," Eddie says in his soothing voice that I'm quickly growing tired of. "No different than you ever have."

"That's not true," I say. "I'm a flabby mess from three months of stuffing my pie hole with cheese and peanut butter and midnight glasses of milk. It was okay with me when I knew I'd get bigger, but now I hate how I look."

"Give yourself a break, Lem," is his constant refrain.

"I'm not sure that I know how to do that, Eddie."

"Just be nicer to yourself. Don't expect so much. Ease back into things."

"Oh," I say sarcastically. "Is that all I have to do?"

He lets it go.

After breakfast, I can't stand the thought of going back to the apartment with him. With his syrupy voice, constant hugs, and endearing looks. They've gotten on my last nerve.

"I'm going to take a walk," I say.

"Great," he says. "I'll come with you."

"No," I tell him. "I need some time alone."

He looks hurt, but I don't care.

"I'll be home later," I say and head into the park, leaving him on the sidewalk.

Surrounded by nature, I see that it's becoming fall. September's golden light colors the trees. The day is balmy with the first whispers of winter in the breeze. I've always loved autumn. The weather usually makes me want to hole up in the kitchen, slow-roasting meats, baking apple pies, simmering soups, and pickling the last fresh produce. Cooking is joyful, promising. It's about life and living. I have the feeling that anything I'd touch right now would turn sour and bitter.

My walk through the park is another mistake. I smell meaty, musky, and strange dogs sniff my crotch. The only other people out on a weekday afternoon are pregnant women and their babies. Fifteen-year-old Puerto Rican girls push their big bellies in front of their tiny hips. Twenty-nine-year-old Hasidic women are trailed by nine children under four years old. Forty-five-year-old yuppies in comfortable shoes carry their one precocious darling in Baby Björn packs. Hipsters sling chubby jerking infants sporting DKNY onsies across their backs. I watch them from the corners of my eyes with my lips pressed tightly together, and secretly I hate them all. How dare they parade their fertility and good fortune around as if it were nothing? How dare those groups of mommies with their milky-eyed infants sit on park benches comparing breast pump advice? I wish I had saved the bloody blob that I expelled so I could walk right up to these smug women and show them my baby, too.

Of course, I can do no such thing. There is no way for me to talk about what's happened. It's a hushed-up affair. There are no social conventions for grieving this loss, no ceremonies, no Hallmark cards. At least when my parents died, everyone expected me to be sad. Now all I can do is wander through the park with the squirrels, trying to figure out how to get back to my life.

TWENTY-TWO

I don't think I can do this," I say to Eddie from the bed where I'm sitting, still in my underwear. My nice salmon-colored linen dress lies beside me. I hate that dress. It's the most girlie thing I own, and I feel far from girlie at the moment.

"Do you want me to come with you?" Eddie asks as he pulls on his tennis whites. "I can cancel my game."

"Boys aren't invited."

He tugs a T-shirt overhead. "So don't go. They should understand. For God's sake, it's barely been a week."

I shake my head. "Believe me, my family wouldn't understand if I missed Trina's precious baby shower. These are people who could lose limbs, and they'd still show up for family functions."

Eddie leans down and hugs me. "They just want to see you."

"I didn't buy her a present." I tried. Even walked into a baby store, but I couldn't stay. Couldn't finger the soft fabrics of the clothes or look at the teeny-tiny socks. I turned around immediately, as if I'd walked into the wrong place. I don't tell Eddie this because I'm embarrassed by how easily undone I still am.

He shrugs. "So, we'll send her something later."

"Maybe a supply of nicotine patches," I mutter. I think of

Trina after her welcome home party, slinging her leg over her smarmy boyfriend's motorcycle, then lighting up a cigarette.

"Hey, now." Eddie gives me an extra squeeze.

I hate it when he does that. As if I'm behaving like a child who needs correcting. Makes me want to jab him in the ribs. That would be mature. I yank my dress over my head.

"You look nice," Eddie says as I struggle with the zipper up the back. He reaches out and zips it for me. "Great color on you."

I glance at myself in the mirror. "I look like a giant hot dog."

"I think you look good."

I should say thanks, of course, but I've had enough of his studied kindness for one morning. I grab my shoes and leave the room.

The steps up to my grandmother's house are crisscrossed with pink and yellow crepe paper. The ends of the banisters are festooned with huge bouquets of helium balloons and big floppy bows. Over the green door hangs a banner proclaiming "Baby Shower Here!" complete with goofy long-legged storks in delivery-man hats, wobbly ducklings, and large-eyed kittens romping through Easter-egg-colored grass. I stand on the sidewalk, looking up at the hideous decor, and have the strong urge to rip it all apart, leaving the street strewn with pastel destruction. I take a breath and march up the steps, determined to sit through at least an hour of this affair before making my excuses to get the hell out of here.

Inside, I smell sugar cookies and fruit punch, deviled eggs and ham. The soft comfort food of impending motherhood. Why not a spit-roasted suckling pig with baby corn? Have these people no sense of humor? From the living room, I hear the squeal of women's voices cooing over rubber nipples and car seats. As I peek in on the scene of my slavering aunts and cousins gathered around Trina in full bloom, I wish that I had the technical knowledge to construct a bomb out of a Diaper Genie, Enfamil, and tiny plush toys. I imagine the whole place exploding into one giant poof of confectioner's sugar and me escaping through an open window, shimmying down the drainpipe to freedom.

Which would be a great idea. Because watching Trina perched on the sofa lapping up the bounty of attention and loot, I want nothing more than to punch her as hard as I can in the center of her giant pregnant belly. How could she possibly deserve this more than I do? Before I can find the answer to that question, my cousin Sophie spots me lingering in the doorway.

I know my face is twisted into some horrible grin, the look of a banshee trying to pass as a woman in the daylight hours. I'm sure I'm drained of color, and my knuckles have likely grown white from gripping a box of cookies I bought. Sophie slips away from the group and quietly comes to me while Trina rips into another pink-paper-covered box. I shove the cookies toward Sophie to avoid some cloying hug and kiss, but she pushes it out of the way and drapes her arms around my shoulders.

I stand there like the Tin Man as she pats me and coos, "Lemon! How are you?" in a voice way too high for an adult. "We're so glad you're here." And then, nightmare of all nightmares, she clutches my hand in hers, turns around, and announces, "Hey, everybody! Look who made it!"

Christ, Lord Almighty, have mercy on my soul and kill me now, I silently beg. Strike me dead with a giant lightning bolt as punishment for all my sins. As if I'd ever be so lucky. My aunts and cousins are on their feet in a nanosecond, surrounding me. "How are you?" Pats and squeezes. "Feeling okay?" My hands are held, my arms are swung. I'm nearly spun around like a little doll. "You look great!"

And for some reason, I answer them as if I've only been away on a fabulous vacation to the Bahamas. "I'm great! Just fine! Feel good! Glad to be here! Nice to see you." Because, really, what the hell else can I say?

"How about something to eat?" As always, my grandmother rescues me with food. She cuts through the wall of love by handing me a plate filled with thick slices of ham, a glob of potato salad, two deviled eggs, and several cookies in the shapes of rattles and bears. My aunts, always reverent at the sight of sustenance, quickly leave me and move en masse to sit at Trina's puffy feet again.

"Come over here by me," Grandma says, and I obediently follow her because I'm completely shell-shocked and would walk in front of a train at the moment if she told me to.

A cheer goes up as Trina unveils a fourteen-in-one play center for the tot, and I think of handy things nearby on which I could impale myself. The fireplace poker. Obvious choice. The plastic serrated knife on the edge of my paper plate. If I tried hard enough. Or if I get really desperate, the sparkly purple ballpoint pen my cousin Angela uses to record the gifts in a special flowered book called "Baby's First . . ."

Aunt Mary gets to me first. She wrenches herself between Grandma and me. I realize then that the overdose of baby-related paraphernalia must've softened my brain, because normally, I wouldn't let any of my aunts corner me like this.

Mary grabs me by the forearm; her talons gouge into my skin. "You know this is God's way," she says quietly to me while Trina holds up an itty-bitty crocheted hat in the shape of an eggplant. And I wonder, What's God's way? This shower? All these stupid shades of pink? Women sitting around blathering over tiny socks?

"I highly doubt any of this is divinely inspired," I say dryly.

Mary looks at me straight and steady with her most Catholic stare. "Because that baby would have been deformed," she informs me. "God was sparing you a lifetime of heartache."

Oh, I get it now. My baby. The one I thought I had so carelessly lost. Turns out God was being nice. Before I can respond, Aunt Gladys has positioned herself on the other side of me. "Lots of women lose them," she tells me in a whisper. Trina has two little booties on her fingers and makes them dance the can-can. Everyone twitters with delight at her clever antics.

"And some women can't even get pregnant," Mary adds.

"That's right," Gladys says. "Uncle Stan works with a woman whose granddaughter had to inject horse hormones into her tushy every night for weeks, then have her husband's you-know-what injected into her with a syringe. And it still didn't work. Poor thing."

Both my aunts shake their heads.

"They're going to adopt," Gladys tells me. Then she lowers her voice and says in a sorrowful tone, as if she's confiding a sad secret like cancer, "From China."

I glance at my grandmother, hoping she'll rescue me again, but she's completely engrossed in watching my cousin Angela demonstrate for Trina how to connect a breast pump to maximize milk production. "You are breast-feeding, aren't you?" Angela asks.

Trina shrugs. "I don't know," she says. "Chuck thinks it's disgusting."

A general murmur of disapproval rattles through the crowd, but Trina seems oblivious as she rips into the next gift. I'm amazed. How can she be so calm? I would have been livid had my family so publicly objected to my plans.

When I look back at my plate, Aunt Joy kneels at my feet, and Adele has wedged herself behind me. This is too much. All four of them at once? Haven't I gone through enough the past few weeks? Maybe this *is* God's way. Maybe it's some horrible punishment for all my transgressions in life. Perhaps the nuns at my elementary school were right all along, and this is the day I'm paying for all those years of ditching mass and never confessing any of my immoral acts.

"Now, Lemon," Adele says, her cold hands resting on my shoulders. "My neighbor Loretta's daughter lost her first one, too."

I'm completely appalled that she's telling me this in the middle of a fucking baby shower. I try to show my revulsion as clearly as I can. I twist my face into a mask of horror, but she takes no notice and plows ahead, my other three aunts nodding their encouragement for her to yammer on about some other woman's misfortune, as if somehow that will make mine less dire.

"She walked around for eight weeks, thinking she was perfectly pregnant," Adele says. "I'd even given her some of Beth's old maternity clothes. But when she went to the doctor for her first sonogram"—and here she pauses for effect—"there was no heartbeat."

Joy gasps. "What a shame! Thank God that didn't happen to you."

I stare at her with pure disgust. Is she joking? In her mind, what happened to me was better?

"Broke her heart," says Adele. "The doctor called it a blighted ovum," she says with a serious nod.

And then I lose it. I've had it. I can't take any more. The whole thing—the gifts, the food, the specter of my irresponsible cousin happily carrying her daughter full-term—each and every reminder of what I've lost crashes down on me, and I'm a goner. Only this time I'm not angry or sad, bitterly gnashing my teeth and crying. This time I'm delirious with the cruel hilarity of it all.

"Blighted ovum?" I ask too loudly. "Isn't that a Girl Riot band from Seattle?" I snort into my plate. My aunts look at each other, clearly puzzled. "I think I have their first album," I tell them. A giggle bubbles up from my throat. *"Spontaneous Abortion!"* I nearly yell, and then I crack up. Double over and roar. I laugh and laugh, slap my knees, suck in huge raw breaths while tears leak from my eyes, spilling onto the deviled eggs. It's the funniest fucking thing I've ever heard, and I can't stop. Blighted Ovum! *Spontaneous Abortion!* What a cutup. Every part of me quakes and shivers as I guffaw. I know the room has gone from excited chatter, to nervous twitters, to completely confounded silence as I'm lost in this sick uncontrollable laughter.

I feel a hand on my back, then an arm around my shoulders. I recognize that strong touch. My grandmother lifts me from my seat and leads me from the room, cradled against her body as my laughter breaks into aching sobs.

Grandma takes me into the kitchen and closes the door. This is our sanctuary, the place she has been bringing me to ease whatever ails me since I was very small. And when I'm in here with her again, I feel like that same kid, small and scared and raging inside, who ran away from her parents' funeral and hid in the pear tree until my grandmother coaxed me out with a pie.

I remember that part of the day clearly. After the service, I'd had enough of all the tears and stares and glance-aways, as if all the sadness in that room was my fault. My cousins all looked at me sideways, squinting as if I were the sun, too bright and hot to stare at. I was a figure of tragedy then. A real live orphan with a just dead mother and father sleeping with the fishes. But I was sick of the formalities, of the muted mourning, of the black velvet dress way too hot for a muggy late summer day, the severe braids in my hair, and too-tight shoes on my feet.

So I took off when no one was watching. I slipped out the door, bolted across the parking lot, dodged between cars, snuck through the school-yard fence behind the funeral home, shimmied past the swings and beneath the slide to the side gate, which was open. I heard voices close behind me, yelling my name. Heard feet smacking the pavement. I tripped and fell. Crashed to the hot black tar on hands and knees. Tiny rocks pressed into my palms, and the skin on my knee opened up. I rolled over to look at my hurt leg. Blood ran down my shin and soaked into my sock, turning it pink. But I didn't stop. I scrambled to my feet and ran.

My heels ground into the cement, my knee was a balloon, and my hands stung as if I'd smacked someone hard. People on the sidewalks watched me zip by. "Hey, hey!" they yelled. And some people reached out their arms to grab me. But I imagined myself a blur, running so fast in my black dress and frilly white socks that I looked like a zebra with a river of blood down my shin.

At my street, I took the corner too sharply. Slid on loose gravel and leaves. Tumbled off the sidewalk, rolled over the cracking yellow curb, and flopped into the street. I heard the car first. The screech of brakes and tires and the shrieking horn. Then I felt its heat down my back and the shuttering of the metal from the sudden stop right behind me.

"You goddamned kid!" The driver leaned out the window and banged on the car door. "Watch where you're going! You could get yourself killed!"

I used the front fender to pull myself up and limped to the other side of the road, ignoring the guy and completely unconcerned with how close I'd come to being flattened. He drove off, berating me.

The block was quiet then. Everyone was at the funeral. No one out to ask me what I was doing. Why my dress was ripped. Why I was bleeding. Why I cried as I crawled up the stoop on all fours like a tired dog. I threw my weight against the front door. The glass rattled, but it didn't budge. I did it again and again, as if I could break it down with my tiny, determined forty-five-pound frame. Then the door opened, and I tumbled into the foyer. I landed at feet, looked up legs, baggy pantyhose, and a frumpy skirt to find Aunt Livinia holding open the door. I have no idea why she was there. She probably couldn't have handled the funeral. I didn't stop to ask her to explain, though. I scurried across the slick wooden floor away from her. The throw rug tripped me up, and I crawled down the hall, toward the kitchen, leaving bloody knee prints behind.

I ran straight through the house to the back door, then out into the garden. My mother's pear tree gently rustled its bright green leaves in the hot humid breeze. Rotting pears littered the ground and filled the garden with the intoxicating scent of fermenting fruit. My mother had shown me two knobs on the back of the trunk, near the chain link fence. Using those as toe holds and the fence to balance myself, I could easily climb into the lowest branches, then work my way up high into the densest part of the tree so that I was hidden.

As I sat in the silent tree with my back against the rough bark, everything went away. There was no funeral. No priests. No angry grandmothers and sad cousins. No weird aunts opening the door as if I'd just strolled in from the playground. There was only the smell of pears and the memory of my mother and father, standing below the tree, looking up at me, smiling. Encouraging me to be daring. To climb up and throw down soft, ripe fruit to them. All of this calm was shattered a few minutes later when I heard the banshee shrieks of my aunts as they came into the house.

"Oh, my God!"

"Blood!"

"She's hurt!"

"Lemon!" they called in frantic tones as they searched from room to room. I watched their shadows pass by windows, but kept myself hidden.

Then I saw my grandmother, standing in the back door, hands on hips, looking straight at the tree. Had Livinia ratted me out? I climbed up higher, probably shaking the branches and giving myself away. But when I looked again, Grandma was gone, and I thought that I had outsmarted her, which disappointed me a little bit. Would any one ever find me? How long would I have to stay in the tree? I resolved to eat pears forever and drink rainwater. I'd never come down.

The next time I peeked through the leaves, my grandmother was walking slowly down the back steps, carrying something in her hands. My aunts crowded in the doorway, one behind the other. A four-headed monster ready to devour me. Grandma held up her hand and shot them a stern look before any of them could open their mouths or come out to the garden, then she shooed them away with a flick of her wrist. They slunk back, whispering to one another as they retreated into the dark hall.

Grandma stood beneath the tree and looked up. "You're pretty high," she said. I didn't answer. "I'm too old to climb up there after you." I stayed quiet, pretending not to hear. She sighed and kicked a few pears away from the base of the trunk, then lowered herself down to her haunches, still holding the thing that was covered in a blue-striped dishtowel.

After a few minutes she said, "I went to Staten Island a few weeks ago. Before—" She stopped and I peeked down at her. I could see the top of her head. Blonde strands wove through the gray. "I took the ferry to Aunt Poppy and Aunt Livinia's house. You remember what grows out behind there? Where nobody else but us knows?"

I knew what Grandma was talking about. Secret black raspberry bushes grew up along the old railroad tracks. Grandma took me there every year in early July just before my birthday, when the berries were first ripe. Aunt Poppy and I loved to pick the berries because we were just the right height to find the best ones, hidden deep in the bushes. We filled up plastic buckets and ate every third berry. We worked until our fingertips were the same inky black as our tongues and we were covered in mosquito bites.

"I picked the last black raspberries special for my little lemon girl," Grandma said. "I made a pie crust with cold butter and a pinch of salt, just like I taught you. I put the berries inside with some sugar and cornstarch and pats of butter. Then what'd I do, Lemon?"

She brushed the top with milk so the crust would get toasty brown. I knew the answer, but I couldn't say it.

"If you come down from up there, I'll give you the pie." She looked up, but I didn't budge.

Then she took the dishtowel off and showed me the pie, with a pinched crust and four steam holes that looked like a star in the center. I knew how that crust would feel on my tongue. Crumbly like sand. Flaky like snow.

"See how tiny it is?" she asked. "The perfect size for you. You want it?" Grandma smiled up at me, sad. I loved that smile. It melted my heart and it made me ache, because my mother had that same exact smile with the crinkly nose and ears that moved up even when the smile meant that she was sad. That was the smile my mother gave me every time she stood at the front door, ready to leave, and now I knew that I'd never see it again.

I lowered myself from branch to branch until I could reach out my hands toward my grandmother. She quickly grabbed my arms and pulled me out of the tree, then held me tight against her chest. I inhaled the scent of flour and salt and sugar from the pie as she rubbed my tight back, kneading it like bread, trying to get all those knots of anger out.

God, I wish it were that easy now. I wish my grandmother could soothe all of this anger and frustration and disappointment away from me with the perfect pie. Instead, we sit across from one another and stare out the window at the tree where I found solace during the other saddest part of my life.

"It was too soon," my grandmother says without looking at me. "I shouldn't have expected—"

"It's my fault," I say.

"Hush," she says. "None of this is your fault."

I nod, but I don't believe her. Outside the kitchen, I hear the rest of my family whispering, uncertain whether to continue. I feel bad for interrupting. For trying to be a part of this celebration when I should've stayed away.

"Want me to call Eddie to come get you?" Grandma asks.

"No," I say. "I think I'll walk home. I need some time to myself."

My grandmother reaches out her hand and covers mine. Her skin is soft and smooth, her touch warm. "You take your time," she says to me. "I mean it now. Do what you need to do for yourself."

"Okay," I say and squeeze her fingers in mine. "I'll try." I stand up from the table and bend to kiss her cheek. "Please tell them good-bye for me."

As I leave, I don't look back at the silly decorations on the front steps. I need to get away from all these reminders and move on. The only way I can imagine doing that is by going back to work.

CHAPTER
TWENTY-THREE

On Monday I go to Dr. Shin, alone. I don't want Eddie with me, and he seems happy not to come. We've organized our lives into a polite exchange of civilities and small domestic matters. "Do you want to order Chinese or Indian for dinner?" "Shall we watch a movie or a sitcom?" "Is there a reason the milk is on the counter?" This seems to work well for both of us now. He doesn't have to see me upset, and I don't have to worry about his reaction to my perpetual dolor.

At the doctor's office, I sit in the reception room and fill out the form that asks me if anything has changed in my medical history since the last time I visited. Oh, no, nothing much, I want to write. Just a tiny thing. A one-word thing. A miscarriage. No big deal. We're all over that now. Moving on!

Across the room two women chat. One is hugely pregnant, and the other holds a toddler on her lap.

"Didn't he just turn one?" the pregnant woman asks.

"Last week. We had a party. My parents came from Chicago. When are you due?"

"In three weeks. I'm so ready."

I nearly laugh and think, What kind of cruel joke is this that

I have to sit here and listen to them talk about their babies? But what else can I do? I learned that lesson when my parents died. Stood with my forehead pressed against the leaded glass window of the funeral home and watched kids play at the school across the street. How could they be happy? Jumping, dancing, singing, tossing balls, when something so bad had happened to me. It's the truth of the world, though. Life goes on. Just because I've lost my baby, or fetus, as Eddie calls it, doesn't mean that no one else will have joy. I watch them smile fondly at the kid squirming on his mother's lap. Assholes, I think, but I wish like hell I was one of them.

In the exam room, the nurse draws blood and takes my urine, then Dr. Shin slips me the ultrasound one last time. "This is great!" she says cheerily as she scans my insides. "Good news for you."

What possible good news could there be in this situation? I wonder as I lie flat on my back, looking at the empty space inside me. Did she find my baby with that sonar machine? Is it still alive and living somewhere in Jersey? I imagine my tiny twelve-week fetus, sitting on an overturned shot glass at a seedy bar, smoking an itty-bitty cigarette, and grousing to the bartender about the hardships of being embryonic in this world.

"You passed the pregnancy beautifully," Dr. Shin says. "No clots left. Your have a clean uterus. Your blood work looks good. You could start trying again as soon as you have a period."

I snort and shake my head as she pulls the wand out. "No way," I say. "That's it for me. By the time I'll be ready to try this again, I'll be fifty, and my ovaries will be as dry and shriveled as currants."

Dr. Shin pats me on the knee. "What you went through was perfectly normal."

"Oh, yeah?" I say. I wish that I could ask her for a certificate proving that I'm perfectly normal, because so far I only feel like a fat, ugly, stupid loser.

"Lots of women lose their first one," she assures me.

Every time she says this, it makes me feel worse. As if somehow I'm totally overreacting to my miscarriage. What do other women do? Drop their half-formed fetuses into trashcans on their way to power meetings on Wall Street and never miss a beat? Could someone else have gone through this and been tougher, stronger, better? Is something wrong with me?

"It's a common thing," she says.

"But we had the heartbeat," I tell her as if I'm pleading my case. "You said an eighty percent chance."

"The body's very efficient. When it decides it's time, it shuts things down quickly."

When she says "the body," she means mine. My body quickly and efficiently snuffed out another little life. "What did I do wrong?" I ask. I mean it to come out calm. A simple question. But the words are thick with my sadness, and it comes out as a pathetic plea.

She pats me on the leg. "You didn't do anything wrong. It was probably a chromosomal defect. Down syndrome, most likely."

The words make me shudder. I think of the woman with no arms that I saw on the train, and I wonder why she made it through. Did her mother love her any less? I think of the tiny creature that grew inside of me. "I would have loved her anyway," I say angrily.

Dr. Shin looks at me for a moment, then she scrawls something on my chart. I imagine her writing, "Hysterical woman, not to be trusted with infant," on my permanent records.

After I leave Dr. Shin's office, I walk toward Lemon with a sinking sense of dread. I should be happy to be going back to my sparkly kitchen, my six burners, my two ovens, my shiny sinks, my gleaming counters, my frosty walk-in, my oddball staff. But mostly I feel overwhelmed by all the tasks ahead of me. What I'd really like to do is go home, crawl into my bed, and sleep like I've done for the past ten days. As I round the corner to the restaurant, I see Ernesto out front, putting a bag of garbage in the apartment bins.

"Buenos dias," I say to him.

When he turns and sees me, he breaks into a huge grin. He reaches for me and pulls me into an enormous hug. "I didn't know you were coming back today. How're you feeling?"

I'm sure Ernesto knows. Franny must've told him. Or maybe she didn't. Her reaction to the whole thing has been bizarre. Whatever he knows, I don't want to talk about it. And I don't want my coming back to be full of sap. And I don't want to be treated any differently because something sad has happened to me. So we stand and smile at one another for a moment, then I ask, "You prepping this morning?"

"I'll come down in a little while," he says. "I'm painting the bathroom right now."

I search for my keys. "Franny got you doing her house-work?"

"It was my idea," he says.

I find my keys in the bottom of my bag. "You stay here a lot?"

Ernesto looks at me quizzically. "I live here," he says.

This is news to me. "You mean you live here for real? You pay rent? All your stuff is here?"

"You know me, I don't have much stuff."

"Since when?" I ask.

"I've never had a lot," he says.

I'm still stuck on the fact that Ernesto and Franny are living together and nobody bothered to tell me. "No, I mean how long have you been living here?"

"More or less since you moved out, I guess."

I'm stunned. Shocked. Which is stupid. What did I expect? And why would it bother me? But it does. Mostly because they didn't tell me.

"You okay?" Ernesto asks.

"Sure. Yeah. Fine," I say as I fumble with all the locks and open the front door.

"Good to have you back," Ernesto calls after me as I disappear into the dining room.

Franny is in the kitchen, chopping onions and singing along to some sappy Spanish ballad. She is glowing. Pink and pretty. She moves her hips to the rhythm and accentuates the beats with her knife.

When I see her, I immediately think of her sleeping with Ernesto in my old bed. Mixing her clothes with his in the dresser I bought at the Salvation Army years ago. Both of them eating at the little beat-up table I found on Avenue C one summer. Keeping all these intimate details of their lives from me. I stand in the doorway, staring at her. As soon as she looks up, I blurt out, "Why didn't you tell me Ernesto is living with you?" I throw my bag down on the counter. "Is it some kind of secret?"

"Well, hello to you, too," she says.

I stomp across the room and stand on the other side of the counter from her. The vapors from the onions seep into my eyes, making them sting and water. "We had this whole conversation about you taking my place. I gave you the keys. I watched you haul your crap upstairs. Even held the door for you. You never once said that Ernesto was going to live with you. In my place!"

"First of all." Franny lays down her knife and scowls at me. "It isn't your place anymore. It's mine. And secondly, what do you care?"

"I don't care," I say snippily. "Do whatever the hell you want. Don't tell me." I stomp off toward the office.

"Nice to have you back, Lemon," Franny sneers. "What's up your ass this morning?"

"Nothing's up my ass," I snarl at her.

"You walk in here, don't even say hello, we had no idea when you were coming in again."

I march back toward her. "You're the one who's keeping shit from me."

"I'm not keeping anything from you. I've barely seen you lately or talked to you. If you hadn't noticed, I've been busy running your restaurant."

"Oh, well, sorry, Franny. I've been a little preoccupied," I say sarcastically.

"You know what? This is stupid." She walks out from behind the counter and stands in front of me. "It's not your fucking place anymore. I can have orgies up there with the entire prep staff, and it's none of your goddamned business."

"I know that!" I scream.

"Then why are you yelling at me?" she screams back.

What is my problem? I should be happy for Franny and Ernesto. They were both in awful living situations with long commutes, and now thanks to me they have a great place above the restaurant. I helped out two of my friends. I just came back to work. This is the first time I've seen either of them. So why am I starting out like this? Why is my heart beating so fast? And why are my palms moist? Why am I so furious with both of them, especially her?

"Because!" I yell. "You have my life!" Suddenly, looking at

Franny, it all seems so clear. Everything I've lost. Not just that little life growing deep inside of me but an entire life that had taken me so long to carefully construct.

I pace the floor, gesturing wildly and yelling at the pots and pans and knives hanging on the wall. "I had exactly what I wanted for about five minutes in my life. I worked my ass off to get it. Everything was perfect. And then this." I jab myself in the gut. "One careless stupid fuck ruined all that!"

"Lemon," Franny says and shakes her head at me.

"No. Stop. I'm so sick of people shaking their heads at me. Looking at me with so much pity. Telling me to stop. This is the truth. I got pregnant, and everything changed. I changed, for God's sake. I walked around for three months, convincing myself that I wanted a baby. That I could handle bringing another person in my life. That I could mold myself into the perfect mother and keep this place going. Only it was a joke. Clearly I couldn't handle it. Then, I couldn't even have the kid. I lost it, and now everything is falling apart in my life."

Franny stands, staring at me, but she says nothing. I'm not surprised.

"And you didn't even call me," I say quietly, evenly. "I lost this baby, and you never once asked me if I was okay or how I felt or what I needed."

She sputters. Looks down at the stained dishtowel tucked into her apron. "I didn't know if I should call. I didn't want to wake you up or bother you if you were in pain."

"That's bullshit, Franny. You just didn't want to deal with how sad I was."

She looks up at me, defiant again. I know that look in her eyes. The way she holds her mouth. I've seen it in every fight we've had since we first encountered one another. "I was busy trying to keep this place going. For you! You don't even appreciate that!"

"Right," I say. "Because I'm just so selfish."

"You know what?" she yells at me. "You are. Everything comes so easily to you. Always has. In Europe, you got every job you asked for."

"So did you!"

"They'd only hire me after they hired you. I was always second."

"What's it matter who got hired first? We both had jobs."

"And every guy."

"Not this again," I say. "You cannot hold a grudge about Herr Fink for this long. He was such a jerk, Franny. You were lucky not to get mixed up with him."

"That's not the point!" Franny screams.

"Then what is the point?" I scream back.

"The point is that you knew I had a thing for him, but you didn't care. You couldn't stay away. You went ahead and started screwing him and left me in the back of that hell hole peeling potatoes with some shell-shocked Nazi who couldn't even form a sentence. I was miserable, and you didn't care as long as you were having a good time."

I have no answer for this, because it's true. But it wasn't that I wanted to hurt Franny. I just didn't know how to tell her that our friendship was smothering me. That I needed time and space away from her. Herr Fink was a very convenient way to make sure that I got it.

"Then you came back here," Franny goes on. "And you sauntered from gig to gig while I fucked around in catering and corporate dining rooms, working my ass off to find any crap job."

"My life was not that easy," I say.

"Then you started this place, and well, look at that, surprise, surprise, you're immediately The Shit. Do you bother to share any of it with me? With Ernesto? No. It's your name in every article. Your face in every picture. On top of that, you've got a great guy who loves you and bankrolls your dreams. A family that adores you. And all you do is bitch about it."

"How can you say all of this to me after what I've just gone through?" I ask her.

"Look, Lemon." Franny holds out her hands to me and shakes her head. "I'm sorry that you lost the baby. I really am. But you can't use that as an excuse to come in here and scream at me because I finally have something good in my life."

I don't want to listen to her words anymore. Don't want to see her face. I turn and run out of the kitchen. I don't know where I'm going, but I have to get out. Only I'm stopped because I smack into Ernesto, coming through the front door.

He catches me against his body with an *ooph*. "Whoa!" he says. "Hey, slow down. What's going on? Where're you going?"

I'm enraged and wild and need to get out. Need to get away from this place, from Franny, but Ernesto hangs on to me. Holds me tightly and pats my back. "Lemon," he says quietly and sooth- ing. "What's going on? What happened? Why are you so upset?"

I'm in his arms, and I remember this position from years ago. Ernesto would hug me after long, hard days of work when I thought I'd never make it. When I questioned every decision I'd ever made and wondered if I should give up trying to be a chef and move back to Brooklyn to live the life my family expected. No matter how bent out of shape I was about my job or my family, Ernesto would ease everything. He never told me condescendingly that I was okay or tried to convince me that I was pushing myself too hard or talked to me with false patience. He just held on to me until I was calm. This is the thing that Eddie has not done for me. He hasn't let me cry without offer- ing me pity, advice, or his anger in return.

As Ernesto gently rocks me back and forth, I cry, and for the first time in weeks I start to relax a little. I've been working so hard to be strong (for my aunts, for my grandmother, for Eddie, for myself) that all my sadness has turned to rage. But now, here in Ernesto's hug, I can do whatever I need to feel better.

I look up into his face. His expression holds no judgment or expectation like Eddie's lamenting grimaces these days. No anger and resentment like Franny's hard stare. Ernesto is the only person who understands what I need. The only one who really cares. I close my eyes and I tilt my head. I should've known this all along. Ernesto is the one to turn to. Ernesto will make things better. I rise to my tiptoes. I find Ernesto's lips. I press my mouth against his and cross my arms against his back, pulling him closer to me.

"What the fuck do you think you're doing?"

Ernesto pushes me away. I stumble backward and see Franny stomping through the dining room. She rips the Cubs hat from her head and throws it against the bar. "You get the fuck away from him!" she yells at me.

Ernesto holds up his hands, an innocent man, framed. "Franny," he says softly.

"You!" She points at him. "Don't fucking say a word to me." She turns to me. "And you," she says with disgust and hate. "You might get everything else you want in life, but you do not get him! Now get the fuck out of my way." She pushes past me and out the front door, slamming it behind her.

I look at Ernesto. I'm horrified. What the hell have I done? What a stupid, thoughtless, juvenile thing! "I'm so sorry," I whisper with my fingers pressed against my stinging lips. But he's gone. Out the door behind Franny, calling her name.

CHAPTER
TWENTY-FOUR

I close Lemon for the rest of the week and try to regroup. I come clean to the staff about losing the baby. It's a convenient excuse for why we're closed temporarily, since I'm not willing to admit what I've done to drive Franny and Ernesto away. Everyone feels sorry enough for me that they don't ask questions. To Eddie I simply say that Franny blew up over long-held resentments, and we've decided to take a break. He thinks it's a good idea and encourages me not to rush back into work until Franny's calm and I'm ready. I figure by the end of the week, I'll either have talked Franny into coming back or I'll have found a new kitchen staff. Either way, I plan to open for Sunday brunch.

I spend long days in my office making calls, trying to line up new cooks, just in case Franny stays mad. The New York restaurant world is a transient universe full of vagabond chefs always looking for the next good thing, but I can't find anyone I'd want to share my kitchen with. The more people I talk to, the more I realize how difficult it will be to re-create what Franny, Ernesto, and I had.

As the days pass and I get more desperate, I leave Franny contrite messages, practically begging her to call me or stop by so we can talk. Although I suspect Ernesto understands that what I did was a momentary lapse of judgment with no more true emotion attached than if I had kissed one of the dead trout in the cooler, I know that his loyalty is with Franny, and I can't blame him. Neither one of them calls me back or answers the buzzer when I go to their door. One day, I sit in the dining room for hours, watching for them to come out of the building, but I never see them. I'm beginning to suspect they've taken off.

The rest of my time I spend grappling with the books, going over a year's worth of finances, trying to figure out why Lemon's never gotten on its feet. When I see how much money Eddie's really sunk into my restaurant, I'm appalled. He's the only reason the doors have stayed open. The scary thing is, I can't figure out why. I'm sure there are efficiency experts who could come in and make this place profitable. They'd recommend a set menu with particular pricing points, cheap vendors who deliver food in industrial-sized cans, and watered-down drinks at double their cost. I've worked in those kinds of restaurants, and I hate them. I won't own one.

By Friday night, I'm in a panic. I've got no cooks, no menu, no supplies. The ovens are cold, the countertops are desolate, and the pantry is bare. But I have a staff that's planning to come back in for Sunday brunch and a sign on the door that says I'll be open. As I stand in the middle of my empty kitchen, I feel an overwhelming sense of doom.

Maybe if things were different. If I had more gumption, more wherewithal, more stamina, I'd pull through. I'd find a way to persevere without Franny and Ernesto and let this be another story about how Lemon made it when so many other restaurants failed. The thing is though, I keep expecting Franny to come back. To walk in the door and berate me for kissing her boyfriend so I can give her hell about never calling me when I needed her most. Then we can forgive each other and get back to work.

What I realize now as I stand here with only the wheeze of the walk-in and the buzz of the lights for company is that Franny's not coming back. She isn't going to forgive me this time, because her anger isn't simply about me kissing her boyfriend. She thinks I'm selfish and uncaring. Always has. Maybe she's right. That's the kind of single-minded determination it would take to get Lemon on its feet again, but I don't have it in me anymore.

I slump down to the cold tile floor and rest my head against the hard edge of the reach-in. My reflection in the stainless steel appliances around me is vague and blurry. Nothing is in my control anymore. I think of my parents' train. Of the brakes surely squealing. The passengers pressing themselves against the windows to see what the conductor could see. Jamming their feet into the floor to mimic brakes. The reeling lurch when the train made its final descent toward the river. How long did they fight against the inevitable? Did they try to kick open windows? Find a back door? Swim to the surface? When did they know it was over?

I sit here, and I cry. For myself. For what I'm losing. For all the years of cooking for other chefs, biding my time, gathering recipes, plotting, and planning. All the money Eddie and I sank into this place. All the press, the promise, the potential of what I could have been. And for how I've pushed away Franny's friendship by lashing out at her in my anger. I cry until I'm exhausted, and as I try to calm down and catch my ragged breath, it dawns on me that I could let all of this go. The bills, the worry, the constant rush to keep up, stay on top, be the best, make everybody around me happy. It would be such relief to drift away, leaving the wreckage for someone else to clear.

Then the back door opens and I look up, half hoping and half fearing that it will be Franny. I don't know what I would do. But I don't have to decide, because it's Makiko standing in the doorway.

"Lemon? Is that you? Are you crying?" She squints into the half-dark.

I rub my sleeve across my eyes and nose. "Yeah," I say. "It's me."

"What's the matter? Are you feeling sad?"

"We're not going to open Sunday," I tell her.

"That's okay," she assures me with a gentle pat to my shoulder. Makiko smells like sweet cake batter, and I regret all of the desserts she won't be making. "There's no hurry," she says.

"Franny and Ernesto quit."

"They wouldn't do that," she says and looks around the kitchen as if she'll find them hiding in a corner.

"We had a fight on Monday," I tell her. "Then they left. I've tried to get in touch with them but they haven't called me or come by since."

"Franny's just mad at you," says Makiko. "You know how she is. She'll calm down."

I shake my head. "She's definitely not coming back. And if she's not coming back, neither is Ernesto."

"But why?" Makiko asks, blinking with disbelief.

I shake my head wearily. "It's too much to explain." I know this is a cop-out, but I'm too tired to admit any more.

"But what are we going to do?"

"Well, actually, nothing," I say. "I mean, there's nothing we can do now. The finances are a mess. I'm weeks behind. I lost my kitchen staff."

"I'll help you," Makiko says. "Eddie will too. Melanie. Kirsten and Lyla. We can make it work."

I shake my head. "I'm sorry, Makiko," I say. "I feel terrible for letting you down like this. All of you. Lyla. Kirsten. Mel.

Manuel. I even feel bad for Mona. You've all been so good to me." I cover my face with my hands. Franny's words hit me again. I am selfish.

"You've been through a lot, Lemon, and Franny has a horrible temper."

"Actually, I don't want to do it anymore." I look up at Makiko and shake my head. "I just can't."

"Do you really mean that?" she asks.

"Yes," I say. "I really do."

Makiko slouches down beside me, and we sit silently for a long time. The only noise is the gentle whir of the walk-in. The old beast. "I used to love the hours after we closed for the night," I tell Makiko. "When the place was empty and quiet, but the smells of what we cooked still lingered."

"Like ghosts were eating," she says.

"I'll miss that."

"I'll miss a lot of things," she says.

I look around at my kitchen. She's right. There's a lot to miss, but for me it'll be a relief to let it go.

"What will you do?" I ask.

"Well," she says and pauses thoughtfully. I watch her face as the reality of the situation gradually hits her. "I've been thinking for a long time about going home to visit my family. I haven't been back to Japan in over two years. We were so busy here, I never wanted to leave."

"You could've asked me for a vacation," I say, and Makiko giggles. "Yeah, that was stupid," I admit and laugh a little, too. "I would've fallen apart if you left. You'll come back, though, right?"

She looks up at me. "Of course I will. I want to work for you again."

"You're far too nice to me, Makiko," I say.

"You're not nice enough to yourself, Lemon."

CHAPTER
TWENTY-FIVE

Aunt Livinia and I watch Montel at four o'clock while we crochet. She insisted I learn to make doilies, and I'm getting
pretty good at it. Otherwise, to her addled mind, watching television is a waste of time. I've found I like keeping my hands
busy. Today I'm working on a star design. I'm thinking of starting a tablecloth.

For the first week after I closed Lemon, I moped around
Eddie's apartment, moving from bed to couch to refrigerator
and back to the bed while he paced, talking on the phone,
selling his latest press of oil and small batches of vinegar to my
old competition. When he wasn't on the phone or the computer, he usually followed me around and asked me what I
was doing, what I was going to do, and what I'd do while he
was gone.

The other problem was his mother. She still calls every few
days and asks to talk to me. Mostly I've avoided it by being
asleep or going on walks or by conveniently locking myself in
the bathroom when I hear him say, "Hello, Mother!" A few
times I simply refused to take the phone when he shoved it
toward me and begged me to talk to her. I don't need to listen to

'Scilla's subtle scorn and inanities about how to get back up on my horse.

Most days, I mosey over to my grandmother's about mid-morning. I walk the back streets from Park Slope to Carroll Gardens, through the little hidden neighborhoods forbidden to me as a child. Past the ironwork shops and warehouses, over small bridges crossing the Gowanus Canal. When I was a kid, my aunts led us to believe these neighborhoods were rough, full of Dominican and Puerto Rican hoods who'd sooner slit our Italian throats than let us walk their streets.

Once, to prove that no one was in charge of me, since my parents were dead, I ran all the way down Smith Street and crossed the invisible line from good to bad. What I found was a neighborhood exactly like mine. Old men still sat outside in their undershirts, but these guys played dominoes. Women still yelled out of apartment windows for kids, but they yelled in Spanish. The shops sold avocados and plantains instead of tomatoes and bananas. When I got back, I told my cousins that my aunts were right. I said that bad kids with knives chased me all over the streets. I didn't want to share my discovery with anyone else.

Now these streets are undergoing the same quick gentrification that happened in my grandmother's neighborhood a few years ago. Odd boutiques and small restaurants are taking over the old ninety-nine-cent stores and bodegas. Hipsters in their grubby chic clothes walk to the subway stops, carrying cups of steaming lattes. Dozens of storefronts are for rent. I pass it all and wonder where all the people went who used to live here, and who will replace them.

So now, Livinia and I spend the day watching TV. *Montel* is our favorite show. Although *Judge Judy* runs a close second. I'm not sure why Livinia loves these shows so much, but for me, any chance to see people who are bigger failures than myself makes me nearly giddy with pleasure. Today the show is about men who secretly marry more than one woman at the same time.

"Oh, come on," I yell at the big blond woman who claims she thought her husband worked overnight shifts at the car factory every other week. "How could you be so stupid!"

"She's a whore!" Livinia yells as the show cuts to a commercial for teeth-whitening strips. I giggle at hearing my weird old aunt scream the word *whore*. When Montel comes back on, she mutters, "The baby wasn't yours!" I have no idea what she's talking about, but the anger is clear in her eyes, and her jaw trembles.

"You okay?" I ask.

"I told him that, but he didn't listen."

"Who?"

She stares at me blankly, then goes back to her doily. I lay mine aside. I need to get out of the stuffy room for a while. In Livinia, I see too many things that are becoming familiar in myself, and the combination of our hostility scares me. I leave her grumbling and crocheting as I climb the stairs out of the dark basement.

The rest of the house is quiet. My grandmother must be out. I browse through the kitchen, opening cupboards and staring into the fridge. I'm not hungry, so I wander through the other rooms until I end up in my old bedroom. Everything is in its place. My shelf of angsty novels that I loved as a teenager—Virginia Woolf, Sylvia Plath, Kate Chopin. A shoebox filled with mixed tapes made by long-ago friends. Yearbooks and albums of pictures from high school. All of it covered in dust and left undisturbed for over a decade.

I catch a glimpse of myself in the mirror above the empty dresser. It's odd to watch myself snoop through my old life, as if

I'm trying to ascertain who the girl was that used to live in this room. In this same mirror, I examined that girl's adolescent face over and over, looking for traces of my mother. I felt forever clumsy and dopey next to the memory of her, perpetually cool and beautiful in her low-waisted red dress, slim cigarette between her long elegant fingers, a squat glass of whiskey sweating on top of the piano where she teased notes and flirted with melody. She has always remained an enigmatic woman to me, drawn away from her riverbed to the depths of the ocean by the suck and pull of tides.

I'm older now than she was when she died, but I've hit my own less literal version of rock bottom. As I look at myself in the reflection, I catalog every tiny crease etched into the skin of my face. I look nothing like her. I am jaundiced and puckered, a sour little person. (More like Livinia, I think with a shudder.) I'd always assumed that I'd live longer than my mother did, but in my mind, I intended to glide through my adult life as one of those people who was stronger, smarter, and more empathetic for her early grief. How many people can claim the simultaneous deaths of their parents at the tender age of six?

I'd always assumed that experience had filled my lifetime quota for sadness. But I've never become a Zen master of the moment with a preternatural sense of the futility of hanging onto the past. I can't slough off sorrow like dead skin. I cling to indignation. So maybe Franny's right. Maybe my false sense of entitlement to a happy ending has made me selfish.

Clearly I'm not one of those heroic people, like some blind one-legged hiker hopping to the top of Mount McKinley, who plants a flag in memory of my long-dead mother. The truth is, I resent my mother for dying. Nor have I been able to dauntlessly redirect my anguish over losing this baby to better humanity in the name of my lost daughter. I resent her for leaving me, too.

And, somehow in all of this, I've lost the person I thought I was. I ask myself, What happened to that self-sufficient, world-weary woman I worked so hard to become? The one who would never give up. Maybe my parents glimpsed my future when they looked into my infant eyes. Maybe they had some inkling of what I'd become. Perhaps that was their consolation prize for never knowing me past that grubby six-year-old trying desperately to make them stay. Well, thank you, Mom and Dad. You must be very proud. Finally, I've lived up to my name.

I fall asleep, facedown, on my old bed, something I do frequently these days. When I wake, the sky has gone gray. I roll over and breathe in deeply. The smell of stuffed bell peppers wafts up the stairs—the brawny aroma of browning beef with garlic, onions, and tomatoes; the starchiness of the rice; and a vibrant whiff of blanched green peppers. My grandmother has been cooking all my old favorites lately. Chicken and noodles. Linguine and sausage. Minestrone with beans. Scalloped potatoes and salmon patties. I'd forgotten most of these simple old dishes, made from recipes that have been circulating through the able hands of my maternal line for decades. A lot of them are the first dishes that Poppy taught me to make.

I drag myself off the bed and venture down to the kitchen to sit on a stool and watch my grandmother work her alchemy of ingredients. She is the picture of efficiency in the kitchen. There are no wasted motions, no extra steps. She is a one-woman assembly line. The rice goes in the meat, the meat goes in the peppers, the peppers go in the oven, the dirty dishes go in the soapy water. I've watched her cook this way for so many years that it seems natural, normal, the only way to do it.

As I sit here now, I think back to the kitchen at Lemon. The anarchy of every meal. Ernesto, Franny, and I built each dish as if it were an architectural feat. We swirled sauces on the bottom of every plate. Towered potatoes, beets, roasted squash, anything that would stack up to dizzying heights and teeter beneath bouquets of fresh herbs. We used squeeze bottles, molds, Parisian scoops, and sifters. Our goal was to make the most complex and gorgeous food we could imagine. We had no order, no structure, no overarching plan except to outdo everything we'd done before. No wonder we were continually exhausted and over budget and irritated with one another.

"Didn't Poppy put raisins in her stuffed peppers?" I ask my grandmother as she finishes up the dish.

She thinks for a moment. "Sometimes," she says. "And pine nuts. She liked pine nuts when she could afford them."

I think about Poppy's gnocchi. Those little pillowy puffs of potato, so delightful on my tongue. Sometimes in the late fall, she would make them from butternut squash out of her garden and coat them in brown butter. Once she made a creamy gorgonzola sauce with walnuts served over the top of a velvety steamed polenta pudding, and I thought I had discovered the food of nirvana.

"Do you remember her carbonara?" I ask my grandmother.

"Sure," she says. "She made it just like my mother."

"With the raw egg yolk in the middle of that black-flecked pasta. It grossed me out as a kid. I always made her stir in my egg so it'd cook."

"You were missing the best part," Grandma says.

"You know what I loved? Poppy's veal chops. I don't know how she pounded them so thin."

"She used a hammer wrapped in a dishtowel," Grandma tells me. "Or an iron skillet. She was surprisingly strong for such a little person."

"The chops were always so crispy and juicy."

"She put parmesan in the flour."

"And in the summer she'd pull those little bitter arugula leaves out of her garden and chop them with fresh tomatoes and red onions and throw it on top of the veal. God, that was good."

"Poppy was a real cook," says Grandma. "Like you. She loved to experiment."

As my grandmother says this, I realize how incredibly inventive Poppy was. Although my grandmother is an amazing cook, she was always busy preparing meals for her family and didn't have the time or the money to experiment. Poppy, though, loved to be in the kitchen, creating new concoctions. Putting together unexpected combinations or turning out classic dishes to perfection.

When I was a kid, all of the recipes seemed so complicated and time-consuming. Now as I think back through them, I see the beautiful simplicity of her cooking. There were no exotic ingredients. She didn't have access to such things. She used what was available in her garden, at the butcher, or the little greengrocers where she shopped.

"What was in Lemon's linguine?" I ask. That was the dish Poppy said she made up and named for me.

Grandma shrugs. "Probably just some garlic, butter, lemons, pancetta, heavy cream. Maybe a little grappa at the end, if she had it around."

I think back to that taste. The tart creamy sauce and the salty ham sticking to the impossibly long linguine. "She always made it for my birthday," I say.

"That and a black raspberry pie," Grandma says.

"God, I'd love to have one of those."

"I have some frozen berries in the freezer," Grandma tells me.

Our conversation is interrupted by the squeak of the front door. We both turn and look into the hall. "Hey, y'all," Eddie calls from the foyer.

Grandma looks up at the owl clock. "Right on time," she says. It's nearly six.

Eddie and I have come to some sort of unspoken arrangement. I spend all day here, he comes over for dinner, then we go home together and go to bed. It seems to be working well for us, since we barely have to see one another or talk. I wonder how long we can sustain this awkward truce before one of us explodes.

He comes into the kitchen with a bottle of wine. "Smells delicious," he says, then kisses each of us lightly on the cheek.

"You have a good day?" I ask him, rhetorically.

"Yep," he says. "I'll tell you about it later."

This surprises me. He hasn't shared much about his days lately. I take three plates out of the cupboard and lay them on the table. "Anyone else coming?"

"Not that I've heard," says Grandma, but that doesn't mean much. Usually someone else shows up for dinner. One of my aunts, a cousin, a neighborhood friend. There's always enough food plus leftovers to take home or eat the next day for lunch.

As we're sitting down and filling our plates with the peppers, the phone rings. My grandmother rises slowly and answers it. "Yes," she says and smiles. "Oh, that's great. Is everyone okay? Uh-huh. They still there? Going home tomorrow? How much did she weigh?"

I put my silverware down and glance at Eddie, who digs into his pepper. My appetite has vanished.

"Well, send them our best," Grandma says. "I'll put some food together and drop it by tomorrow. Bye now." She hangs up and looks at me uncertainly.

"Trina?" I ask, saving my grandmother from the uncomfortable position of finding the most delicate words to tell me that Trina had her baby. She nods. Eddie stops eating and looks at me. I wad up my napkin and lay it beside my plate. "It's okay," I say with a clumsy little laugh. "She had to have it some time."

CHAPTER

TWENTY-SIX

"So I had a really good day," Eddie says in the car on the way back to our apartment.

"Really," I say absently as I watch the passing storefronts, all lit up and full of people. These streets bustle in the evening. People come and go from the train, walk in and out of shops, line up in front of restaurants. So different from when I was a kid and everything on this strip closed by six o'clock.

"I think I'm going to get that Italian Stallion contract."

"What's that?"

"I told you about it," Eddie says. He may have, but I don't retain much these days. "It's that new chain. They're opening stores on the Upper West Side, in Times Square, and down by Wall Street."

I nod as he talks, but my mind wanders toward Trina. I imagine her in a hospital room, surrounded by bouquets of flowers and bundles of balloons. Her baby snuggled sweetly under her arm.

"These suckers have five hundred seats and horrible food," says Eddie. "But they want good oil on the tables so the customers will think they're getting something authentically Italian with their four-cheese-stuffed chicken breasts."

Eddie looks at me for a response. "Sounds lovely," I say derisively.

"I'll take you there for our anniversary," he says with a laugh. I'm not sure if he's serious.

At home in bed, we lie side by side in the dark. This has become our routine. Not touching, not talking, just lying. Sometimes Eddie reads; sometimes I stare at the ceiling before I fall asleep. Tonight I wonder what Trina's doing. How she was during labor. She's probably psyched for the drugs she's allowed to have and for my aunts gathered around, attending to her every need and whim.

"Did you feel weird when your grandmother told us that Trina had her baby?" Eddie asks me out of the blue.

I'm not sure how to answer because I'm uncertain what he's getting at. "What'd you mean, weird?"

He's agitated and twitchy beside me. He shimmies his legs and chews on his lips. "It pissed me off."

"That she had it, or that Grandma told us?"

"I don't know. Both, I guess. It just seems unfair."

"Unfair for who?" I snap. It comes out harsh, all hard edges, and ready to fight. What's Eddie getting at? More blame?

"I mean, she doesn't deserve it. Neither does that criminal she's marrying."

I'm perplexed. This is the first time Eddie's said anything other than happy shiny things designed to cheer me up. For weeks now, he's gone along as if nothing happened.

"It makes no sense," he says, then he looks at me. His eyes search my face. He seems genuinely confused. "Why did they get to have a healthy baby, and we didn't?"

"Because I lost it," I say bitterly.

Eddie sits up abruptly. "Would you stop saying that!"

"Oh, sorry. I forgot, we don't talk about it."

"I *am* trying to talk about it," he says.

"No, you're talking about Trina, not about what happened to me."

"It happened to us."

"*You* weren't here," I say sarcastically.

"Goddammit, Lemon," Eddie says. He twists his fingers into his hair. "I can't change that, and you can't hold it against me forever."

I sit up and smack my hands down on the bed. "You're such a selfish bastard!" I yell. "I don't get to hold it against you for being gone, but you get to blame me for the whole fucking catastrophe."

"I don't blame you!" Eddie booms. "You blame yourself!"

"Because you said it was my fault!" I scream back at him.

Eddie grabs me by the shoulders and turns my body to face him. "I don't blame you," he says angrily, his grip tight.

I resent his strength and try to squirm away. I flail around, smack him with angry open hands. "You did."

His grip loosens, and he kneads my shoulder. "I'm sorry, Lemon. I'm really sorry." Then his face softens, his lips go slack, and his eyes squint. "I should've been here. I should've helped you. I should've never left or said what I said." He's crying, and I'm stunned. I've never seen him cry, and it makes tears sting my eyes. "I let you down," he bawls. "I let our kid down."

"No," I say and shake my head, but what I mean is yes. Yes, he did, only it doesn't matter now, because what I've needed this whole time is for Eddie to feel the same as I do. To cry because he is as sad as I am. I've felt isolated and alone without that commiseration, but now it's different. I wrap my arms around him. "I miss her so much," I whisper.

"Me, too," he says.

We lie and cry together, twisted up, all arms and legs. Every ridge and bump of his body familiar against mine, and welcome. Fitting together, my hip, his waist, shoulder to shoulder, elbows wrapped. Eventually, we calm down. Our tears dry salty on our faces, and we are shy with one another, but we don't let go. I rest against his chest. Breathe him in. Inhale his scent. It's late, and I'm exhausted. I could drift away in this position and sleep for days.

"What'd you think they'll name it?" Eddie whispers in my hair.

"Who?" I ask dreamily.

"Trina and Chuck," he says. "What do you think they'll name the kid?"

"I don't know," I say. "I don't really care."

"Nicotina?" he says cattily.

I laugh, an unexpected giggle. He laughs, too.

"Sorry," Eddie says. "I'm not helping, am I?"

"Actually, it's nice." I rub my hand against his bare forearm. I've missed this arm. All the curly hair from the wrist to the elbow. "I thought I was only one who had those kinds of small-minded, petty thoughts."

He looks at me and smirks. "I'm a pretty small-minded, petty bastard myself."

"That's why I like you," I tell him. He chuckles and pulls me into a hug. We are happy in our meanness. "But I feel kind of bad," I admit. "I always thought I'd be a bigger person about something like this."

"You expect too much from yourself," says Eddie. "We're going to be pissed off and sad for a while. That's okay."

"Are you?"

"Pissed off and sad?"

I nod.

"Of course," he says.

"You haven't acted like it."

He lays his chin on top of my head, and I bury my face into his shirt. "I was trying to be strong for you," he tells me.

"That's not what I need from you."

"What do you need, Lemon?"

I nuzzle his neck and let my cheek rest against his grizzly face. "Just you," I say.

He scoots my body closer into the folds of his. It's the first time I've welcomed Eddie so close to me in weeks. Now I realize how much I've missed his skin, his warmth, his smell.

"Why do you think we lost it?" he whispers to me. He bites his lip and waits for my answer. I see the uncertainty in his face. I'm sure he's afraid of upsetting me again. But I want to meet him here, straight on, so we can finally look at this thing that's happened to us rather than constantly skirting it, as if it will shrivel up and go away.

"The doctor said it was probably some chromosomal problem with the fetus," I tell him slowly, unsure how he'll react. "Probably Down syndrome."

"Jesus," says Eddie. "How could that have happened?"

"Happens a lot, I guess."

We're quiet for a while. Both of us digesting the reality of what we lost and how it affected us. Then Eddie says, "Maybe we were lucky."

"What was lucky about it?" I hear the edge of anger in my voice.

"I don't know that we were ready to have a kid like that. We'd have to give up a lot."

"I would have loved that baby regardless."

"Maybe it's lucky that you didn't have to."

These are the words of someone who's never known bad

luck, but maybe he's right. Maybe I am lucky. I can't help but wonder, though, if luck evens out. Maybe I lost this baby as karmic retribution for having it too easy lately. For having Eddie in my life, for having been at the right place at the right time to start Lemon.

Who do I think I am to evade bad luck anyway? How very middle-class of me. Dead parents, and I think I'm off scot-free. What about the chronically unlucky? The stupid, ugly, poor people? The homeless? The insane? Ride the subway for five minutes, and you'll spot them. They ride with looks of regret etched onto their faces. They shuffle in and out of the cars. They rock with the rhythm of the train. They never put up a fight. They sit on their fat haunches and wait for the day to end.

Am I on a run of bad luck? Has it streaked me like a skunk? Is it something that suddenly befalls a person? One minute you're on top of the world, fated for a better life, a higher calling, a bigger cut of the pie. The next minute you're plunging over the side of a bridge toward an icy river or crawling on your hands and knees to the toilet, losing the baby that you thought would be in your life forever.

"Well, no matter what you think," Eddie says to me, "I know that I'm lucky to have you."

"You sure you still feel that way?" I ask.

"Of course," he says and kisses me. "I've never doubted it for a second."

CHAPTER
TWENTY-SEVEN

I stay away from my grandmother's house the next day. I know each of my aunts will be by to tell their version of Trina's daughter's birth. The story will be repeated over and over again until every detail has been formed into some coherent piece of family lore. And somewhere in there will be a footnote about how poor Lemon had a miscarriage and cracked up at Trina's shower, then had to stay away.

In the morning, after Eddie leaves, I realize that I'm sick of wandering around in my ratty sweatshirt and cargo pants, eating bright orange Cheeze Doodles from the bag. I don't even have Livinia and my crochet hook to distract me. I want to do something today. I want to make something. I want to cook.

The cupboards are as bare as the fridge. We've got exactly one brown banana and two slices of moldy bread plus some condiments that are just crusty layers around the rims. I shower before three o'clock for the first time in weeks, put on clean clothes, throw all my dirties in the laundry basket, and leave the apartment in search of inspiration.

I've never shopped in Park Slope for groceries. I'm looking for simple ingredients, good organic produce, fresh mozzarella, decent cuts of meat, some herbs. I find what I need at a good cheese shop on Union Street, a couple of Italian delis, a little butcher, and by browsing through the bodegas and organic markets. I come home with sacks stuffed with the makings for a feast that Poppy would have loved.

As I'm mincing garlic in the kitchen, the phone rings. I'm distracted, so I answer, forgetting that I don't want to talk to anyone, until I hear a familiar southern voice say, "Well, Jesus, Mary, and Joseph, you're home!"

I cringe. "Oh, hi, 'Scilla." I drop my knife on the counter and begin to pace, looking for an out. "Actually, I'm just on my way . . ." Where? Where could I go?

"Lemon, dear, I've been trying to find you for weeks now. Didn't Eddie tell you?"

"Well, we've been sort of, you know . . ." I could fake the door buzzer ringing or tell her I have a doctor's appointment.

"Honey, I've been so worried about you. Just thinking of you all time. This whole thing has put me in a state. An absolute state. I had to take to my bed."

Of course, this conversation has to be about her. Well, I'm not going to apologize for ruining her luncheon schedule with my ill-timed miscarriage. "Listen," I say firmly. "I've got to be at—"

"Honey, what you've been going through is pure hell," she says, and I wonder what makes her think she'd know. "And I'm sure Eddie has been no help at all. God love him. I know he tries, but men, darling, believe me, men are not capable of understanding what it means to lose a baby like that."

"Oh," I say and shut up. 'Scilla is the first person to come out and confirm that I did in fact lose a baby. A baby that I may have never seen or held alive, but a baby in my mind, in my body. I drop down into a kitchen chair.

"Pregnancy's a funny thing for men," 'Scilla says. "When they're not lusting over your ever-expanding bosoms, as if it's all for them, they're turning into Mr. Safety, pecking around for any ounce of control they can find in the situation. Bucky was awful. Just awful. Always telling me to sit down, drink water, hold onto handrails, as if I was some kind of moron who would tumble blindfolded and dehydrated down a flight of stairs."

I snort a little laugh, thinking of Bucky trying to boss 'Scilla around. I'm sure he had no more luck than Eddie does with me. I dab my finger over toast crumbs on the tablecloth as 'Scilla keeps on yammering.

"Oh, but they're sweet," she says with a sigh. "And how are you, darling? How are you holding up?"

"I'm okay," I tell her. I make a little pile of the crumbs in front of me.

"Well, I don't know that I believe that, Lemon."

"Why?" I ask defensively. "What'd Eddie tell you?"

"Nothing," she says. "That's the problem. He says you're fine, too. But you went through something tough. Takes a lot of time to start feeling better. And you don't need to rush yourself for anybody's sake. Certainly not my son's. He needs to be taking care of you right now."

"He's trying," I say. "It's just that—" I stop. I'm not sure what I want to say, or if I want to say it to 'Scilla.

"What, hon? It's just that what?"

I add more crumbs to my pile while I search for words.

"Listen, I'm not trying to pry. You don't have to tell me anything," she says. "You have your whole family to listen and support you."

"They don't really understand," I say, and am surprised that I've admitted it. "Even though they're very sweet, and they really try."

"Sometimes that's the way it is. The people you think are

going to be the most helpful just aren't, for whatever reason. Either they're too caught up in their own lives, or they only tell you how to get over it."

"That's just it!" I say to her and scatter the crumbs across the table again. "Everyone wants me to be all better now, but I can't seem to get over it. Sometimes I'll feel okay. I'll almost forget for a while. I'll feel like me again. And then it'll hit me, like a sucker punch in the gut, and I'll remember."

"Oh, honey," she says. "This isn't something you get over. It's just something you get through, and then you carry it around with you for the rest of your life. It's part of your story now. Part of your history. It'll always, always hurt. Just not quite as bad someday."

We both sit silently and breathe together. I am grateful for this covenant. For this unexpected moment of understanding and connection from so far away. She's the only person who's said anything that's made sense to me lately.

"'Scilla?" I ask her after some time. "Did you lose one, too?"

She's quiet, then she says, "The past was a long time ago, honey. And we're not talking about me right now. We're talking about you."

"I'm sorry," I say, because I know from the sound of her voice that she's been in this exact same position.

"Me, too," she says. "I'm sorry, too. But let me tell you something. Someday you will have a child, and when you hold that baby for the very first time, all this sadness will shrink down to an itty-bitty pea."

Then the door buzzer really does ring. It startles me out of my chair. "'Scilla, I'm sorry, but someone is at my door. Can you hang on?"

"Oh, well, I should be letting you go anyway. I know you have things to do."

"I'm really glad that we talked," I tell her. I walk to the front of the apartment and peek out the window. I can't make out who's on the stoop. I think it's a woman with dark hair, but not one of my aunts. They almost always travel in a pack. Maybe it's a Jehovah's Witness. "You've been incredibly helpful," I say. The buzzer rings again.

"Any time, darling. Any time at all. You just call me up, and we'll have ourselves a little chat."

"Thank you," I say.

"You take care of yourself, now."

I hang up the phone and push the intercom for the door. "Who is it?" I ask warily.

"Hello, Lemon? This is Makiko."

"Makiko!" I nearly yell into the intercom. "When did you get back? Come on up!" I jab my finger against the button, then yank open the door and scurry down the stairs to greet her.

We meet on the second landing. Makiko looks great in a little vintage plaid swing coat and red woolly scarf around her neck. I open my arms and hug her. She's stiff but allows this outpouring of American affection to be visited on her.

"Sorry to barge in," she says. "I should've call you first, but I couldn't find your phone number."

"Shut up," I tell her. "It's great to see you. I'm glad you came. Come upstairs."

"I won't stay long. I wanted to bring you some *omiyage* from my trip to Japan." She holds up a big box by a string handle.

"You didn't have to bring me anything," I say, but of course I'm dying to know what it is. "Come up and have some tea so we can talk. I want to hear all about your trip."

"It smells so good in here," Makiko says when we walk into my apartment. "What're you cooking?"

"Just some old recipe for cannelloni with artichokes that Little Great-Aunt Poppy taught me."

"You have to teach me some good American home cooking," Makiko says.

"I'll teach you some if you teach me how to cook Japanese food." I take her coat and toss it over one of the chairs in the living room. I glance around and see how unkempt the place is. Magazines and newspapers slump off the coffee table onto the floor. Empty mugs and crumby plates cover the end tables. My shoes are kicked off and abandoned in random places around the room. For the first time in weeks, the disarray annoys me. "Sorry for the mess."

"Your apartment is nice," she says. "Homey. Cozy."

"You mean messy and filthy," I say and laugh.

In the kitchen she sets the brown box in the center of the kitchen table while I heat up water and slice an apple and some cheese.

"Was your trip home okay?" I ask.

"It was fine. Very busy. Too many people to see. I'm tired now."

"Was your family sad to see you leave again?"

"Yes, it's very hard on my mother. She's so old-fashioned. I'm an only child. And not married. Such a disgrace," she says, rolling her eyes. "Not a good Japanese daughter."

I bring the tea and food to the table on a tray. "Did you see old friends?"

"Not really. I lost touch mostly. They think I'm strange for leaving Japan and moving to New York. But I was always a little different from everyone else, so I don't mind."

"I know what you mean." I pour Makiko a cup of tea. "I don't have any friends from my neighborhood anymore, either."

"But it's important for me to go back," Makiko says.

"For your mom?"

"Yes," she says, then pauses. She stares down into her tea,

lets the steam tendrils curl around her face. "And another reason." She looks up at me. "I want to give you this." She pushes the box toward me.

I lift it off the table and onto my lap. It's heavy, probably ten or fifteen pounds, and solid. "What is it?" I ask.

"Please open it," she says.

I grab a knife off the counter and cut through the string binding the box closed, then through the tape holding the flaps together. I pull out handfuls of shredded newspaper and Styrofoam packing peanuts, then dip my hands inside and pull out a small stone statue. It's about a foot tall, with a placid face and arms down against its body. I'm not sure what to make of it, but I say, "It's lovely, Makiko. Thank you."

"This is a *mizuko jizo,*" she tells me. "A water baby statue. Many people have these in Japan. We put them at the temple and visit them often." She looks down at her tea again and bites her lip. "I have one in Sawara, where I'm from. I went to visit it while I was home."

"Does it bring you good luck or something?" I ask.

She shakes her head and is quiet, as if she's trying to figure out how to explain it to me. Then she takes a breath and says, "We think that when a baby dies, it's too young to have a soul, and so it gets stranded on the banks of the river that separates life and death. So we have these statues to remember the babies and to try to make them feel better."

I look down into the tiny expressionless face on the statue. Where is my baby now? I imagine her by a river, peering into the water at her reflection. Would my mother look up from beneath the cloudy surface and find her?

"We have these for many reasons," Makiko continues. "Maybe an infant dies too soon. Maybe some women are like you and lose the baby before it's born. Or maybe . . ." Her voice falters. She clears her throat and tries again. "Like me, they decided not to have a baby, and they feel guilty."

I look up at her suddenly. "You mean an abortion?"

"I'm sorry if this makes you angry," she says. "Maybe you feel like it's unfair of me to compare my situation with yours."

I reach across the table and lay my hand against hers. "I don't think that, Makiko. I thought I was pregnant once before when I was twenty. If I had been, there's no way I would've kept it." I shake my head at the memory. I was so immature then, and such an asshole to Franny.

Makiko watches me for a moment, then she says slowly. "I was seventeen."

"You were so young."

"My boyfriend wanted me to have it. He wanted to get married. A lot of girls in my town got married young. But I didn't want that. I knew I wanted to leave."

"Did your family know?"

She nods. "I told my mother. She was devastated, but she helped me. I don't think she ever forgave me, though. To her, having a child anytime would be a wonderful thing, because she never wanted anything else in her life."

Makiko's words make me think of my own mother and everything she wanted in her life. All these years, I've questioned whether I was one of those things. Looking back, though, I realize how much she had loved me. How hard it was for her to leave me each time they went on the road. The sad smile on her face as I looked out the window, waving to them. Now, I'm glad that she got to do what she wanted. Her life was so short. She deserved to make herself happy.

I've spent my life expecting some kind of payback for losing my parents. Now, as I listen to Makiko's story, I understand that sorrow is a part of life. Rather than letting injustices weigh me down, like carrying around little stone statues in my heart, I could let them create some space, open me up, and become as empathetic and magnanimous as Makiko has been for me.

"The thing is, Makiko," I tell her, "I know the difference between a pregnancy you don't want and a baby that you do." The weight of the statue is heavy on my legs. I like it there and cradle it closer to my body. "But the point is that both of those things are terrible losses. You have every right to be sad."

"Thank you," she says quietly. "No one's ever said that to me before."

"No, thank you. You've been a good friend to me," I tell her.

She smiles kindly at me, then looks down into her teacup. "So have you," she answers.

I pick up the water baby and hold it near the window. Tiny specks of mica embedded in the stone glint in the sun. "I'm not sure what to do with this," I say. She looks immediately apologetic, but I hurry to reassure her. "I'm really glad to have it. I just want to find a special place for her. Some place where she'll be safe. Where I can visit her whenever I want."

"I hope you find that place," Makiko says.

"I will."

CHAPTER
TWENTY-EIGHT

Eddie and I stand in the foyer in Lemon's dining room. It's quiet except for the rumble of delivery trucks passing by on the street. My eyes roam over the empty tables, each one holding dinner plates and silverware as if waiting for happy eaters. It's hard for me to imagine that just a few weeks ago these tables were full of people, and the air was perfumed with the aromas of daring food.

"You're sure you want to do this?" Eddie asks me. "Nothing's final yet."

I try to conjure up the feelings I used to get when I walked through this door every day—optimism, excitement, enthusiasm. Now, as I stand here surveying the place, I simply feel disheartened.

"Is the landlord being a jerk about breaking the lease?" I ask as I walk by the bar. The sleek dark wood is covered in dust. Sunlight dances off the liquor bottles and teases a dead flower arrangement in Poppy's green cut-glass vase.

"You'll take a hit, but not too bad," says Eddie. "He knows he can rerent the space in a nanosecond and probably get more money out of it anyway."

I stop in the middle of the room and sigh. A deserted restaurant with no future is one of the loneliest places in the world for a chef. "Who's taking what's left in the pantry and the freezer?"

"City Harvest is supposed to come tomorrow," says Eddie. He shuffles through the room with his hands shoved deep in his pockets. "But I can tell them not to."

"Did you find an accounting firm to close the books?" I ask.

"They can come Friday."

A menu from our last night lies abandoned on the edge of the bar. I pick it up and scan the dishes. Spicy crab cakes over guacamole, braised hanger steak with semolina dumplings and mustard greens, quail roasted with port-soaked figs. We were so ambitious. No wonder people loved us. And no wonder we were exhausted. I leave the menu where I found it and push open the kitchen door. Clean surfaces sparkle; the smell is antiseptic, more like an operating room than a busy restaurant kitchen. Eddie comes in behind me and puts his hands on my shoulders.

"You can change your mind," he says.

I think about the long nights in this kitchen with Franny and Ernesto. Our interdependence defined Lemon and made it shine, but we'll never get that back. Franny and I have hurt each other too badly at this point. Everything I did here reminded her of some long-held resentment over my despicable behavior in Europe. Sometimes I think I hired her to make up for that. But then I blew it again. This time, I was the one smoldering with resentment over her abandoning me when I lost the baby, and I lashed out in a way I knew would hurt her terribly.

I turn around to face Eddie. I could try to resurrect Lemon without Franny and Ernesto, but it would always pale in comparison to what it once had been, so it's best to let it go. "I'm sure this is what I want to do," I tell him.

"Okay," he says. "I'll take care of it."

I wrap my arms around his waist. "Thank you for doing this for me."

"Of course," he says. "I'll do whatever I can to make it easier."

I let go of him. "I'm going to wait out front while you make the calls."

I don't stop in the dining room for one last nostalgic look around. I know how restaurant closings go. It's too much like cleaning out a dead person's house for me to sigh wistfully and romanticize the end. I've made my decision; now I need to leave so all the details can be taken care of by someone less emotionally attached than I am. I do want one last look, though.

As I stand on the sidewalk in front of the restaurant and shade my eyes from the glare off the front window, I hear the door open to the apartment building next to the restaurant. I almost don't want to look, but of course I do, and I see Franny. She's backing out the door, her crazy red curls flashing in the sun. I have a chance to duck away, turn and run, cross the street and hightail it out of there before she sees me, but I stand my ground and wait.

She doesn't notice me as she turns away from the restaurant and heads down the street, preoccupied with stowing her keys inside her shoulder bag. I consider letting her go, taking it as a sign that we're not meant to hash out our differences or reconcile this time. But then she turns around abruptly, as if she's forgotten something. She startles when she sees me standing on the sidewalk watching her.

"Oh," she says and jumps. Her body is pensive, guarded. "What are you doing here?"

I point to the restaurant. "Taking care of a few things."

"You opening again?" she asks.

"No," I say.

We stand ten feet apart on the sidewalk, uncertain whether we're going to have a conversation or just a quick exchange. Then the bell above the door at Lemon jingles, and Eddie steps out onto the walk. He stops when he sees Franny and me facing each other warily.

Franny's eyes cut to Eddie. If she's still angry with me, then this is her chance to get me back by launching into every sordid detail of my ill-timed kiss with Ernesto. For a moment I regret not confessing everything to Eddie before she has a chance to make it sound like I was screwing her boyfriend on the bar. But Franny's face softens when she sees Eddie, and she waves to him.

He greets her with a friendly peck on the cheek. "I haven't seen you forever," he says as if we're simply running into a dear old friend. "You look good. You're tan."

"I went to Ecuador with Ernesto," Franny says proudly and cuts her eyes toward me.

"I hear the fruit there is amazing," says Eddie. "And the coffee. Was it outrageous?" He's a master at disarming awkward situations with idle chitchat about food.

"Yeah," says Franny. "But the best thing was the fish! Ernesto and his brothers caught fresh stuff every day. At night we wrapped the fish in banana leaves and cooked it over open fires on the beach."

"Sounds great," says Eddie, then the three of us stand in an uncomfortable silence. "Well, it's great to see you, Franny," Eddie says. "Tell Ernesto that we said hi." He turns back to me. "I have to make one more call and check the doors, then we're all set."

After Eddie goes back in the restaurant, Franny digs her keys out of her bag again. She walks toward the apartment building and says over her shoulder, "I heard you were closing, but I didn't believe it. It's not like you to give up just because you lost two cooks."

I could be cheesy and tell her that I lost a lot more than that, but I don't. "I'm sick of this place," I say. "It was too much work. No fun anymore."

"And the management was crappy," she adds as she unlocks the door.

"Yeah, well, some of the staff was a real pain in the ass," I say, immediately pissed off at her again.

She turns around and scowls at me before she pushes open the door and disappears into the foyer. I watch her jog up the stairs, and part of me thinks, Good riddance. I could leave now, and I know that someday Franny and I will run into one another at a restaurant. We'll be perfectly civil. Have an insipid conversation to catch up on the broad strokes of our lives, and that will be that. Until we see each other a few years later and do the same thing over again. She'll be one of those people that I see and think, I used to be really good friends with her, what happened?

But that's not what I want. That's what the old stupid, immature Lemon would have done. After everything I've been through recently, I'm tired of letting things go in my life without the proper kinds of good-byes.

The door to the apartment building has made a wide arc and is slowly closing again. I take two quick steps and catch it before it latches. Inside, I hear Franny's fast footsteps a few landings up, and I begin to climb.

It's strange to be back inside my old building. It hasn't been that long since I was in here, but so much has happened to me that I feel like I'm revisiting a part of my distant past. I was a different person when I lived here. One with a promising

restaurant, a vague commitment to my boyfriend, a baby growing inside of me, and little regard for anyone else. None of those
things are true anymore.

I pause on the fifth landing outside my old door, which is
ajar. I put my hand on it and stop. This is probably a bad idea.
Ernesto could be home. Clearly Franny is in a hurry to get
somewhere, and she doesn't want to talk to me. But I'm not
willing to leave. I push the door open a bit. "Franny?" I call quietly and step inside.

The apartment is immaculate. They've painted the walls rich
jewel tones. Ruby in the kitchen, gold in the living room, and
plum in the hall toward the bedroom. Little wooden figurines
of farm animals dance around the fruit bowl in the center of the
kitchen table, and a gorgeous Ecuadorian tapestry covers my
old ratty couch. Everything has a place, and it even smells good
in here.

As I'm gawking at the transformation, Franny strides into
the living room and stops short. "How'd you get in here?" she
demands. "Did you keep keys to this place?"

"The door was open," I quickly explain and back up against
the kitchen table. "I wanted to talk to you."

"About what, Lemon?" She throws her bag onto the counter
and opens it. "What's there for us to talk about?"

"The reason why were not talking," I offer.

She shoves her wallet into her bag and cinches it closed
again. "I know the reason we're not talking," she says.

"So do I, but maybe we should talk about it."

"What?" she asks, confused. "That makes no sense."

"I just mean, maybe we should talk about what happened."

She drapes her bag over her shoulder. "You were a jerk.
That's what happened."

"Yeah, that's true," I admit. "But so were you."

She starts to protest, but then she stops. She fidgets with her bag, and we look past one another.

"Look," I say. I pick up a green pig with yellow polka dots from the table. I concentrate on it instead of looking at Franny, but I make myself talk. "I came up here to tell you that I'm sorry for how things ended with us. I regret how I behaved. I mean, specifically, I'm sorry that I kissed your boyfriend. I mean Ernesto. It was a very stupid and thoughtless thing to do. Especially after how I acted in Europe. With Herr Fink. That was terrible. I don't know if I ever told you how sorry I am about that. But I am. Sorry, I mean."

I realize that my apology is terribly jumbled and incoherent. Like someone just learning how to atone, which isn't far from the truth.

"I don't give a shit that you kissed Ernesto," Franny says. "It meant nothing to him, and it was just a way for you to get under my skin."

"No." I shake my head and squeeze the little pig in my hand. "It was more than that for me. I was really hurting, Franny. Ernesto was the first person to truly console me. I shouldn't have kissed him, but it wasn't just to spite you. It was a way to comfort myself."

"See!" Franny says and throws up her hands. "That's just like you. So selfish. No thought to how your actions would affect anyone else."

"You're right," I admit. "It was selfish. And I'm sorry." My words stop Franny. She probably never expected to hear me apologize. Frankly, I'm a bit surprised myself by how easily I'm owning up to my mistakes. I'm not done, though. "I'm sorry that I hurt your feelings. Again. But you weren't exactly there for me, Franny. At the worst time in my life, you never called, you never asked how I was, you never asked me what I needed. I felt totally alone."

Franny closes her eyes and bows her head. After a few moments, she says, "I just didn't know what to say. I kept trying to call you, but I was afraid I would make it worse. The only thing I could think to do for you was to keep the restaurant going." She looks up at me. Her eyes are red. "I threw myself into it. Then it was like you didn't even appreciate it. You showed up at work one day, yelling at me for moving in with Ernesto."

I remember all the fury I had toward Franny that day. The hurt festering below my skin. "I never cared that you moved in with Ernesto," I tell her. "I was just afraid that I'd already lost your friendship." Then I shake my head. "God, we've made such a mess of things."

"We should've never worked together," says Franny.

"Or lived together," I add.

"Or tried to date the same guy."

When she says this, I laugh and quickly cover my mouth. I look at her to apologize, but she's got a grin on her face, too. "Yeah," I say. "That's hard on friendship."

"I'm sorry, Lemon," Franny says. "I should've been there for you."

I shrug. She shrugs back. Neither Franny nor I is the type to fall upon each other, professing our undying friendship now. But what we've got is a start, and I'll take it. I put the pig on the kitchen table between a rooster and a frog. "These are nice," I say and touch each one lightly.

"We brought them back from Ecuador."

"Did you meet his family?" I ask without looking at her.

"Yeah," she says uncertainly. "But his mother hated me."

"Who could hate you?" I gently tease.

She grins a little again. "It's shocking, I know."

I take a small step closer to Franny, as if I'm inching my way toward a skittish animal. "Is Ernesto okay?" I ask.

She nods. "He's good. He got a consulting gig with a hotel chain. He'll travel around the country setting up their restaurant and bar menus. It's only for a year, but it pays a lot, so he's happy."

"What about you?"

"What about me?" she asks.

"Do you have a job?" My heart pounds as I ask her. If she doesn't have a job yet, she might blame me, and we'll be right back where we started a few minutes ago.

"I got a gig at a new Mediterranean place on the Lower East Side," she says proudly. "Head chef."

I smile at her fully. "That's great, Franny. You totally deserve it."

"Yeah," she says. "I do." She readjusts her bag across her back, then she says, "I have to go to work now, Lemon. I'm already running late."

"Okay," I say and open the door. "This place looks great, by the way. Better than when I lived here."

Franny follows me into the hall. "We love it," she says.

"I'm glad you guys are happy."

We walk down the stairs single file, me in front. I want to turn around and look at Franny's face. I want to know that this isn't the last time I'll see her, because the thought of not having her and Ernesto in my life anymore makes me very sad.

"Hey, did you know Mona got a job at Coyote Ugly?" Franny asks.

"Oh, my God!" I look at her over my shoulder, and I laugh. "That's perfect. All she'll have to do is let drunk guys slurp tequila out of her belly button."

"Maybe you should've made that a specialty at Lemon."

"That would've gone over well with the foodies. Do you know what Lyla and Kirsten are doing?"

"Lyla got a gig touring with an off-Broadway production, and Kirsten's teaching dance at some private school in Brooklyn."

"What about Manuel?"

"He's fine," Franny says. "I hired him as a line cook at my restaurant. He's awesome. Just like Ernesto on the grill."

"Tell him that I said hi."

We reach the bottom of the stairs, and I push open the door. Eddie stands on the sidewalk, looking down the street, bewildered. "Hey," I call out to him. "Here I am."

"Oh," he says when he sees me coming out with Franny. "I wondered where you went."

"Sorry," I say. I'm getting good at the apology thing. "We were upstairs talking."

"You heading out?" Eddie asks Franny.

She nods as she locks the door. "I'm a working woman."

"We should all have a beer sometime," says Eddie.

Franny turns to us. "I'd like that," she says. "I really would." Then she starts down the street. "Come by the restaurant sometime if you have a chance," she yells over her shoulder. "I'll cook you up something good."

I wave to her as she walks away. "We will," I call after her. "We'll come."

CHAPTER
TWENTY-NINE

Closing Lemon and making things a little better with Franny has unleashed a mad desire in me to cook again. I spend the next five days re-creating nearly every dish Aunt Poppy ever taught me to make. By Friday, Eddie and I are both sick of gorging ourselves on the heavy, garlicky dishes of my past, and I wake up with a hankering to bake something light.

After Eddie leaves for the day, I take my daily jaunt through the local markets and find the most beautiful crate of perfect organic lemons. I cart two dozen home and spend my morning juicing, zesting, and thickening. Rolling out flaky crusts. Whipping pearly white meringue into stiff peaks. I build two pies with tall waves of meringue over the bright yellow filling and bask in the sweet smell of burning sugar and baking lemons. When the pies are cool and I'm freshly showered, I carefully wrap one pie and head over to my grandmother's house.

I love these long walks. They started out as necessity. A way to clear my head of all the grating sadness, anger, and confusion. Now, being alone on the streets is pleasant. I know the people and businesses on my path. I stop for a café con leche at the little Spanish coffee shop, where the cashier with red lipstick watches Mexican soaps on the TV above the counter. Sometimes I pop into the ancient Ferdinando's Focacceira, still in the same tiny space since my grandparents were born, for a rice ball or scungilli salad. I browse the newer shops on Smith and Court for handmade tote bags, funky pottery, and vintage coats. I almost never buy anything, but I love to look.

Today, with my pie tucked against my hip, I stop in front of an empty store on Smith and Second. The door is open, and the lights are on. A realtor stands in the center of the main room, gesturing to the light spilling in from the large front window. A couple stands, faces sour, shaking their heads at the old exposed brick on the walls and the wide-plank floorboards.

"It would need a lot of work," the guy says. He's wearing sunglasses and Prada shoes. I can't stand him already.

"We'd have to do something about these floors," the woman says. She scuffs her pointy-toed boot against the mellow oak. I want to step on her dainty foot.

"But the light!" the realtor exclaims, desperately.

"It's an exclusive champagne bar," the guy says. "We'd have to cover the window anyway."

Oh, Christ, I think and try to imagine my aunts and uncles sipping overpriced bubbly while some obnoxious twenty-two-year-old deejay named G-Lover Flash spins a Cocteau Twins remix. I step aside when the couple walks out. They look up and down the street and shake their heads, clearly unimpressed. The realtor runs doggedly behind them. "I have a gorgeous urban space in DUMBO," she says. "Very industrial. Exposed ductwork. You'd love it!" When they are around the corner, I peek in the window again. As soon as my mind starts conjuring up a floor plan and a menu, I jump away and walk quickly toward my grandmother's. This is not what I need right now.

•   •   •

My grandmother isn't home, so I leave the pie on the kitchen table. From downstairs I hear a man's voice say, "I'm sensing a child. A small child. Blond or strawberry blond or reddish hair."

It's coming from Livinia's living room. I walk downstairs to see what she's watching and see a teary-eyed woman nodding her head on the TV screen. "My son," she says. "Joseph. He had the most beautiful red highlights in his hair during the summer."

The camera cuts to James Van Praagh. "Joseph is here," Van Praagh says. "And he's okay. He says to tell you it wasn't your fault. You did everything you could. And he loves you."

Livinia sits with rapt attention, her hands paused from her constant crocheting. I shake my head at the poor gullible woman on TV, so desperate for the spirit of her dead son to reveal himself to the studio audience. Maybe old James could conjure up my dead baby and my long-gone parents from the great hereafter so they could have a panel discussion about what kind of mother I would've been. Now that would be a show worth watching.

A commercial for floor wax comes on, and I step into the room. "Hey, Aunt Livinia," I say softly. She looks at me uncertainly for a few seconds. "It's me, Lemon," I say as I drop onto the couch.

"I know who you are," she says and turns back to her crocheting. "Aren't you supposed to be at work?"

My half a doily and abandoned hook lie on the arm of the couch where I left them a week ago. The tension is all wrong, one side tight, the other loose and sloppy. "I don't really have a job right now," I tell her.

"That's good." She draws a long length of baby blue yarn from her basket and begins working it into a tulip pattern. "It's better to stay at home. Let your husband work so you can raise the baby."

"I'm not going to have a baby," I say. "Remember? I lost it." I'm surprised by how easily I admit this to Livinia. Then again, this is the woman who surrounds herself with photos of dead children. She continues to work the yarn as if I've said nothing.

I pick up one of the photos from the end table and look at it carefully. It's a baby in a long christening gown with tatted lace edges extending far below where its feet would be. Its little cheeks are sunken, and its closed eyes look like dark hollows. Poor tiny creature looks more like an old man than an infant. What could have ravaged a baby that way? Some old wasting disease, dysentery, cholera? How did mothers stand it? So many babies died.

As I study the picture, I think of the water baby Makiko gave me. I still haven't figured out what to do with it. I've kept it in the living room for the past few days, on the mantel, next to pictures of my parents. This feels a little weird. Slightly creepy. Only I love to see it. Every time I pass by, I watch it watching me with those stone dead eyes. I find it oddly reassuring. Sometimes I touch it. Trace the outline of its face. Cup my hands around its head. Or hold it close to my body. And I talk to it. In my head. Like I talked to my baby when she was inside me. I tell her how much I miss her.

Now Livinia's photos don't seem quite so weird to me. I can understand the appeal of having a picture of a deceased child. Some tangible reminder of the soul that so quickly left. Even the poor woman duped by James Van Praagh doesn't seem so pathetic when I think about my own ways of hanging on to what I've lost. I show Livinia the picture I'm holding. "Do you know who this was?" I ask her.

She peers at it. Her lips work in and out as she studies it. "That was my son," she says.

I know this can't be true. The picture is way too old.

I pick up another one of a little girl, maybe two years old, with soft brown curls around her face. She wears a dark wool dress with a wide sailor collar and sits stiffly upright in a high chair. "How about this one?" I ask. "Do you know who this was?"

Livinia narrows her eyes and concentrates. "That was my daughter," she says.

I set the picture down and take Livinia's hands in mine. "Why do you have these pictures?" I ask. She looks away from me. I have no idea what Livinia's been through in her life or if she'll even remember, but I figure there has to be some explanation for her fascination with the photographs and claiming the children as her own.

"Did you ever lose a baby?" It's a bold question, but I can't stand the thought of her carrying around that kind of sadness and having no one to talk to about it. "I did," I tell her. "I had a miscarriage."

She nods. I'm not sure if this means she knows about my loss, or if she's acknowledging her own. Either way, it feels good to talk about it.

"Most people don't understand how much it hurts," I say. "To lose a baby when you're pregnant. They think it's not really a baby, and they move on so fast. They think you should, too. But they don't know what it's like. They don't want to hear about how sad you feel or how much you miss that baby. But I'll listen, Livinia. I'll listen if you want to tell me."

She stares at the photos with tears quivering on the bottom lids of her rheumy eyes, but she says nothing. I wait. I'll be patient. I know how hard it is to find the words. I watch her face, and nothing changes. No teardrops fall, no hint of recognition glimmers in her face. Maybe I'm wrong. Maybe Livinia and I have nothing in common, and she is simply an odd old bird.

Just as I'm ready to give up, to accept once and for all that Livinia is far too strange for me to understand, just as I'm letting go of her hand and straightening to a stand, she grips my fingers and says, "I lost five of them."

"Five?" I whisper with horror. I lower myself in front of her again. "Five?" I repeat and shudder.

"I buried them behind the house," she tells me in her dry raspy voice. "Beneath the rosebushes. I named them after saints. Catherine, Jerome, Philip, Anne, and Christopher." She pauses. Twists the unraveling doily in her fingers. "Then Tony left me for that whore. He was so stupid." She spits the words. "It wasn't his baby. I told him that. They didn't deserve to have a baby."

I'm startled to hear my words in hers. I've said that exact same thing about my cousin Trina. And although I understand Livinia's anger, hearing it from someone else's mouth, I'm struck by how horrible it sounds. How does she know if that woman deserved a child or not? How does she know what kind of life that child had?

"Did you tell your sisters?" I ask. "My grandmother? Did they help you?"

Livinia looks at me, dead on and serious, as clear as I've ever seen her. "They wouldn't have cared," she says coldly. Then she puts her face close to mine. "They were all whores!" she spews. "All of them and their daughters. You, too. With your loose morals. Not saving yourself for marriage. I'm the one who waited. I'm the one who should've had a baby. None of you deserved it!" she screeches.

Her words startle me backward. I stumble to catch myself against the chair. My cheeks are hot, as if she's smacked me.

"Yes, I do!" I yell at her. "I deserve to have a kid as much as anybody else!"

"You're going to hell!" she screams. "All of you!"

I don't need to listen to this. Senile or not, she's a wretched old woman. I turn and run up the stairs. Slam the door behind me. Tear through the hall and rip open the front door to find my grandmother standing on the steps next to her red shopping cart full of groceries. She has her keys in one hand and jumps when I explode out onto the porch.

"What the hell happened to you?" she asks me.

"Livinia!" I sputter.

"What about her?"

"She's such a horrible, awful, mean old bat!"

Grandma shrugs as she pushes past me through the door. "You're just now figuring that out?"

"She called me a whore and said I didn't deserve to have a baby."

"Aw, don't listen to her nonsense." My grandmother pats me on the shoulder. "She's just an unhappy old woman."

I wipe my sleeve across my sweaty face and shake my head. "I was trying to be nice and talk to her about those baby photos."

Grandma pulls the cart down the hall. I follow her. "Why would you want to talk to her about that?" she asks me.

"Because I thought maybe she'd had a miscarriage, too." In the kitchen, I drop into a chair and watch my grandmother unload her groceries.

"Were you right?" she asks. "Did she have a miscarriage?"

"She had five," I say.

This stops my grandmother. She stands with a jar of olives in her hands and looks at me with her eyebrows raised. "She never told me that."

"Apparently she didn't tell anyone. Not even Tony. She thought no one would care."

"Well, that's her own damn fault," says my grandmother. "We would've helped her, but she never asked."

"It's not that easy," I protest.

"I didn't say it was easy, Lemon." Grandma pulls two industrial-sized cans of crushed tomatoes out of her cart and sets them on the table. She leans over and stares at me. "Your whole family loves you and cares about you. You know that, don't you? They might not always understand you or say the exact right thing, but their hearts are in the right place, and they want to help."

"We're talking about Livinia," I say snottily.

"And if you don't watch out, you'll end up like her. Sad, old, bitter, and alone."

I snort a little disbelieving laugh at my grandmother's straight talk. "I don't suggest you write a self-help book or volunteer at a suicide hotline any time soon," I say, but of course I know she's right.

She just shrugs. Hauls her cans of tomatoes off the table and stows them in the pantry, already fully stocked with soup, canned vegetables, spices, boxes of pasta. I remember my parents coming home from the road and raiding these cupboards for something good to eat. My father would make us grilled cheese sandwiches and tomato soup, or my mother would scramble eggs with diced onions. These shelves were never empty, nor was a meal missed. My grandmother never slowed down for a moment after my parents died. "How did you get over my mother's death so easily?" I ask her.

She turns to look at me. "I had you to take care of, and I had the rest of the family to deal with." She dumps a head of lettuce and several zucchini into the crisper drawers of the refrigerator.

"Sometime you just have to keep moving. It's not such a bad thing to distract yourself so you don't get mired in sadness and end up in a chair in front of the TV." She looks at me pointedly.

I'm quiet for a moment, seething a little at the sharpness of her criticism. But again, I know she's right. "I made you a pie," I say sheepishly and nudge the pan in the center of the table.

My grandmother smiles at me. "I love your pies. What kind is it?"

"Lemon meringue," I say begrudgingly.

Her face brightens as she uncovers it. "You haven't made me a lemon meringue pie for years. It's one of my favorites. Did you have this on the menu at your restaurant?"

I shake my head as she sets it on the table between us. The meringue has held up nicely. No slumping or weeping. I could take advice from the pie as easily as from my grandmother.

"Well, you should have." She takes two small plates from the cabinet and hands me a knife.

"It didn't seem fancy enough." I score the meringue to make the pieces even, then cut deeply across the middle. "Everything at Lemon had to have sixty-five different ingredients. Tahitian ginger bosc pear crème brûlée with sugared violets and Thai vanilla bean ice cream over a puddle of pomegranate quince coulis blah blah blah blah. Jesus." I lift a large firm piece of pie out of the pan and slide it onto a blue dessert plate for my grandmother. "Our menu read more like a Dean & DeLuca shopping list. No wonder the whole thing collapsed under its own pretense."

"Do you miss it?" my grandmother asks me as she digs her fork down through the fluffy peaks of the pie.

I cut a piece for myself and shake my head. "Honestly, no. I miss cooking, but I don't miss the constant chaos and headaches of trying to keep that place going. I made everything so complicated for myself there. Between Franny and me fighting and trying to compete with every other Manhattan restaurant to be the best at everything and get all the attention for us, I nearly drove myself insane." I point my fork at her and say, "I'll tell you this, the next time I have a restaurant—" Then I stop myself.

Grandma laughs at me and puts a large bite of pie in her mouth. I do the same. The crust crumbles, the lemon filling is velvet across my tongue, the meringue dissolves into silk.

Grandma closes her eyes as she chews. "Perfect," she says. "The next time you have a restaurant, put this on the menu."

CHAPTER
THIRTY

I've decided what to do with the water baby statue. Having it stare at me from the mantel seems a bit too Aunt Livinia-ish, and after her last outburst, I want to disassociate myself from her as much as possible. Plus I don't want to explain to visitors that it represents a baby I lost once when I was pregnant, as if it's some curious totem to be revered. Yet it's too intimate a part of my life to put away in a shoebox at the top of a dark closet. Since we don't have special graveyards in this country for the souls of lost children, I need to find my own sacred space to rest this part of my past, and suddenly I know the perfect place.

Eddie agrees to come with me. He's been shy about the water baby. I've caught him a few times standing several feet away from the mantel with his hands in his pockets, staring at it. I wonder if he's silently talking to it, like I do. Or if he's trying to comprehend what this object means to me. I think his mother's right; despite all his effort to comfort me, he'll never quite understand what I've gone through. I realize now that he has his own version of sadness and anger over this, and ours don't have to be the same for us to get through it together.

I wrap the water baby in a soft silky scarf, the same sunny

yellow as my mother's wedding dress. I'm tempted to swaddle it like an infant, but I don't. Eddie and I take turns carrying the water baby as we walk the Brooklyn streets that have become so familiar to me. It's a gorgeous fall day, warm except for the blustery breezes that stir up orange and gold leaves around our feet. We hold hands, and neither of us says much, but the silence between us is comforting just now. I don't need any more words.

My grandmother pops her head out of the kitchen when we come in the front door. "You need anything?" she asks us.

"No," I tell her. "We're fine."

She nods, then leaves us alone as we make our way into the garden. The mock orange is long faded—the brown shells of its buds now litter the ground—but my mother's old pear tree is in full glory. Vibrant green, yellow, and red leaves form a mosaic on the branches and a soft bed underneath. I crouch down and brush the leaves away from the base of the tree, looking for the perfect spot where my water baby will be safe. On the left side of the tree, near the corner of the fence, two rocks sit together at an angle, leaving enough space between them for the statue to fit comfortably.

Eddie unwraps the water baby. He holds her for a moment in the dappled sunlight coming through the leaves before he hands her to me. I cradle her briefly against my body one last time, then set her down. She fits snugly in the crook between the rocks. She is lovely beneath my mother's favorite hiding place, and I hope that they know one another like they've known me, intimately, from the inside.

Eddie and I stand together, our arms wrapped around one another as we look down on her. We've both said good-bye to the thought of this child many times over the past few weeks.

Since she was never here with us, we have no smile to forget, no smell to linger over, no memory of her soft skin against ours. What we have is the lost potential of this life. Something taken from us before we had a chance to know it. There is no finality of a burial for our child, just the slow drifting away of what we thought we'd have.

As I stand with my hand in Eddie's and look at the statue, I realize how afraid I was to become a parent. I thought since I hadn't known my own mother very well, I wouldn't know what to do with my child. But in this backyard, where most of my childhood took place, I realize that I've had many mothers. My aunts, Little Great-Aunt Poppy, and my grandmother have taught me well how to love. I look forward to bestowing those gifts on my own children one day.

My grandmother offers to feed us when we come in from the garden. "I have some nice amaretti cookies from Monteleone's. I can make coffee. Or maybe you want some lunch?" She wipes her hands on a dishtowel and scans the interior of the refrigerator.

"That's okay," I say and lay my hand on her shoulder. "We're not hungry."

"Well, here." She opens the box of cookies anyway. "Take a few with you, then. You'll want something later." Her offer has nothing to do with hunger, but everything to do with feeding our souls, and we gratefully accept.

She hands a foil-wrapped packet of cookies to Eddie, and he pulls her into a deep hug. For the first time since my miscarriage, I see my grandmother's eyes well up with tears. She buries her face in Eddie's shoulder. Wipes her eyes against the fabric of his shirt. Something inside of me swells at the sight of this. They've been beside me all along, two pillars, so that I wouldn't fall too far. To watch them collapse against each other now, I know that I am strong enough to support myself.

"Now, get out of here," my grandmother says, completely composed. She gently pushes Eddie away. "I've got work to do."

"Thank you, Grandma." I kiss her on the cheek, then take Eddie's hand in mine.

From the stoop, I see Trina before Eddie does. She is walking down the sidewalk, Chuck beside her, pram proudly out in front. My first reaction is panic. I want to flee. Run back inside the house and hide.

She spots me before I can make a plan of escape. "Lemon!" she yells and waves her arms as if we're drifting out to sea.

"Hey, Trina," I say reluctantly.

"Oh, Christ," Eddie mutters beside me. "Just what we need." He takes my hand, and we walk down the stairs together.

Trina abandons the baby carriage and runs to greet us. She throws her arms around my neck and squeezes tight. "I haven't seen you since," she whispers in my ear, then stops.

I'll save her the trouble. I disentangle myself from her grip. "How's the baby?" I ask.

Trina beams at me. "Oh," she says, full of reverence. "She's so beautiful."

Chuck pushes the stroller closer to us. He even grins a little as Trina carefully pulls the blankets away from her daughter's face.

"Her name is Delilah," Trina says. "Hello, Delilah, hello beautiful girl," she coos.

The baby blinks up at us with her unfocused blue-gray eyes. She has incredibly fat cheeks and a perfect little rosebud mouth with bubbles perched on her lips. She reaches out, and Eddie lays a finger in her gripping hand.

"She is beautiful," I say, and I mean it.

Trina doesn't take her eyes off Delilah. She looks genuinely happy, and as much as I'd like to begrudge her this contentment, I can't. I have no idea what this child will bring into the world. Or how her experience with Trina for a mother and Chuck for a father will shape her. I have no idea what the bigger picture is. Call it luck or fate. Mine will come later.

"Well," I say. Even though I can be happy for Trina, I don't want to linger over this kid. I'm still too fragile for such a thing. "It's good to see you guys."

Trina turns to me. "You, too," she says. "You take care."

Eddie takes my hand, and we walk away.

At the end of the block, he slings his arm around my shoulders. "Were you okay with that?"

"Yeah," I say. "It's getting easier. How about you?"

"It's hard to be pissed off when you see a baby."

"She was pretty cute," I say. "But I still like the name Nicotina better." Eddie and I both laugh.

We stroll down Smith Street, past all the new restaurants. Half of them are fake French bistros; two Indians sit side by side; a sushi shop and a burrito place share an awning.

"How long do you think these places will last?" I ask Eddie.

"I think they'll do okay," he says. "I was talking with one of my buyers the other day, and he said these neighborhoods have boomed. So many people are moving out here from Manhattan. It's a great place to be trying something new, because the rent is still relatively cheap and people are hungry for great food."

"But don't you think some of this stuff is too trendy? How many French bistros can one strip support?"

"You know what this neighborhood needs?" Eddie asks me. "Something simple."

"A little rustic even," I add.

"I remember when we first started going out and we'd come over here to your grandmother's, there were all kinds of old-school Italian restaurants. Family places."

"There's a few left," I point out. "But they're not going to attract that Manhattan crowd. Those people want something more daring, more fresh. Butternut squash gnocchi or arugula ravioli."

Eddie stops and looks at me. "What would you call it?" he asks.

"Call what?"

"That restaurant you're describing."

I laugh. "I'm not saying that."

"Come on," he chides. "You've thought of a name already, haven't you?"

I face him in the middle of the sidewalk. We're only a few blocks from the space I saw the other day. Eddie leans forward and watches me with a big grin. This is the look he gave me on the night I told him about my grand scheme for Lemon. The look that means he completely believes in me and he's willing to do anything to help.

"Poppy's," I tell him. "And I've found the perfect place."

"Show me," he says and reaches for my hand again.

I lead him down the street. "You should see the way the sun comes in the front windows," I say. "And it has these wide-plank floors and exposed brick walls. I know exactly how I'd do it. There'd be an open kitchen. And no futzing around with the basics this time. I'd get a manager so I could just be head chef. I'd hire one sous-chef, some line cooks, and Makiko to do desserts. The menu would be simple. We'd have signature dishes and a few specials every night."

As we're crossing the street in front of the building, I see the same realtor from the other day locking the door.

"Hey," I call out. "Excuse me. Wait." I jog across the street, Eddie close behind me.

She turns around, startled, and drops her keys.

"Is this place still available?" I ask. Eddie presses his face against the window.

"Yes," she says eagerly as she retrieves her keys.

"Lem, it's great," Eddie says. "I think it even has a garden."

"Can we see it?" I ask. "Right now?"

She looks at her watch. "I only have about fifteen minutes."

"That's fine," I tell her.

After we walk through, the realtor leaves us with hearty handshakes, her card, and all the specs. We promise to call her in the next few days after we sit down and look at the possibilities of financing the deal.

"One of my stocks just split," Eddie says as he paces in front of the building. "So I could easily generate some start-up cash. And according to the accountant, the finances at Lemon weren't as bad as you thought. But this time, I really think you should hire a bookkeeper and a manager. It was too much for one person to handle. I could write up a business plan." He stops and looks at me. "I'm sorry," he says. "I always do this. It's your place. I'm supposed to be a silent partner."

I look at Eddie, and my heart revs, my palms sweat, my mouth goes dry. I see the excitement in his eyes, the way he truly believes that I could pull off Poppy's. I'm ready for Eddie to truly be my partner. And I realize for the first time, that means I have to be willing to let him help rather than trying to prove that I can do everything myself. "I want you to be a part of this," I tell him. "My full partner, not silent. But I'll only do it on one condition."

"Okay, what?" he asks.

I know without a doubt that this is what I want. I can't

explain my certainty, except to say that standing across from Eddie, I realize that I want him in my life. I don't know that everything will always be okay between us. I don't know that we will never go through more hard times. This restaurant could fail. Parents will die. Friends will come and go. We could lose another child. All I know is that whatever happens, I want Eddie with me.

"You have to marry me first," I say.

The silly grin on his face dissolves, and he reaches out his hands to take me by the shoulders. He shakes his head, and I panic, certain I've made a mistake. Misread the situation. Irrevocably damaged our lives together with all the blunders I've made in the past few months. I can't stand the thought of more hurt, and just as I'm ready to backpedal, to withdraw my offer and slink away into some other version of my life, Eddie pulls me close to him. He holds me against his body. "I can't believe it," he says. "Are you serious? Do you really want to marry me?"

"Yes," I say simply. I pull in his olive oil scent and wait for his answer, wait for this moment to define our lives.

"Of course," he says to me. "Of course I will."

WATER BABY

You reach out from the depths through murky cloudy water. Part the seaweed and jellyfish tendrils with your dry and brittle finger bones. Cross atolls and coral beds to get back to the river edge, where you thought you'd never go again. She waits for you.

You recognize her instantly. That soul, a piece of you once, endlessly splitting and dividing the way only love can infinitely replicate itself while gaining strength. She is your daughter's daughter who's come to the water now.

You emerge and taste the air, redolent with verdant life. Savor hints of what you had before. Then you lift that little lost soul from the shores and hold her as you once held your daughter. You whisper all the secrets of your time on earth. She tells you everything she was going to do in life. And in between was Lemon, the life you both missed. Now you know everything, before and after.

The river crosses over from death to afterlife, but neither of you will make that trip. Together now, you wade into the deep. Let the water wash over you and carry you out again to the in-between where souls are never forgotten, but swim forever in the minds of those who love them.

UP CLOSE AND PERSONAL

WITH THE AUTHOR

Okay, look, here's the skinny. Most authors write their own back-of-the-book interviews. We try to come up with insightful questions and clever answers designed to clarify our work and foster an up-close-and-personal connection between our readers and ourselves. But I'm not going to do that here because frankly it makes me uncomfortable.

If I wanted to tell you a lot about myself, I would write a memoir or a thinly veiled autobiography in the form of a first-person novel. That's not what I do, though. I purposefully write fiction because it gives me a place to hide—behind characters and scenarios, inside narratives, crouching beneath the surface of the story. I also get to spy on people, eavesdrop shamelessly, steal stories, and adopt histories that are not my own. Yet I can pop up anywhere in a novel or fade away, and you, my dear reader, won't know the difference. I do this because for me, fiction is a way to get at parts of life that aren't accessible through a recounting of reality.

Reality is so very messy. All loose ends, no clean clear arcs or tidy endings. So many superfluous details have to be stripped away, like peeling an artichoke, to make real life as palatable as a book. And then what's left? The heart. I'm not so sure I want to lay myself bare like that.

I could use these pages to tell you about how I write. What time I get up, where I find my inspiration, how long I sit at my little red desk every day. But honestly, none of that is very interesting. Besides, I think what you really want to know is how much of this book is true.

Am I a chef? Are my parents dead? Are the experiences, attitudes, and feelings I portray my own? Am I writing from the heart?

As for the last question, the answer is yes, I am writing from the heart. The story that I've told is very dear to me, but that doesn't necessarily mean that it's true. I will tell you, however, what's not true.

I didn't grow up in Brooklyn. I was not raised by my grandmother and four nosy aunts. Nor do we have a weird old woman living in my family's basement. I've never been a chef or worked in any restaurants in Europe, and my husband's only relationship to olive oil is putting it on salad. I have no fruity nicknames, I'm not a blond, and I've never lived in the East Village of New York. I did, however, have a sweet little Italian grandmother and a large extended family in which food and love were inextricably intertwined.

And yes, I am sidestepping the biggest question of them all. This book centers on the loss of a pregnancy. The isolation and hidden grief of that all-too-common experience that we skirt around and don't address well in our tidy western world of happy babies and child rearing. By some estimates, nearly a third of all women who get pregnant will miscarry. For something that touches so many people (not just the women themselves, but their partners, family, and friends), there is very little literature or information out there. So I figured, why not write a book that deals honestly with one woman's loss, hoping that it will bring some comfort or understanding or empathy to others?

Of course this entire diatribe begs the question, have I experienced such a loss? The answer to that question, my dear reader, is in this book.

Then don't miss these other great books from Downtown Press!

Scottish Girls About Town
Jenny Colgan, Isla Dewar,
Muriel Gray, et al.

Calling Romeo
Alexandra Potter

Game Over
Adele Parks

Pink Slip Party
Cara Lockwood

Shout Down the Moon
Lisa Tucker

Maneater
Gigi Levangie Grazer

Clearing the Aisle
Karen Schwartz

Liner Notes
Emily Franklin

My Lurid Past
Lauren Henderson

Dress You Up in My Love
Diane Stingley

He's Got to Go
Sheila O'Flanagan

Irish Girls About Town
Maeve Binchy, Marian Keyes,
Cathy Kelly, et al.

The Man I Should Have Married
Pamela Redmond Satran

Getting Over Jack Wagner
Elise Juska

The Song Reader
Lisa Tucker

The Heat Seekers
Zane

I Do (But I Don't)
Cara Lockwood

Why Girls Are Weird
Pamela Ribon

Larger Than Life
Adele Parks

Eliot's Banana
Heather Swain

How to Pee Standing Up
Anna Skinner

Look for them wherever books are sold or visit us online at www.downtownpress.com.

doWn
tOwn
press

Great storytelling just got a new address.

PUBLISHED BY POCKET BOOKS

10403